CHINALIVE

BOB JONAS

For Meg

VAGABOND LIBRARIAN PUBLISHING

First edition.

ISBN 978-0-9892744-0-1

For the lovely Susan.

Dragon Heroes

Prologue

An ancient Chinese tale tells of a time when a millennium rainstorm poured over China. With nothing to stop unending rains and rampaging floodwaters, the Chinese people watched helplessly as their greatest river, the Yangtze, was about to break free of China's borders.

In a desperate attempt to control the path of the river, the Emperor hired a mysterious, magically talented government worker named Yu. After assembling a team of dragons, Yu soared through the skies of the Middle Kingdom, cracking his whip on the thundering herd, to assess the task before them.

The job would not be done in a month — or in a year. For decades Yu guided his powerful dragon team, fearlessly harnessing their might. Canals were dug, rivers blocked, streams diverted, mountains and lakes created. Never once did their dedication waver.

It was said, that on at least three occasions while flying over the town where his family lived, Yu heard the mournful cries of his wife and children begging him to return home. Sadly, he could not. Had it not been for the Emperor's decision to hire Yu, the floodwaters would have roared out of the Middle Kingdom and changed China's history forever.

Of all the tasks he and his host of dragons completed, the most important was the placing of Cloud Mountain directly in the path of the Yangtze. The *Chang Jiang*, as the Chinese respectfully called their river, coursed a savage thousand miles down from its origin on the Tibetan plateau. For hundreds of miles it ran alongside the Salween and Mekong Rivers. If not for Yu, it would have joined the Red River as it flowed 600 miles south through Vietnam on its way to the Gulf of Tonkin.

At the small town of Shigu, in central Yunan Province, the waters of the *Chang Jiang* slammed into Yu's mountain, forcing the river to take a 300 degree hairpin turn to the north. In its northbound fury, the waters began carving out the famous Tiger Leaping Gorge. After another sharp turn to the east, and a twenty-six hundred mile journey to Shanghai, the river finally emptied into the South China Sea.

So great were things that Yu accomplished that when his flood control efforts ended, he was crowned Emperor. Before assuming the duties of Emperor, which would leave him no time to himself, he searched for a place to rest—a place where no one could find him, a place he could return to again and again when the pressures of being Emperor were overwhelming.

It was said, but never proven, that he and his dragons created a secret chamber under Cloud Mountain, expansive enough that they could fly free beneath the mountain without fear of being discovered. For centuries after Yu's rule ended, the chamber and dragons remained undiscovered, but the legend lived on, and the work the dragons did with the Great Yu was immortalized.

The chamber would have stayed hidden for another thousand years had it not been for a young, angry, patriotic government worker from Shigu.

Chapter 1

Charlie knew they weren't going to hurt him unless he did something stupid. How he knew was his only edge—he understood and spoke Chinese. From the things he heard them say, they didn't have a clue—a western-looking kid from the States who spoke fluent Chinese? No way. Charlie thought they sounded like a couple of dim bulbs from the country.

"Not hurt him," one of them said, in Chinese.

Everything about the day had been routine—everything except the driver. Charlie's antenna should have shot up when the man who usually picked him up at school wasn't there.

"My brother sick today."

"I didn't know Tony had a brother," Charlie said. The new driver didn't reply.

"I said, I didn't know Tony had a brother."

"Yes, brother."

The man didn't turn around to look. Charlie could see him staring in the mirror. "My brother send apologies for being sick."

Charlie relaxed for the first few miles—no big deal, people got sick. When the driver took an abrupt turn away from the usual way home, Charlie moved to the edge of his seat.

"What are you doing? This isn't the right way."

"Big accident. Traffic. Very bad traffic."

"I don't care. Please turn around." The driver didn't respond. Charlie grabbed his cell phone. In a lightning move, the driver turned, grabbed Charlie's cell, and threw it out the window. Idiot. His mother and dad warned him—the government kept a close watch on all Internet use. But he was only working on a school project. Why had he ignored his mother's warnings? The driver floored the accelerator.

"Stop the car!" Charlie grabbed the door handle, waited for the car to slow, and got ready to jump. After a quick swing into a gravel alleyway the car slammed to a stop. Before he could right himself, the door flew open, two men pinned him down, and a cloth was shoved over his mouth and nose. Everything went black.

Hours later Charlie struggled awake. As he woke, his head felt tight. His eyes wouldn't focus. He had no idea what time it was or how long he'd been out. The air was hot but Charlie felt himself shivering in a cold sweat. This must be a dream. He forced his eyes open, shut, open—he was living it. He realized he'd been sleeping outside in a tent, maybe near the old Hongqiao airport.

Surrounding the airport was urban farmland, home to hundreds of pig farms. Tony had often taken a shortcut to school, and many times they found themselves behind a three-wheeled bike, outfitted with a small platform, piled high with severed pig heads. From the roar of the planes and the stink in the air, he was sure he knew where they were. What could these men want with a fifteen year old American kid?

Charlie held his breath when he heard voices close by. With the jets in the background it was difficult to hear what was being said but he thought he heard one of them say something about a boat. "Safest to wait here, until... transfer soon to boat."

Could he escape? His head felt like it had been flattened under a ton of concrete. When he tilted it up, rotating it gently in his hands, the pain lessened. Could he move any part of his body without being noticed? The tent was a tiny A-frame, big enough for one person—no place to stand, and not much space to move.

Were the men close by? The voices stopped. Still holding his breath, he gradually brought his knees up to his chest. So far so good—pain under control. He straightened out and rolled from one side to the other—painful, but still okay. At the edge of the left side, he cautiously picked up a piece of the tent to look out.

Immediate, suffocating, darkness.

In one frightening instant, Charlie's breath felt like it had been sucked out of him. Two men had collapsed the tent and rolled it up with him inside. When he tried to scream, his cloth cocoon smothered the sound. The men each grabbed an end and quickly walked him to the back of a waiting truck. After being unrolled, his hands were tied behind his back. When the men backed out of the truck, he caught a quick glimpse of his captors—cheap, black leather coats, dangling cigarettes, and on one of their t-shirts was written the slogan, *Impossible is Nothing*. One of his captors was the driver who had picked him up. Before the doors were shut, the other man said in poor English. "You no escape." His voice sounded more like a mild warning than a threat.

Whatever they had used to drug him was slowly wearing off. The bouncing, the heat, and the leftover stench from whatever had been in the truck before, made him nauseous and his headache worse. They hadn't traveled for long when, with one uncontrollable spasm, he wretched up what was in his stomach. The man sitting next to the driver screamed something through the open window that separated the cab from the cargo area. Pretending to know a little Chinese, Charlie yelled a word he knew wouldn't give him away. Stop—"*ting, ting, ting*."

The driver shrugged. A few minutes later he slammed on the brakes, opened the door, and Charlie was let out. While they hosed down the back of the truck, he doubled over and let loose again. He was still doubled over when they told him to get back into the truck. Exhausted, barely able to stand, he dropped to his knees, pantomiming his need for a few more minutes. They grunted in disgust, but he knew they were giving him more time. Desperate to get his head straight, he took several deep breaths. Charlie begged in simple Chinese for water, *"shuǐ, shuǐ."* They handed him a bottle half filled with tepid green tea. It tasted so bad he almost let loose again. Gargling with the tea helped clear the hot, horrible, vomit from his throat.

From the way his captors kept checking their watches, Charlie knew he only had a few seconds before they got going again. He quickly looked up to see if he could figure out where he was. They were off the main road in one of the small, ramshackle neighborhoods in the shadow of the city's skyscrapers. That didn't tell him much though. Nearly everything was in the shadow of the enormous, modern buildings in downtown Shanghai.

In a moment of clarity, an unsettling thought—the science fair. It must have something to do with the science fair. Before he could build on the idea, the men shoved him back into the truck. By pushing his feet against the opposite wall, he could brace well enough to keep his body upright. When the road smoothed out, he felt his strength returning. With a clear head and a calmer stomach, he could think. The science fair, the chat rooms, his dad, and the terror he felt after his last online encounter. And now this…

No one would believe something like this could happen in the Evers' adopted country. China was safe. You could walk the streets without a care. Except for an occasional backpack slashing, or pick pocketing at a local market, serious crimes against foreigners didn't happen.

Freedom from fear was something Charlie's family had not anticipated as one of the best fringe benefits of living in China. During their first years in Beijing this feeling was always reinforced. When they moved to Shanghai it was the same. But as Charlie reached further into his memory, he remembered recent discussions with his parents—things were beginning to change. When his dad disappeared a few weeks before, there was no doubt—the change had come.

Chapter 2

Charlie's family acted like it was his birthday the day they announced they were moving to China. *What was the big whoop? Where were the presents?* Charlie was five and he didn't care about a world 9,000 miles away. He cared about Robert, his friend next door, Patty, his preschool teacher, and life in Salt Lake City—his home at the foot of a snow capped mountain range. For weeks, all his parents could talk about was China, China, China. They showed him a map and talked like cheerleaders. In the end, he didn't mind that much.

From one of his secret hiding places, he overheard them brag to friends how easy the transition was going to be for him—bright kid, easy going, liked everyone and was liked by everyone; and more than a bit precocious. *That's me,* he said to himself. *I'm cool, oh yeah.*

They had read all the books about third culture kids. Charlie would have no trouble adapting. The first culture was his own; peewee baseball, a house in the suburbs, riding his bike on a safe, tree lined street. The second culture was the one he was moving into; 1.3 billion people, the Great Wall, a culture thousands of years old, and chop sticks. The third was a twilight zone most expat kids struggled with at first. In his new life he would not be in the first or second, but somewhere in-between—a hybrid, a mix, but a wonderful mix according to his parents. He would be going to school with kids from around the world in one of the world's oldest countries.

#

Charlie never forgot the sweat-soaked August night they arrived in Beijing. His mom and dad tried to tell him what humidity was like—hot steamy air, the kind you find in the bathroom after a shower. But their descriptions had in no way prepared him for the rice cooker they walked through on their way to a taxi stand. After hours and hours on an air-conditioned plane, the twenty-minute wait for a taxi was like nothing Charlie could have imagined.

Crowds, pushing, shoving, and so much noise—and what was that smell? Everyone was speaking super-fast; screeching, barking—incomprehensible. Men kept coming up to his dad, "Taxi, Mr.? Taxi, cheap, over there, no wait. Where you go?" Like buzzing flies, they wouldn't stop. When it looked like his dad was considering one of their offers, Charlie's mom stepped in.

"No, John. Remember what they warned us about? Take only the marked, regular taxis—the ones with meters. Leave," she said to the drivers. "No. No taxi. Go away." Charlie was surprised to see his mom get so mad, but it was a relief to see the men move on.

When John Evers lifted his son onto his shoulders, Charlie felt safe. For their first few years in Beijing, this perch would be his lookout—protected, secure, and what a view. As far as he could see, a forest of black heads surrounded them wherever they went. With so many people, it took Charlie months to realize that Beijing was not China, but only a city filled with millions and millions of people. Years later, when they moved to Shanghai, or visited any other big city in China, the idea of a country with 1.3 billion people became more understandable.

The Evers family arrived in China as it was opening up to the world and the site of a cute, blue eyed, blond haired kid, on top of his 6'4" former football player dad, was an amazing novelty. Unlike many annoyed foreigners, Charlie and his dad loved posing with friendly, camera-toting locals. There wasn't much in Utah to compare to this.

#

After only a few days, Charlie had seen some of the strangest sights. Their fifty-story hotel was all glass, steel, and ultra modern. On the broad boulevard in front of their hotel, old ladies were sweeping up—no street sweeping machines, just old brooms.

Beautifully dressed people in the hotel café were drinking coffee while ragged people across the street were cooking outside in big blackened woks. A bunch of men were sleeping on cots getting ready to sell crates of watermelons. Charlie was curious about some little old ladies pushing carts with big brown pots.

"What's in those pots Dad?"

"If I'm not mistaken Charlie, those are chamber pots. The ladies are collecting night soil." After John Evers explained what that meant, Charlie said, "No way. Poop?"

"Hard to believe Charlie, even in this big, modern city. Not everyone in the world has indoor plumbing." It took Charlie a minute to think, to understand. And that was only the beginning. Every day rocked his mind with more unimaginable sights and situations.

Charlie couldn't wait to see his new school. On their way there, the Evers found themselves on a forty-five minute drive from downtown, on a four-lane highway with a name that none of them could pronounce. Past hundreds of farms and miles and miles of newly built factories, Charlie's eyes bugged out as if they had landed on another planet.

"There," said the driver pointing to the middle of an approaching cornfield. Charlie stared at what looked like a mile long, concrete tomb. The building stood out in stark contrast to the mud bricked houses of the neighboring village and surrounding fields.

"Is that it? Is that the school?" It was big, ugly, and looked more like a factory than a school. The lady who was assigned to show them around walked in a fast, stutter step way. Charlie's dad had to pick him up to keep pace.

"We have fifty-six nationalities at this school—four gyms, two libraries, an Olympic sized swimming pool, two theatres, two cafeterias," and on and on. Charlie noticed she never stopped smiling, and talking, and walking. She wore high heels that clicked as she walked down the tiled hallways. When they went outside to see the track, baseball fields, soccer fields, tennis courts, volleyball courts and newly constructed million-dollar playground, Charlie looked across the road.

"What's that over there?"

"That, young man, is a real Chinese village," she said, as she kept walking, and talking, about the state of the art this, and state of the art that. The Evers noticed that Charlie was still looking through the fence as their tour guide was about to lead them back inside. "Charlie, come on."

"Do those kids get to play on this playground?" Charlie had noticed many dirt-covered kids playing in the road that separated the village from the school.

"Oh no, hardly. But our students do take field trips once a year to bring those children Christmas gifts."

"That's nice." Charlie said.

On the way back to their hotel, his mom and dad tried to get a sense of Charlie's feelings. All he would say was, "I liked it. Fine. It's okay." So they left him alone.

"What's an expat?" he asked.

"That's what we are," his dad explained, "a special breed of foreign person."

"What's that mean?"

"Expat is short for the word expatriate. And that refers to any person who lives temporarily, or forever away from their home country." Charlie liked it. In addition to being an American, he was now an expat. Expat Charlie—Charlie the expat. It sounded cool. His mom and dad were relieved that his amazement continued, not only the rest of that day, but from that day on.

"Look at that," he kept saying everywhere they went. Balanced on either side of a passing cyclist were indeed things Charlie could not believe he was seeing. "That man has a refrigerator on his bike—and a stove. And look at that." It was a bike carrying more wicker chairs than he could count.

"I counted twenty, Dad."

"I counted twenty-five, Charlie."

"While you two were counting chairs I saw a lady on a bike with two dozen straw cages filled with squawking chickens," his mom added.

The newly constructed highway was built to be shared with thousands of bicyclists. Bikes were still used for personal transportation and movement of every kind of product or material imaginable. Bike lanes that had been built on either side of the highway were jammed with people who routinely traveled for miles, in every kind of weather, on the only kind of transportation that made sense. But bicycles weren't the only means by which goods were transported.

Charlie gawked with glee every time he saw some combination of wheels and platforms, propelled by rusted, ancient engines, challenge 60 mph modern trucks for highway supremacy.

"I can't believe it. I just can't believe it." He said over and over throughout their whole first year.

Charlie's never ending observations delighted the Evers. "I don't think they take weekends off. They can make anything work. The whole family helps." Every time he saw something out of his world, he immediately made comparisons. His appreciation of their new culture grew quickly and developed way beyond what his folks had imagined so soon in their new life. In the years that followed, Charlie would never have guessed how someday his initial impressions would be shredded with a much harsher reality.

Chapter 3

After John Evers had been missing for three weeks, Charlie started believing the worst. His dad often flew out of Shanghai for a week or two—sometimes longer. It always had to do with his job. Charlie was afraid what to think when his mom sat him down after his dad's most recent two-week absence.

"This is different," she said, "no communication whatsoever—no calls, no emails, nothing. When I tried to call his cell, it was dead. A recorded message said the number was no longer in service." Even though the PSB (Public Security Bureau) said they were doing all they could, neither Charlie nor his mom could understand the lack of results. Their only official contact had been an interview at a nearby PSB precinct–unnerving, unproductive, and as far as Charlie and his mom were concerned, a big waste of time.

Two policemen showed up one night at dinnertime and urgently requested they come to their station house for an interview. Unsure what to do, they climbed into the back seat of a black, unmarked car. The dark plastic film on the windows made what was left of daylight even more ominous.

After waiting for over an hour in a cold, dim entrance hall, Jill Evers called the US Consulate. Other calls to the Consulate over that past few weeks held out such little hope that she hesitated. In this case, she was relieved when they promised someone would be right there. As she returned the cell to her purse, a guard pointed to a sign and demanded that she give him her phone. When she refused, two other policemen showed up to make the same request.

"I will not give you my phone," she said. Two of the men again pointed to the sign as one of them stepped towards her with his hand out. Looking beyond the sign, she saw more cops walking up and down stairs at the end of the room, but no other civilians. Defiantly, she wrapped her arms around her purse. When they could see their request was going nowhere they stepped back, but did not leave.

In the dim light of the few florescent bulbs that worked, and the greenish glow of a fishless aquarium, everything looked dirty and old. Together with the annoying squeak the men's shoes made on worn out linoleum flooring, the overall effect gave Charlie an eerie, morbid feeling. The Chinese Communist Party insignia hung over a double doorway in the back, along with fading, colored pictures of high-ranking party officials. Warning posters featuring cartoon characters committing some sort of crime had circles around each with a line through them. I'd better not do that kind of stuff, Charlie mused, or someone who looks like Comrade Donald Duck Wong will come for me wearing a rumpled, blue uniform.

Before the situation escalated, a US Consulate official, accompanied by two United States Marines, walked in.

"Are we ever glad to see you gentlemen." Jill said. Charlie thought he had seen the man somewhere before.

"Hello Mrs. Evans, don't worry, we'll straighten this out immediately. And you must be Charlie." The man stuck his hand out to introduce himself. "I'm Winston Roper son. I've worked with your dad before. He says great things about you." After a few minutes of talking to the Chinese police officers, a polite man in a perfectly pressed uniform walked in and invited them to his office. The Marines were asked to wait outside.

"My name is Captain Fan. I am sorry if we caused you alarm, Mrs. Evers. We do things a bit differently here. I hope you believe me, getting your husband back is our highest concern." Winston Roper replied by stating rules that applied to American citizens and told Captain Fan that he would greatly appreciate the courtesy and consideration due Charlie and his mom.

"Of course," Captain Fan agreed. "I only have a few questions."

"Please begin, Captain. Mrs. Evers is anxious to get on with it." Charlie thought the Captain looked annoyed with Winston Roper, but immediately focused his attention on Jill Evers.

"Where was your husband going? Who was he with? Had he traveled there before? What kind of project was he working on? When was the last time you heard from him?" Captain Fan asked the same questions again and again. Jill Evers answered them in the same way, again and again. After an hour, Winston Roper interrupted.

"I think Mrs. Evers has answered your questions, Sir. If you have nothing new to ask, this meeting is over." In an abrupt departure from his previous questions, the Captain turned to Charlie.

"Do you ever log onto the Internet using your father's account?"

"What does that have to do with anything?" Jill Evers said, as she stood to leave. Charlie's breath stopped as he looked at the man. He followed his moms lead but it was too late. Charlie knew this cop was smart and could see the way he was trying to hide his feelings. The next question cemented his fear, and his mom's.

"Is your husband in the employ of the United States CIA?" Jill Evers had to fight back her anger. She was well practiced at staying cool, and she knew it would only look worse if she overreacted to such a question—one she suspected might be asked. Captain Fan pulled an official looking file from a drawer, folded his hands on top of it, and waited for a response.

"No, he is not. Please do your job Mr. Fan. Find my husband."

"Captain Fan, Mrs. Evers. Captain Fan." Charlie could see the man's eyes tighten as a slightly twisted smile appeared on his face. "I am doing my job, and one more thing - it would be best to let us find your husband. These criminals could be extremely dangerous. Please be available if we need to talk again." Charlie tried to get his mom's attention as they started walking to the door, but she was only focused on one thing—getting out.

"They love to play games Jill," said Winston Roper, as they walked out of Captain Fan's office. "Don't worry. Let us know—you or Charlie—if anything strange happens. I told Captain Fan he had to contact our office if he wishes to speak with you again. Don't hesitate to call any time—my cell, or the emergency line at the Consulate."

#

Uniformed patrolmen did not show up again. The Evers received no more phone calls and no other attempt was made to contact them. The Chinese government, according to the Consulate, was paranoid about what the world would think—that such a crime could be committed in their tightly controlled, heavily policed city. It became the assumption in the expat community that it would be up to them to find John Evers.

They were also warned that the Public Security Bureau might try to find a foreigner to take the blame.

When a British lady living in one of the expat compounds was found murdered a few months back—the first real sign that things were changing—the husband was told to keep company with at least two friends or fellow workers at all times. Consulate officials warned that the man could be arrested and presumed guilty by local authorities in order to save face, until the real murderer was found—if ever. A person lost in the Chinese legal/penal system could take months to find.

"Charlie," his mom began one night at dinner. "You're fifteen and you've lived long enough in China to know about the growing unrest and anger throughout this country." Charlie would often take home conversations he had had at school and his mom and dad were always happy to continue those conversations.

He read it in the foreign press and he could see it daily on the streets. Thousands and thousands of displaced people were brought in from the countryside to build huge new projects. Inefficient SOE's (state owned enterprises)—giant businesses created by the CCP (Chinese Communist Party)—had been used to guarantee jobs for life to millions of people. Once these inefficient businesses became a financial burden to the government, they were shut down. The CCP guaranteed that replacement work and homes would be found for everyone, but there were too many people.

In the past, the government was able to control the movement of millions by using an internal passport, a green ID card every citizen had to carry. As the number of homeless and unemployed grew, the government lost control of these people. With the promise of a job and a better life, workers were easily recruited to help build the infrastructure of the new China. When they came to the big cities, they were paid a bare minimum, housed in temporary dormitories, and had a front row seat to a fabulous life that would never be theirs. Charlie and his friends walked by these people everyday.

Observations about what was happening on the street were always fair game for Charlie's Humanities class. His teacher Mr. Fathom was a man who never backed away from controversy.

"The friction is mounting," he told them. "The explosion is coming." Charlie was never content when Mr. Fathom didn't have time to follow up with remarks like these—obviously outside the school's curriculum. The simple questions Charlie asked in his first years in China grew in complexity to ones that were much more sophisticated and insightful.

And now, dangerous.

Chapter 4

The interrogation left Charlie and his mom unnerved. With little hope from the Chinese authorities, they had to believe representatives of the company where John Evers worked—he would be found. But why should Charlie believe their promises? What was this company neither his mom nor dad would talk about?

For the first few years, Charlie had no idea what to tell his friends about what his dad did. After living in China for a decade, he still wasn't sure. Supposedly, John Evers worked for what was called an NGO, a non-governmental organization. They told Charlie it had to do with helping the Chinese government solve critical, environmental problems.

When he was younger, Charlie told his friends that his dad was helping save the environment. Although he wanted to believe this, he was sure they were holding something back. As he grew older, his mom and dad knew it was only a matter of time before they would have to tell Charlie the truth—the NGO was a cover for a top-secret government agency of the United States.

For years Charlie tried to get at the truth. "Hey Dad, it says on the Internet that a lot of people believe some NGOs in China are covers for other organizations – information gathering organizations."

"You mean spies? You still think I'm a spy?"

"That would be cool. Are you?" This discussion came up many times over the years. Unfortunately for Charlie, it always ended in about the same way. Politics, world affairs, the environment, and even failings of the Chinese government—all out on the table, but never a direct answer about what John Evers did for a living.

As they left the police station Charlie could tell from his mom's guarded, worried look, she was keeping something back. He hesitated to ask the question. Her face looked drawn and tired, her rock-solid self-confidence, gone. Was this an unfair time to ask? The question was burning in him.

"Is Dad a spy?"

"Charlie, we've said it again and again. His work is complicated. When he gets back…" she paused and thought, perhaps this is the time to tell him what they had been putting off for far too long—but she stopped herself.

"From this moment on," she continued, "until we find your father, I want you to be careful. I want you to tell me if anything out of the ordinary happens." Sure thing, Charlie said to himself—must be a family trait. They had held back for years. With the information he had recently uncovered...now it was his turn to keep secrets.

For weeks after his dad's disappearance, a flood of people came to visit. Some of them were friends. Most he had never seen before. Charlie worried what his mom would think of his covert Internet adventures. Would she be mad? He knew his dad would be furious. But would telling what he had discovered help find him? Had Charlie held on to this information too long?

Charlie suspected his dad had been kidnapped days before his mom told him—but he couldn't be sure. The information had come to him while visiting a Chinese chat room to find information on the Yangtze River for his science fair project. Many of the places he visited were forums for discussions on current political topics. During some of his recent visits, the chatter had risen to great intensity from people making reference to the *laowai*, meaning outsider, or the *meiguoren*, American, who had disappeared. No news had emerged anywhere in the expat community. But here it was, on the Internet, in Chinese. The missing person referred to in the chat rooms—could it be John Evers?

Why didn't he tell anyone? Why did he hold back?

A frightening message came directly to Charlie a week after his mom told him her worst fears. As soon as he entered the chat room, the message jumped at him, "Charlie, say nothing or he die. We watching you."

Charlie froze. There on the screen, his name, Charlie Evers. How did they know his name? His hands hovered above the keyboard as he stared at the computer screen.

"Where's my dad? What do you want?"

"We get back to you. Keep mouth shut, tell no one about Internet chat." Charlie wanted to tell this creep to bite the big one, but instead, picked up a piece of scrap paper, squeezed it into a ball, and threw it at the computer. His digging into the darkest part of the Internet finally confirmed what his father warned him about—what he was doing was extremely dangerous.

It started innocently enough, with his research for the science fair. It was still innocent. But his dad was gone, and whoever sent him this warning was real. He stared into a small mirror in his room. Idiot, he thought. Not so innocent. He had been logging in using his dad's account—no easy feat, but his dad had been strangely careless. How did they find out it was him? And why had he put his dad at such risk? Was this the reason John Evers had been kidnapped—someone had thought it was his dad who asked all those questions. He looked in the mirror again and stepped back in his mind. I screwed up. Boy, did I screw up.

Charlie grabbed a legal pad and furiously started to write. He tried to remember every question, every risky place he should have avoided. After filling an entire page, he realized he could revisit some of the chat rooms and find strings of the conversations he had had. He typed in the locations. The message strings weren't there. He continued, trying to remember if he had returned to the right places—he knew the addresses. It was no use. Every place he could remember, gone. He jumped when the next message appeared. "Told you funny boy, leave it alone or he die. Back off." Charlie's fear was now joined by another emotion—anger. Something about the choice of words—leave it alone…funny boy…back off...

"…or he WILL die. We ARE watching you. Your English sucks, idiot." He couldn't help himself. His response flew off his fingertips like flames at the end of a match. Throughout his life, reminders of his impulsive behavior were never in short supply. He liked to think some of his pinball reactions were a good kind of spontaneous—inspired ways to express how he felt. In the unreal, anonymous world of the Internet, especially in some of the insane chat rooms he had recently visited, Charlie felt less and less able to resist. During every imagined conversation with his dad, he could guess his dad's response. Spontaneous expression? Bull. Recklessness? Absolutely. No inspired expression here, only idiotic risk taking.

It didn't matter what his dad said now. To feel so helpless at the hands of morons whose English sucked big time, brought out Charlie's swashbuckling side. He sobered up quickly when the next response came: "see how funny this when father's finger arrives in mail. Be smart Charlie." As quickly as the anger joined the fear, this message brought him back to reality. It took Charlie only a second to regret what he wrote. Not because he felt bad for saying it, but for possibly putting his dad in greater danger.

Chapter 5

None of this mattered now as the truck rattled and twisted through the streets of Shanghai. His immediate goal was to stay upright and not hurl again. After he stabilized himself, all he could think of was his mom and how worried she must be. His dad always described her as a tough Montana girl—ready to rope and hogtie anything on four feet. In the years since they had moved to China, she took over more and more of the household responsibilities. Although his dad's job kept him away from home a greater part of each year, his mom never complained.

"Your dad's job is important Charlie. We need to support him by showing how well we can get by when he's gone." Charlie seldom questioned her, but he missed his dad. He missed their long talks, and especially the things his dad shared with him about China. Charlie was constantly amazed at his dad's encyclopedic knowledge of their host country.

Knowing how much Charlie longed for his dad's company, Jill Evers was thankful for Charlie's school friends, strange as they were.

"Eclectic bunch," her husband reassured her. "They all checked out."

"You didn't?"

"Why wouldn't I?"

"John, they're only kids."

"So were the Red Guards, Sweetie—too much at stake. Sorry."

There were usually six of them, sometimes as many as ten, depending. Jill could never tell for sure how many were in what Charlie called *his bunch.*

"It's a loose confederation, Mom. They're all pretty much independent types, do their own thing. We enjoy talking, computing…hanging out. Each of them know their families are only here on temporary assignment."

Zhiang Wan was one of these kids. He hung on the fringes. Wan was his first name although Charlie and his friends called him either Zhiang or Wan. Charlie knew that in China the family name was always used first. Neither Charlie nor any of his group ever got to know Wan well at all.

They often kidded him, "you speak pretty good American. Where are you from Wan?"

"Nowhere, everywhere."

At times Charlie thought it strange how Wan kept himself two steps outside the group. The kid seemed content, but lonely, thought Charlie. Almost as if he wanted their friendship, but not only for his tech skills. He was holding something back, but none of Charlie's group could figure out what. They were all a bit odd, displaced, and socially challenged. They all knew it, so the mystery of Wan was easy to let go.

"Want to go listen to music with us tonight."

"No thanks, too loud for me. Okay, what kind of music?"

"Take a chance Wan. We'll have fun," said Charlie. Wan stood quietly, as he always did, thinking and evaluating. Charlie stared at his reluctant friend.

"Wan, we're only going to listen to some music, not hold a demonstration."

"No thanks, maybe another time." Charlie could hear a hesitation in his voice. The expression on his face might have given Charlie a clue, if Wan hadn't turned so quickly and walked away.

Although Charlie wasn't convinced, some of his group thought Wan was one of the rich, privileged kids who got into their school because his family had connections. He might have been a local, but Zhiang Wan was brilliant in ways that gave him the credentials needed to be a player in this odd mix.

Chapter 6

Rita Zhiang liked to brag about her little cherub—the computer whiz kid whose brain worked like a microprocessor. From the first time his fingers made sense of a keyboard, he absorbed and stored everything he learned about computing. She and her friends thought this natural as Wan's father was a computer engineer. He did something for a living most people couldn't understand—something to do with satellites and fibers and optics. Once, in a light-hearted way, he told his son that he was helping change the world. Wan made the mistake of repeating this to kids at school. From a boy who already wore his pants way too high, and spoke like a little adult, with absolutely no playground smarts, words about a father saving the world were perfect ammunition for class bullies. Although his mom and dad admired his formal, confidant way, their concern escalated after more than one teacher told them how Wan's behavior came off as arrogant and stuck up to other kids.

"He is confident of himself," Rita and Bill Zhiang assured his teachers.

"But it seems like bragging to the other kids. He needs to be more aware of what he says and how others perceive him."

After too many skirmishes on the playground—ones he tried to hide from his parents—together with his longing for friends, the Zhiangs became much more concerned. Jerry's immediate reaction was not exactly what they had in mind, but it was a start. By lowering his profile, the number of playground incidents decreased and he finally found a few computer nerds who would hang out with him.

During Wan's first ten years of life, Bill Zhiang faced an ever-increasing barrage of questions from his young computer genius. As the boy grew older, his questions became more insistent and more specific. He also begged his parents for a western name. Wan might have been in a league by himself when it came to technology, but they knew how important it was for him to fit in—Zhiang Wan became Jerry Zhiang. Admiring his emerging genius, the elder Zhiang began to explain details he thought the boy could comprehend—telecommunications, radio signals, television, cellular phones, and wireless technology. These were things Jerry and his friends knew about, even if they didn't understand them yet. Bill Zhiang suspected his son's understanding was way beyond that of his friends.

Jerry enjoyed going to the homes of classmates but he was seldom given permission to have them over to his. One day, after all the difficulties he had had finding friends to hang out with, his mom relented. This wasn't an unusual weekend for Jerry but it was for his computer buddies. It was the first time he started to understand the special household in which he had been raised. The weekend began with a flight from their home in San Francisco to Los Angeles on the Zhiang's private jet. At a mooring in Newport Beach, they boarded their 50-foot yacht to a private villa they owned on Catalina Island.

"Wow," the boys said when they saw his dad's computer stuff on the jet, and then on the yacht. Jerry couldn't help but notice their growing, jaw dropping amazement. He had always taken the plane, the boat, the houses, and the computer gear, for granted. Kids who lived near or in Silicon Valley and whose families worked in the technology field generally weren't poor. After this weekend, there was no doubt—Jerry's family was more than a little bit richer than most of the kids at his school.

Chapter 7

Charlie kept thinking how he had kept his word to the punks who threatened him online. He hadn't said a thing about his Internet exploration—nothing to anyone. He did what they asked. So why was this happening? Were these the same creeps who had kidnapped his dad? If they were, was he being taken to the same hiding place? They said they'd be in touch but he never dreamed they'd grab him too.

The questions came to an abrupt end when the truck made its next stop. His nose instantly filled with another of the city's nastiest smells—they were next to one of Shanghai's canals. The men lifted Charlie under each arm and guided him out of the truck, up a ramp, and into the hot, cramped cabin of a canal barge. With a quick look over the side, Charlie could see every imaginable kind of garbage suspended in a layer of thick, green scum. He held his breath to avoid feeling sick again.

As soon as his captors left, the engines rattled to life. Slowly, the barge started chugging through one of Shanghai's most polluted waterways. After the barge was under way, the rope binding his hands was removed, but his relief was short lived. Handcuffs—not the dime store variety—were slapped around his left wrist, while the other half was snapped to a rail inside the cabin. When he looked up, a family was staring at him—a teenage girl, a small child, an old woman, and an old man. The adults looked much older than they probably were.

"You will only be in our home for a few hours until you are transferred."

"You speak English? What am I doing here? Why have you kidnapped me?" In Chinese, the man told the woman to give Charlie something to eat. He then stepped outside to pilot the boat. The woman stirred some vegetables in a wok and served them to Charlie with a handful of steamed rice. None of them took their eyes off him while he struggled to use the chopsticks. He had to hold the bowl in his handcuffed left hand, while bending over far enough so the chopsticks in his right hand didn't drop the food on the floor. The little girl giggled as the others stared. Charlie paused for a second to look at the giggler. He couldn't help but smile.

"What's your name?" he asked, in English. She looked to her mother. Charlie could see the woman gesture to the girl. In a low voice, with her eyes turned to the side, the girl answered in English.

"My name is Mei Lin."

"Happy to meet you Mei Lin. My name is Charlie." He leaned toward her to see if she would look at him. As she was lifting her head, the girl was told to go finish some work.

"She speaks English well," Charlie said. The mother scowled, but as she and the others headed back to work, he could tell the older woman was proud of the child's language skills.

Charlie had studied the Grand Canal—an eleven hundred mile waterway from Beijing to Hangzhou. He always hoped he would get to go on a canal trip but never dreamed his wish would come true in this way. Begun in 456 BC, it was the longest canal in the world and second only to the Great Wall in scope and complexity. Over six million workers had been used in its construction. The canal system in Shanghai was one of many smaller systems that fed into the main canal artery. Like most of the system, it was used to transport much more than the grain it was originally intended to carry. Charlie knew there must be areas, somewhere in the eleven hundred mile stretch, that were beautiful and picturesque. He had seen pictures. But from what he overheard, this trip wasn't going to take him outside Shanghai's polluted boundaries.

For the next few hours, the family went about their lives as if he wasn't there. Laundry was hung from two clotheslines—one in front of the cabin, and one in the rear. Charlie counted four externally mounted tractor engines. They belched out a ton of smoke with a deafening roar—tightening the vice on his throbbing headache. Tall piles of something that looked like sand—but smelled like something much worse—rose from a sunken cargo area and crested under where the laundry hung. The path the father had to take around the edge of the cabin, to get to the front of the barge, was a narrow sliver of decking that required careful navigation. The boat sat so low in the water that Charlie could see only a few inches between the water's surface and the deck.

He watched in disbelief as the family washed their clothes in the filthy water. When they used the same water to brush their teeth his disbelief turned to disgust. Although their intent might have been to ignore him, every time he looked at one of them they quickly averted their eyes.

For a time, he pretended to sleep, desperately trying to figure out why he was there and maybe how to escape. Detecting the sound of whispering in Chinese, Charlie held his breath.

"How long to the transfer?"

"They will come for him soon."

"Not soon enough. Are they taking him to where his father is?"

"Yes. I am glad they did not want us to help with that leg of the journey. This is dangerous enough." Charlie's heart began to pound. His dad was alive. He had to calm down, breathe quietly. Go along. Then he heard a tiny noise. The little girl was sitting across from him, staring.

"Were you sleeping?" she asked in Chinese. Before Charlie could think, he answered no, in English. When she jumped up to go he wondered if she realized he had understood her Chinese. Would she tell the others?

"Wait," he said, as she skipped away. Minutes passed, nothing. When his language screw-up produced no further attention, he relaxed. More minutes passed and there she was again.

"Help me with these," she asked, in Chinese, handing him a set of flash cards. Then she said it again, in English.

"Please help me?"

"I would be happy to help you. Where did you get these?"

"From a man we know." Charlie was impressed how well she knew the words on the cards. With every compliment her smile widened. After a couple of rounds her mother's voice rang out. Without answering, the little girl jumped up and left.

"I told you to leave him be. You are not to disturb him again. Go help your sister." Charlie was sad to see her go but thankful for the company.

He couldn't help wondering how this ordinary, hard working Chinese family was caught up in a plot that involved a United States citizen. China was opening up to the world, the Olympic Games were only a few months away—how could this be happening?

Chapter 8

For Herny Liu, the son of another hard working Chinese family, life in a small village in southern Yunnan province was never exciting. It was as it should be—school, home, friends, and a part time job on the river. That had all changed after a frightening instant—discovery of a secret he would be forced to keep for a teenage eternity. In other words, as his mother repeatedly reminded him, not an eternity, but not right away—her way of trying to keep his curiosity from killing him.

Returning home from his summer job on the river one night, Henry stopped at one of the public toilets near the boathouse. The guide boats in his care were safely tied up, tourists had all returned to Lijiang, and only a few people were on the street. After finishing up, he hesitated a minute when he heard an unusual sound from the stall next to his. When he entered the bathroom, there was an *out of order* sign on the door next to his. No one should have been in that stall. He quickly washed up, walked outside, and almost tripped over another sign that read, *bathroom under repair, do not use.* This sign wasn't there when he entered. As he walked away, he heard footsteps close behind. When he turned, he saw something that would forever squash the idea that nothing interesting ever happened in his sleepy little town. A big, mud covered workman carrying a tool Henry had never seen before was tracking mud out of the bathroom. The man didn't see Henry as he turned to go to the back of the building. Henry hurriedly found a place to hide. A moment later, another mud covered workman, and another, and after the first half dozen exited, Henry counted twenty more men, each carrying either a personal tool kit, or more pieces of the strange machinery. Each man checked to see if anyone was watching before following the previous workman to the back of the building. How could all these men be coming out of this bathroom? Had his active imagination finally taken him a step too far? He pinched himself to make sure what he saw was real. An inner alarm told him it was probably best to stay hidden until the men were gone.

He knew what his mom would say about such an incredible story—workmen with funny tools? Coming out of a public toilet? He wouldn't have believed it himself. He had to come back as soon as possible. Would the men show up again? The next night, he arrived early and waited. Nothing. No *out-of-service* sign. No one came out or went in. He had to check. The stall was still locked and had the same sign on it. He looked under the partition. Everything looked okay.

"Are you going to use it?" Henry jumped when he turned to find a boy staring at him.

"Yes. Sorry. Go ahead." That was it. Time to go home.

At about the same time the following night, he again found a safe vantage point—still no sign of the men. His surveillance efforts were a week old when his mom started to wonder where he was going every night. "To a friend's house to study," he lied. He felt awful lying to his mother but he couldn't tell her what he had seen. She would accuse him again of having a crazy imagination. These accusations were always followed by a threat to curtail his reading of fantasy books. If she knew the content of his most recent Chinese translated purchase—*The Lion, the Witch, and the Wardrobe*—he would be in deep trouble. He wondered maybe, just maybe, if kids could find an alternate universe by going through a wardrobe, was it too much to imagine a worker's world through a toilet stall?

Henry couldn't wait for his father to come home. Edward Liu was away in Beijing consulting on the building of a new university. He would be gone for a week, maybe two. Henry hated when his father was gone this long, but knew his work was important. It was usually on some project that would benefit the province or town where they lived.

Henry's mom joked about her boy being light in the head, although his father appreciated his son's ability to fantasize and dream things up. It was this kind of creativity his father said that was missing in Chinese education.

Henry knew his father was in a small but growing minority of educated men and women who had new ideas for the direction of their country. Unfortunately, they were often considered thorns in the side of the government. He remembered many times listening to his father's impatience with the rate of change in China. In these discussions, or overheard conversations, he absorbed every word, every detail.

Chapter 9

Charlie had mixed feelings about the new school his parents found for his second year in Beijing. It was in the city, it was much smaller, and it was in what his parents called a "real Chinese neighborhood." In this neighborhood, going to a Chinese school, Charlie would more easily learn the language and develop a greater appreciation of his host country—at least that was his parents' plan.

From the apartment they found nearby, the family could easily walk or bike to school in a few minutes. Everyday the Evers joined the largest human powered commute they could ever have imagined. It was always a challenge to move into and out of a fast flowing river of newly minted mountain bikes and decades old, rusted but working bicycle relics.

Every night for weeks John and Jill Evers used all their parenting skills to keep Charlie on steady ground. Within a week he hated his new school. Almost all the other kids spoke Chinese. All he could do was sit, try not to feel stupid, and try not to get into trouble. At first he didn't want his parents to feel bad so he said nothing. Gradually, after complaining about stomachaches, headaches, school food, and kids stealing his pencils, the Evers knew they needed to do something.

After meeting with his teacher and the principal, things seemed to get better, for a while—until Charlie decided to wander off. A local vegetable seller brought him back the first time. Charlie said he wanted to buy a banana. When his trips to the vegetable stand became daily, the owner started getting upset. How could the school keep losing this kid? Charlie liked the vegetable lady but one day decided it was time to take a different route. A few blocks away, in the opposite direction, there was a retirement home. Everyday Charlie saw older people exercising outside.

"Do you live nearby?" a gentle sounding older man asked him in English, when he saw Charlie watching through a fence.

"Kind of."

"Is your mother or father with you?"

"No. My dad's at work and my mom is probably at home. Hey, you speak English."

"Yes, a few of us do," the man said with a twinkle. "What is your name son?"

"Charlie Evers. What's yours?"

"Rusty Su."

"That's a funny name."

"Yes, it is, isn't it? It's my Western name. I got it from an old American television show. Please call me Rusty."

"Okay. But why is your hair so funny?" Rusty Su laughed at the unexpected comment.

"You have many questions Charlie Evers. Would you like to be friends?"

"Okay Rusty. But would you teach me how to do that exercise you were doing?"

"I would like to. But first, you must tell me more about you. New friends do that you know." Charlie smiled.

"My name is Charlie Evers, I come from Utah, my dad is helping China save the earth, I hate my new school so I ran away. Your turn."

"I see. I am a retired teacher, I have two children, and two grandchildren, and I have been to Utah. And why do you hate your school?"

"Because they all think I'm stupid."

"I can't believe that Charlie. You are a bright young man. Why do you say they think you are stupid?"

"Because they all speak Chinese and I don't."

"How long have you been going to the school there?"

"Not too long, I guess. A few weeks."

"Charlie, Chinese is a difficult language. It takes time. Sometimes students need a little extra help. Would you like me to help you?"

"That would be okay."

"Good. Here, come inside our exercise yard and sit while I go get something." Charlie hesitated, looking at some old ladies staring at him from their exercise equipment.

"Do not be concerned with them Charlie. They are nice ladies. You can outrun them if you have to."

"I know I can," Charlie agreed. Rusty said something to the women in Chinese as he walked away. After he left, the gang of grandmothers gestured to Charlie to come over and have a go on their equipment. When Rusty returned, Charlie was having a great time with the ladies, trying out all their exercise stuff. Rusty Su brought back the largest Chinese writing brush Charlie had ever seen and a bucket of water. After dipping the brush in the water, Rusty made a huge Chinese character on the cement.

"Can you guess what this means Charlie?" Charlie hesitated. "It means we are…friends?" Charlie guessed. Rusty beamed.

"Yes Charlie, friends. Now you try it." Charlie made a number of awkward attempts as the old folks gathered around. The brush was taller than Charlie so it wasn't easy. When he finally drew the character as it was supposed to look, they applauded. Charlie's smile sparked a feeling of affection in everyone watching.

"You have now written a difficult character and learned it in a few minutes." Mr. Su had Charlie say the character out loud and soon they were making a game of it. All the residents joined in.

With the principal's approval, Rusty Su started volunteering at Charlie's school. With Mr. Su's help he found that he liked learning the new language and his parents were delighted. In December, Charlie got an unexpected Christmas present—a new student from the States, a kid named Chris. They instantly became best friends. These welcome additions to Charlie's life came at a time when the Evers were beginning to doubt themselves and their decision to send Charlie to this new school.

Chapter 10

Although their apartment was in the middle of a Chinese neighborhood, the shortest route to school was through an area of diplomatic compounds. Charlie enjoyed his bike ride past these big, fancy looking houses. They were patrolled by dozens of life-sized toy soldiers in green uniforms. Regardless of the nationality, it was the responsibility of the Chinese government to guard all these compounds. Charlie, naturally outgoing and friendly, always said hello to these men. His first attempts at saying hello in Chinese might have sounded awkward, but by the end of his first year, he could speak a number of words like they were supposed to sound.

"The national uniform," his dad called the heavy green coats People's Liberation Army soldiers wore in the winter. The men patrolled around the clock, everyday of the year. They had an esprit de corps like the guards at Buckingham Palace or the Vatican—always at attention, unsmiling. Many carried weapons, but not all. At certain times of the day, a group of the men marched through the streets to replace the shift on duty. As one man stepped out of formation, his replacement would step in, until all those on duty had been relieved. Those coming off duty would then march in formation back to their barracks.

As Charlie and his family went about exploring their neighborhood, they discovered the gated barracks where the men lived. One night when the gate had been left partially open, Charlie stuck his head in. A number of tables were set for dinner outside and all the men were laughing and having fun performing karaoke. Naturally, Charlie joined in at the gate, dancing away. When the men saw him they all burst out laughing and waved. After only a few months, blonde haired, blue eyed Charlie Evers became the local mascot to the People's Liberation Army.

Where do they get those coats, his mom wondered throughout their first winter. The guards who did night duty needed the special, extremely heavy coats to keep them from freezing during their long, nighttime watch. One day his mom passed by a military store that sold the coats and asked, with a joking smile, if they had one in Charlie's size. The man returned her smile then looked at her as if she was crazy.

Keenly aware that sewing and tailoring were China's most common small industry, she asked the man where she could buy the fabric. He told her to wait a moment, and then brought out a bolt of the warm looking material. "One and half meters," he said. "Make sure the sewer uses enough heavy padding to make it warm enough." She didn't understand the Chinese, but somehow, with enough pantomimed gestures and a good sense of humor, they understood each other.

Charlie loved the coat. When the first men on duty saw him wearing it one cold January morning, they almost slipped out of character. A week after his first public outing in the coat, one of the men handed something to Charlie in a bag while pretending not to lose his position on guard. Inside the bag was a set of miniature epaulets, the official looking red things that were worn on the shoulders of the all the guard's coats.

A week later, Charlie and his mom repaid the guard's kindness with huge smiles and steaming bao—a delicious meat-filled bun. Now Charlie was a true PLA mascot. All the kids at school and all his teachers thought he was the cutest and coolest kid ever. Even when the weather turned warm, he wouldn't change to a lighter coat. This was Charlie Evers; funny, flexible, and always ready to accept anyone who smiled at him. At times, it was unnerving to his parents, but it always reinforced their decision to move to China.

By the time he was old enough for middle school, Charlie's parents began to see limitations in the school he was attending. His Chinese was so good now that taxi drivers turned in amazement as he rattled off where he wanted to go. They had to blink twice to believe that it was a Western kid who sounded like their own kids. He had a remarkable appreciation of the culture and the city and he had many local friends. But Charlie's parents wanted to broaden his perspective and his opportunities. During the six years they had been in China, many new international schools had been built. Unlike when they had first arrived, they now had a choice.

As Charlie was about to start his third new school since moving to Beijing, his dad's company wanted him to relocate to Shanghai. The Evers had visited Shanghai a number of times and felt overjoyed to get out of Beijing's horrible pollution and dust storms. Shanghai had its own pollution problems, but they were nothing compared to Beijing. And Shanghai held the promise of even more new schools.

After visiting many of them, Charlie and his parents decided on a school, located in the middle of a Western development. Although it required a forty-five minute commute, they were willing with Charlie's okay, to sacrifice the distance to school to have the best of both worlds—the school they wanted and the urban environment that made them feel like they were living in China.

To make sure the transition went as smoothly as possible, Jill and John Evers were not above tossing in some extra incentive to seal the deal—a small motorcycle for use in their neighborhood. When Charlie turned five they had bought him his first, junior motorized motorcycle. They never would have guessed that from that toy a passion for motorcycles would grow. As much as they wished the passion would cool, it only increased, along with the size of the bikes. Restrictions were set for close-in neighborhoods—restrictions they worried were not necessarily followed.

Charlie was a wide-awake kid in the morning and the private car his dad's company provided for the trip to school gave him time to read, do homework, or play a video game or two. At this new school he could study yet another language, Spanish, play a variety of sports, and continue his Wushu training. Based on traditional Chinese martial arts, Charlie loved the discipline and the moves of Wushu.

Although his teacher constantly reminded the class that Wushu was not about power or hurting someone, Charlie felt what most of the boys in his class felt—evil would be dealt with. Bring on the bullies. He could now study with a Wushu master almost every day.

Chapter 11

Charlie had no idea how long he had been asleep when two strong hands reached over his head with a cloth bag. They walked him off the barge, down a short road, and onto what he could tell was a good-sized vessel. From the ship's movements and the blast of an air horn, this had to be a much bigger waterway as well. The seamen who escorted him, rough as they were, didn't hurt him. After a few minutes, Charlie was guided to a bed in a small, steel walled cabin. The handcuffs came off and the cloth bag was removed. Charlie sat up to find a teenage boy staring at him.

"Where am I? Where are you taking me?"

The boy replied in broken English. "Not sure, but you safe. Better rest. We have long journey." As the boy started to leave, Charlie rushed past him but was stopped by a rough looking sailor outside the door—a painful knee to the stomach dropped him instantly. The boy, with an apologetic look, stared down at him. "Sorry, not good idea."

"Please tell me what this is all about," Charlie begged the boy.

"You stay," he said, as he helped Charlie to the bed, and then turned to go. The sound of the lock made a loud click after the door was shut. For many minutes he sat taking deep breaths, trying to recover. He wasn't trying to escape—he just wanted to see what was happening. Stupid. He needed to play along until he hooked up with his dad.

His newest prison was cold….and again, that smell. In the corner was a squat toilet covered by a board. A lone, wall-mounted light was enough to let him see where he was. Rust streaks discolored the walls from where water seeped in. He could tell, from the dampness and the sloshing sounds all around him, that his cabin was below the water line. After flipping the light switch off, Charlie detected no other light. The blackness, the isolation, the cold in his body—it was freaky. He turned the light back on. The bed was hard, but at least the blankets were warm and heavy. After he covered himself, the cabin's light didn't matter—he was out.

Hours later, Charlie woke with something to be thankful for—no bag over his face, and no nightmarish surprises. The heavy, lumbering movement of the ship confirmed his first impression of the ship's size. He had no idea what time it was but as his stomach started to rumble, the door opened.

The same boy entered, holding a tray of food. A crewman stood behind him. This sailor was short and even more dangerous looking than the one he had encountered before. The ruts on his face looked like they'd been added in layers. He was obviously there to keep Charlie from making another escape attempt. At this moment, Charlie was so hungry that food was the only thing that mattered.

"*Xie, Xie,"* he thanked them as the boy set the tray on the bed. As soon as they were gone, Charlie looked for a fork, a spoon, chopsticks, anything. "Where's something to eat with?" he yelled. "I need something to eat with." Had they forgotten—on purpose? It didn't matter. He attacked the food with his fingers and licked the plate when the food was gone. After enjoying a moment of contentment, he took a deep breath and looked over at the squat toilet. He had never gotten the hang of squatting, so with every ounce of resolve, tried to postpone the inevitable. When Mother Nature won out, he had no choice—his aim needed to be good. He was thankful he had eaten first.

From the walking tours he had taken in and around Shanghai he knew the only river within reach of their short barge ride was the Huangpu, a tributary of the Yangtze. He had no idea which direction they were going, but if they were heading north, toward the Yangtze, they would soon turn east or west. If they steered to the east he would soon smell the salt air of the South China Sea—heading out to sea was the worst option. If they turned to the west, they would be heading up the great river toward the interior, the heart of the Chinese mainland. He was sure he would know the difference.

Charlie snapped to the moment it happened. He was daydreaming when the ship started turning portside, no doubt about it. The Huangpu intersected with the Yangtze a half-mile inland from where the great river flowed into the South China Sea. Slowly, the ship began its journey inland. Where, how far, and why—Charlie's mind kept juggling too many unanswerable questions, but at least they weren't heading out to sea.

Chapter 12

In his last Internet post, Charlie had asked for names of experts who criticized the construction of the Three Gorges Dam. "Find the Red Spears and you will find the truth," came the first reply. What did that mean? Charlie thought. Within minutes, thirty more responses popped up. Some in English, some in Chinese, none of them expressed a middle ground. Some screamed through the screen to kill all PSB. Public Security Bureau cops were often the target of heated debates. Others talked about democracy, and how the dam exposed some of the government's worst flaws. Someone offered to meet for coffee. A few referred him to another blog or website.

After reading all the suggestions to find the Red Spears, Charlie began to follow a cyber trail that led in many directions. Most went nowhere. One or two looked too dangerous to try.

And now, unbelievably, he was heading toward the dam. He wondered if their journey would take them that far. After his first day in captivity, Charlie began to keep track of the days by scratching a mark on the cabin wall with a chunk of plaster that had fallen from the ceiling. By keeping a record he hoped he could keep figure out how far they had traveled. Some of the things he had recently learned for his science project would now come in handy.

Charlie couldn't stop thinking about the Red Spears—who were they? Why were they so important to all these people? It wasn't like any other spam—this looked interesting. In and out, that's all the further he would go. One link, maybe two, then no further. It was for his science project. What could anyone say? The blogs would be a perfect example of an Internet-linked, primary resource. He only had to find the right places to go, the right people to talk to. The river, the kidnapping, and his science project—there must be a connection, especially since the kidnapping had come after his research began. The river or the dam had to be the key.

After living in China for ten years, Charlie's knowledge of his adopted country was impressive. Looking at the long lists of things he knew about China—and things he cared about—the Yangtze made its way to the top of his research list. It began with a childhood love of boats and piqued after a field trip he had made with classmates through the Three Rivers Gorge. But what would be his research question? In both his science and humanities classes they had talked about the river's importance to China. The Yangtze, at 3,900 miles, was the third longest river in the world. Compared to the Nile and the Amazon, it was unquestionably the most important—the lifeblood to the millions who lived along its shore. The Yangtze basin in Szechwan province was home to over three hundred million people. If this area were a country, it would be the seventh most populated in the world. There was no way to overstate the river's importance.

Charlie had been ready the day he was given the assignment. His dad was home—a miracle these days—and right where Charlie had needed him to be. As a primary resource and China expert, John Evers was the perfect go-to guy.

"What do you have in mind Charlie?

"The Yangtze. The dam. The politics. All I have are a bunch of interesting questions, so far." Charlie and his dad loved playing the devil's advocate—questions for the sake of questions—no real answers, the more outrageous the better. It was fun, and challenging, and sometimes so close to being real that Jill Evers squirmed. Their edgy discussions might amuse the Evers men but it usually drove Charlie's mom nuts. No subject was safe from the follow-up questions what if, what if, what if.

"What if China invaded Taiwan tomorrow? What if Tibet has been training a secret army in India for the past ten years? What if China had met with the protestors at Tiananmen Square instead of murdering over three thousand of them? What if Mao hadn't promoted the Cultural Revolution or had taken the advice he received in the Hundred Flowers Campaign?"

"What if the government has this place bugged you big idiots?" Jill Evers said.

"I guess we put on our coats and get ready to be arrested," Charlie's dad laughed.

"I think teenage boys go to the same jail as adults," she warned her son.

Sometimes, when Jill Evers kidded her husband about being under surveillance, Charlie wondered if she was serious, especially after the weird looks she and his dad exchanged.

"What if the two of you put a lid on it and eat your supper?"

"I've studied a good deal of ancient and modern Chinese history," Charlie continued, "but you know how much I love everything to do with the Yangtze."

"So, playing the devil's advocate Charlie, take us back to the issue of the dam," his dad suggested.

"What if the dam doesn't work? Or what if global warming has some disastrous effect and the river dries up? I've read that many of the rivers in China have dried up for short periods in the past few years. Could it happen to a river that big?"

"Maybe you don't quite know the question yet, so think of all the things you would need to learn to be able to answer some of the questions you've asked. Why don't you use these supporting questions and start thinking more about what it is you want to know, and where you might go to find answers?"

"What if, what if, what if?" Charlie's mom chimed in as she brought the two of them dessert. "What if the river never existed?" she said. To which they both said, "good question." She wasn't surprised at their immediate and gleeful agreement. Chip off the old block, she thought. It was the same twinkle in Charlie's eye she was so used to seeing in her husband's.

Chapter 13

Charlie calculated they'd been on the river for four days. He knew the geography so well it was easy to imagine their journey in his head. It was eight hundred miles from Shanghai to Wuhan. Since it always took longer going up river, the current would be a factor.

On the second day, the boy delivered the food by himself. Did they consider their captive less of an escape risk now? The boy appeared more relaxed this time and Charlie was curious to see how much English he spoke.

"What is your name?" Charlie asked. The boy stared at Charlie for a few moments before answering.

"My name is Liu Xianxing. You can call me Henry." Charlie remained on the bed to show that he wouldn't try to escape.

"I'm Charlie."

"I know you," Henry said. "I cannot talk to you." This produced an awkward moment where neither of them spoke. Charlie didn't want him to leave so he tried to keep the conversation casual.

"Your English is very good."

"BS."

"Excuse me?" said Charlie.

"You hear me. BS." Charlie assumed Henry knew what that meant so he said nothing and waited. Charlie thought he saw something strange in the boy's face when he said BS—almost a smile he was trying to hide.

"I know how good or bad my English." Charlie thought quickly before the boy turned to leave.

"No more BS," Charlie said. "This place creeps me out and I don't want you to go. Can you stay for awhile and talk?"

"Okay. But they mad if catch me talking to you. Maybe, I say, practice my English. Not so bad for me." He smiled, like he had solved something important. Charlie could see a bit of himself in this kid—figuring stuff out, working the angles. Charlie remembered what it was like learning a new language while trying to make friends. This boy would never be his friend, but Charlie had to start somewhere if he was going to understand his situation.

Henry looked uneven—short jagged haircut, big ears, and reddish rounded cheeks. He didn't look dangerous. The jeans he wore were a knockoff that had recently flooded the streets of Shanghai. The Converse tennis shoes looked real, as did the North Face windbreaker. Henry looked sensible, like he cared about what he wore and what people thought about him. Small town, Charlie thought.

"Where are you from?"

"Not your business."

"You mean, none of your business." Charlie waited to see if Henry took this as an insult or a friendly suggestion.

"That the way you say it? None of your business?"

"It's better. It's the way an English speaking person would say it." Much to Charlie's relief, Henry thanked him.

"None of your business." Henry grinned broadly as he said the words again. Charlie knew if he could gain Henry's trust by helping him improve his English, he might be able to find out where they were –and maybe even why.

"Do you want to practice your English with me?"

"We practice tomorrow. Okay? You need anything now?"

"A key to the door would be helpful."

"Why?" Henry asked. "You don't need key." Charlie couldn't tell if Henry knew he was half joking or not.

"Tomorrow, see you again." There was no click when Henry left. Charlie jumped up to try the door. It opened. When he stuck his head out, Henry turned from down the hall.

"See, I tell you, don't need key. You go to any deck but not open doors. You be safe."

What the? Charlie sprang into the corridor. No guards appeared. He should do something — but what? His heart was pounding. Frozen with uncertainty he stood motionless, watching Henry disappear up a stairwell to another deck.

"What the hell do you want?" he shouted as he stepped back into his room, and then slammed the door shut.

Charlie's brain was fried wondering what to do next. Why had they left the door open? Were they trying to gain his trust for some reason? Should he be out exploring the ship? Did they want him to explore? A knock came at the door.

"This pillow you need more than a key. Yes?" said Henry.

"Thank you, but why…?"

"You going somewhere? You are welcome. Good night."

What the hell do you want—indeed, thought Henry, as he played Charlie's words back through his mind. Soon you will know. He was on his way back with a goodwill offering when he heard Charlie's question. I hope we both get to know. Henry stood quietly, listening. He felt bad for Charlie. As he had done so many times in the past two years, Henry took a minute to think back. Charlie had been jolted out of his peaceful world for less than a week. For Henry, it had been two years. Not knowing made it a lifetime.

Until a week ago, it had been 729 days of agonized waiting. When they finally confided in him, Henry felt as if his life had started again. But his father's trust came with a price. There was a request, a mission—one of the strangest things ever asked of him. He had to get information from a boy named Charlie Evers.

Chapter 14

If Charlie hadn't overheard on the barge that he would be reunited with his dad, he had no doubt that he could have made fools out of his captors, unless... had they intentionally let him know their plans? Was that the reason they thought it safe to let him roam the ship? There were many cities and towns along the river. With his knowledge of China, his language skills, and a little luck, he could have found his way back to Shanghai.

Charlie had to take some control. It was time to do something—anything. Henry said he could go to any deck, with only a half hearted warning not to open any doors. Charlie waited until he thought most of the crew had gone to bed. The passageway outside his door was clear. When he climbed to the other decks they were clear as well. A few sailors were out on the main deck but it was as Charlie had hoped—quiet. He didn't see any video cameras. They couldn't be watching him.

There were four decks above the water line. He had no idea how many below. As he walked down the passageways, he quietly tried every door. They were all locked. After Charlie had exhausted every twist and turn, he made his way back to the deck where his cabin was located. The hatches at either end of the passageway were locked as well. When he looked at his watch, he was surprised to see he had been at it over three hours. This wasn't going anywhere. He was exhausted and ready to crash.

When he woke hours later, the movement of the ship continued to match the movement in his stomach. Charlie usually enjoyed being on the water, but living in this hole was like being strapped to an airplane seat next to one of the airplane's bathrooms—hours of stink and turbulence. At times, he almost got used to what many Westerners called the China stench. Around any street corner in China, pockets of the foulest air waited in ambush for unsuspecting pedestrians. You never knew. A canal ran parallel to the street where they lived in Shanghai. Depending on the time of year, the height of the water, and the number of canal boats tied up, opportunities to practice holding your breath were unlimited.

Charlie had studied the history of pollution in China—it worsened with every dynasty. This was especially true now. Economic development was considered a major key to modernization. Millions and millions more cars, continued reliance on coal, unregulated industries—all signposts of an environmental meltdown.

Charlie tried not to think about the putrid waste the ship was cruising through. He was practically sitting in it, in a cabin far below the water line. For now, he needed to focus on something other than the smell, the darkness, and his aching loneliness. Again, he thought back to his research project.

As he studied every aspect of the river, his drive to know more deepened. This drive quickly turned into a dangerous treasure hunt. Late night searching stretched into early mornings as hours piled up looking at every link that held promise.

Although his Chinese language skills were considerable, it took a great deal of concentration to filter out the sites that were time wasters from the ones with meat. With so many newsgroups, chat rooms, listservs, and blogs, there were more locations for information than he could ever hope to enter or digest. Much of the interesting chatter was in Chinese. Charlie wondered how many of his chat room buddies would respond if they knew they were exchanging information with a teenager—as American teenager.

The blogs and chat rooms were safe enough. More and more links suggested he go to social networking sites but these could get dangerous in a hurry. In his half-hearted attempt to stay safe, his daily mantra became*, research the river, research the river, research the river.* In a way, he couldn't imagine any real danger to himself. But every day he was drawn in deeper. This was research for a school project, with only an occasional detour. Some online conversations were so detached from real life that they were comical.

KillKid: "Pig brain. Who wants to know what would happen if the river had never existed. What kind of idiot are you?"

Run Die Dog: "Big question—what now, if we blow up the dam?"

Blue Blade: "Too chicken to use your real name?"

CHEVIT: "Who cares what name? Would the government fall if dam were blown up." CHEVIT was Charlie's online name.

MadDog Red: "Tell it to the Red Spears."

CHEVIT: "Who are the Red Spears?"

MadDog: "Go to hell, CHEVIT pig. You figure it out. Maybe go to Hard Rock Café at midnight, this Saturday. Ask for LuLu." Intimidating as some of the discussions had been, Charlie grew more and more bold, cloaking himself, like thousands of others, in the shadowy side of the Internet.

Charlie was taken aback when he ran into some of the filthiest language imaginable. The basic swear words were familiar but many local idioms he had to look up. He steered clear of these sites most of the time, but like any determined voyeur, wondered where the conversations would go—one more link, maybe two, no deeper.

Sometimes he had the impression people were intentionally sidetracking conversations at a site dedicated to politically sensitive issues. If the conversation was about democracy, someone might flame the room about what idiots they were. It didn't occur to him at first, but it would be easy for the government to hide out anywhere they wished. Charlie knew that in some of his explorations, he needed to be extra cautious. PSB could manipulate, provoke, or listen, and no one would know. How could he continue to believe he was safe? Threads of those conversations would not stop spinning in his head.

"Charlie, you know people have been arrested for writing the wrong things," he had heard from his dad, repeatedly. "You know the Chinese government does everything they can to control every corner of the Internet." Charlie knew, but he still couldn't believe. In addition to his dad's warnings had read the same thing in countless newspaper, magazine, and online articles.

"Please son," his dad had pleaded with him. "Tell me we're not going to get a knock on the door. China's security people are smart." Charlie remembered, more than once, his dad stopping to scan his face.

"No way," Charlie said. "How can any government control the Internet?" Before he answered, his dad's scan became more intense.

"Charlie, you're a fairly sophisticated kid; savvy around computers, tuned into China's political climate, and yet, what's with these questions? You've read about it and we've discussed this many times. The government employs as many as 30,000 censors to try and keep track of everything going on in cyberspace." Charlie remembered feeling unnerved. What was he doing? Where had he gone? Why couldn't he stop?

If only he had listened maybe he and his dad would still be safe at home.

Chapter 15

After his graduation, it was decided that the best place for Lieutenant Rong Choi to serve would be in a special branch of the Ministry of Public Security's Olympics division—an area with access to highly classified information. This would offer him a vantage point that was relatively safe, working with 10,000 other cadets, whose sole purpose was to make sure China's great Olympic investment paid off. In addition to the government's 30,000 Internet watchdogs, the purpose of this special division was to focus on any threat to the stability and smooth running of the Games. This new generation of Internet watchers recently graduated from Public Security Bureau colleges. Their responsibility—investigate any irregular or suspicious Internet activity. With only a hint of wrongdoing, special units were instantly dispatched. Keyword searches such as *democracy, Tiananmen, Taiwan, Tibet,* or *overthrow*—tied together with any Olympic reference—became top priorities.

The Chinese government spent millions on a public relations campaign to bring the Olympics to China. They would not be denied as they had been in 2004. Rong was twenty-one and never remembered a time when the Chinese Olympic bid was not headline news. Electronic billboards were erected all over China to count down the last thousand days. Chinese citizens in every major city were incessantly informed of the number of days, minutes, and seconds, left before the Games were to officially begin. It was now down to ninety days.

In addition to their basic training manual, all cadets were given an Olympic preparedness addendum. Rong winced every time he read through the propaganda.

"Every job, no matter how small, is important to assure the success of the Games." *Stripping more people of the freedoms China overtly promised to respect. Eighty-thousand protests last year and counting.*

"This will be the century China emerges as the next superpower." *So what? By ruining the environment so that a few can get rich?* Rong reread the manual many times to remind himself of the special undercover role he had been groomed to play. The patriotism the manual inspired in other cadets only inspired Rong's loathing and determination.

"The nineteenth century belonged to Britain and the twentieth century belonged to the United States. Now it is China's turn." *They still have not learned. How can the century belong to us if the government will not let the people share the power in any way?*

"For the first time in centuries, China is not plagued by an internal war. All foreign concessions are history. Hong Kong, Macau, and Tibet are safely tucked under the wing of the Motherland, and it is only a matter of time before Taiwan returns as well." *They can dream about Taiwan all they want.*

"For the first time in modern history the change in leadership at the Fifth Party Congress went smoothly—no bloodshed, factional fighting, or war. World Trade Organization status was granted to China in 2001. The whole world is knocking down our door to do business." *Because they wish to make as much money as possible from us.* Rong could almost hear the patriotic fanfare seeping into his thoughts.

"The Olympics will be the crowning achievement leading to a brilliant future. It will be our way to prove to the world that China has arrived. We will not be denied our rightful place in the new world order." *Not if ChinAlive has anything to say about it. Tibetan protesters blew out the flame in Paris. Wait and see what we can do in Beijing.*

PLA cadets embraced the party line like a religion. They were there to become soldiers, but were lucky to be serving at a time when their first contribution toward China's welfare would be historic and without bloodshed. Their pride, patriotism, and commitment were unquestionable.

Rong had to be careful. So far none of his comrades suspected him.

When they first thought that their division had a mole, every resource was dedicated to uncovering the identity of the traitor. Rong knew if he were caught, if the PSB discovered his real identity, his family would be charged the price of the bullet used to execute him. The risk was great. Every security bureau continually monitored all activity within their ranks. No one was above suspicion.

Rong's destiny had been set in motion from the moment of his birth. On June 4, 1989, while trying to get the government to listen to their concerns at Tiananmen Square, Rong's father and pregnant mother were gunned down by the PLA. From that day on, the change in Rong's family was a mirror of the pain and anguish that rallied millions of his countrymen. Rong's grandfather vowed that he would do everything in his power to honor the memory of Rong's parents. He was groomed to help fulfill his grandfather's vow. As the Olympics drew near, the truth behind the government's lies had become more and more obvious to the world. *Let the neon clocks glow their inevitable reminders. The world is about to be given a front row seat to join in the real "China Celebration."* All they needed was a little more time, a great deal of luck, and a thousand things not to go wrong.

Chapter 16

The wisdom of placing Rong Choi in his current position was never so evident as it was now. A boy named Charlie Evers had drawn the attention of his unit. The people who had placed him with this top-secret unit now needed to know more about Charlie Evers.

The science fair project became more interesting than anything Charlie had imagined. After only a few more weeks of dangerous Internet searching, he knew he had wandered way beyond a place of no return. When the foul language turned vicious, when death threats became common, the time to stop had passed. But there were still so many interesting, informative places to explore, many of them useful to his research. Inescapably, the dark side of the Internet was always a click or two away. This was not a democratic country. There were no safeguards.

The possibility of uncovering new information, a connection between the river, the dam, and the democracy movement, was too tantalizing to give up. In his heart he knew it was only a matter of time. He would be lumped in like the rest—an un-welcome, law-breaking intruder.

Research the river, research the river—self-deception. He was only lying to himself. There was no use pretending. He was researching the river, but then; every lead, every twist, every new discovery was more interesting than the last. No way was he about to quit.

In the gloomy isolation of his cabin, more memory threads began to unravel; his dad the teacher, Charlie the student, and all the things he wished he had taken more seriously.

"The government walks a fine line Charlie. On the one hand they want and need the Internet. They need the ideas and knowledge from us 'barbarians' but they don't want their people 'polluted' by our ideas. They want the people to use the Internet for what they call 'positive use' not for 'unhealthy trash.'

"I can guess what that means," Charlie said.

"I know you can," his dad replied.

Warnings were not given by just his father—Charlie remembered many similar discussions in his Humanities class with Mr. Fathom.

"They have laws," he told the class, "which include phrases like 'threatening the social order, endangering state security, spreading rumors,' or even 'subverting state authority.' It's pretty scary stuff."

Mr. Fathom was told to tone down his political rhetoric when some visiting Chinese dignitaries observed one of his classes. After taking a vote of his students, he refused. When students returned to class after Spring break they were chilled to find that Mr. Fathom was gone.

One of Charlie's friends said it best at lunch that day, "we're not in Kansas anymore, comrades."

Chapter 17

Charlie had many follow-up thoughts to consider, but before he could formulate the next one, the cabin door opened and in walked Henry. A man in a PSB uniform followed. And then Charlie was stunned to see a face he knew well.

"Good morning Charlie," said Henry. "This is Mr. Liu. And I think you know Zhiang Wan." Charlie stared in disbelief. Zhiang Wan was in his science class and a kid who hung on the fringe with his group of friends. Before he had a chance to recover from the shock, he was asked to follow them. To Charlie's great disappointment, they only walked a short way before entering a larger version of his own cabin. A metal table was set for tea.

"Please sit Charlie," said Mr. Liu. "We are sorry for your inconvenience, but it is necessary for your safety." As Mr. Liu poured them each a cup of tea, Charlie tried to digest what he had heard. And was his classmate, mixed up in his kidnapping?

"Excuse me, did you say 'for my safety'?" All three remained stone faced.

"Yes. Your Internet explorations have put you in danger. We need to know how much you know about a certain matter so we can better protect you."

"Know about what?"

"Charlie, the government wants 'to educate' your father about the seriousness of this subject." This frightened Charlie. He knew enough Chinese history to know "educate" or "reeducate" often meant torture or relocation to the Chinese Gulag.

"Please, do not take this lightly Charlie. It is our intent to protect you and your father, if possible. The communication from the computer in your home involved many discussions of the Red Spears. We must know your connection to them, everything you have found out, and what you have told others."

"Wait a minute," said Charlie. "Why would the government want to kidnap my dad? Do you know where he is?"

"They did not know it was you logging on to your father's account," replied Mr. Liu. "This was only brought to our attention with the help of your classmate. The things you shared with your class helped lead us to you."

Charlie could feel his knuckles pop as his fists tightened. How many ways had he been stupid? At least he hadn't given away his Chinese language skills. How could the idiots who grabbed him not have known he spoke Mandarin? But this was bullshit. Mr. Liu was lying. These people had his dad, not the government. He wasn't stupid enough to believe this Zhiang Wan kid coincidentally blew in from the Gobi Desert. Charlie decided to keep cool – no Chinese, no anger. Maybe he could get something out of them.

"I don't understand, Mr. Liu. You're wearing a Public Security Bureau uniform. Aren't you the government?"

"No Charlie. The uniform gives me certain advantages when I travel. But that is of no concern to you right now. I think we are far enough away that you can be told how deeply involved you are in something we wish you had never discovered."

"Why is being far away important?" Charlie asked.

Mr. Liu ignored the question while he offered Charlie a snack. After sipping his tea, Mr. Liu put his cup down and looked at Charlie earnestly.

"What do you know about the Red Spears?"

"You aren't kidding, are you? This really is about the Red Spears thing." Charlie still couldn't believe it, but no one changed expression. "Okay, here it is, plain and simple. It was an interesting distraction I ran across during my research." Charlie paused for a sip of tea. All three of them waited, staring at him. What is up with these people? Charlie thought.

"I'm not hiding anything. When I saw the name Red Spears repeatedly popping up, I did some research. They're like a gang who came into being because of the rotten way corrupt officials treated the people a long time ago—like Robin Hood and his merry men."

"What else?"

"That's all. They were heroes. People needed them. There were many times in history when people needed a champion, or at least the dream of someone larger than life – like Zorro, or Superman."

"You are quite right, Charlie," said Mr. Liu.

"And your English is perfect. Who are you?" Mr. Liu's face betrayed a degree of respect for Charlie but a greater degree of irritation.

"Thank you Charlie. It would be best if you focused on answering my questions. Please tell us anything else you remember."

"I told you. That's it. Why don't you tell me why I'm here? Why don't you tell me where my dad is and why we've been kidnapped?" Mr. Liu did not back off. He persisted in asking the same questions. Totally exasperated, Charlie started answering Mr. Liu's questions with ones of his own. After many minutes of this quiet confrontation, Mr. Liu stood up.

"Enough!" he said, trying to control his anger as he headed for the door. Before he got there, Charlie stood up.

"Is this the time where the thugs with num chucks and black gloves come in? I know you're lying to me. I know you have my dad and you're taking me to him. The government doesn't have him, you do. Or are you the government?"

"Why do you think this, that we have your father?"

In Chinese, Charlie blurted out, "I heard someone say it on the canal boat." To Charlie's great surprise, Mr. Liu was not shocked at Charlie's language skills and answered him in Chinese, "But did you hear them say who had your father?" Somewhat shocked himself, Charlie answered.

"You know I speak Mandarin?"

"Yes Charlie. Are you surprised?"

"From the way the thugs who grabbed me spoke...sure I'm surprised. And was I supposed to overhear on the barge that you're taking me to where my father is?"

"The thugs—as you describe them—who were hired to kidnap you were told that you spoke Mandarin. Of those on our team, they obviously don't have the best memories. We don't want you to run Charlie. If you think that is where we are going, then the possibility of you running disappears— we hope. Again, the question—did you hear them say who had your father?"

"No. So are you going to tell me?"

"Not now Charlie." Mr. Liu signaled the others to stand. As they were leaving he said to Charlie, "please believe me, we are doing what is best for you and your father."

Charlie watched them as they walked down the hall.

"Wait a minute," he yelled. "Who the hell are you? And what right do you have to kidnap me and my father?" He started after them but only got a few feet before slamming into two sailors blocking his way. As he struggled to get past he heard Mr. Liu's angry voice in the distance. "That got us nowhere. We still have much to learn."

Chapter 18

Although Henry came to visit everyday, Charlie was losing patience—this kid wasn't giving anything up. And where was Zhiang Wan? Was he coming back? Had he really been spying on Charlie? Charlie remembered that Wan had not started at the beginning of the year but joined their class sometime in late fall. From his experience with the local culture, Charlie guessed he was not an expat kid. One of the basic rules for admission to the international school was ownership of an overseas passport. However, Charlie learned that in China, there were always exceptions—if you had enough *guanxi*.

Guanxi was a Chinese custom. The literal translation meant connectedness—who you knew or how much power your family had to get things done—legally or not. Charlie, along with most westerners, quickly learned that this was at the heart of most of the graft and corruption in China. And it wasn't only in business or government. The practice was common in the everyday lives of millions and millions of people.

Admitting someone like Wan to their class came as no surprise to anyone. It was rumored that the boy was the son of a high-ranking Communist Party member. The school's original charter was sponsored by the United States Embassy, but it was known that keeping the government happy was vital to keeping the school open. Thus, Wan got a place. He was reserved in class. During all the times he hung out with Charlie's group, he never revealed much about himself. What a scumbag, Charlie thought. We were his only friends. I sure hope there comes a time…

When the next visitor knocked on his cabin door it was a relief—this time no one came bursting in. When he opened the door to find Wan and Henry standing in the hallway, his first instinct was to slam the door shut. But he hesitated. They were smiling.

"Ready for a little outing Charlie? Time you stretched those legs and took in some of the beauty around here." Charlie didn't move.

"This time you get to see the sun. You look a little pooped after your adventure a few nights ago. Must have been kind of spooky." Charlie still didn't move. "Well, do you want to get out of this stink hole or what? We're not going to throw you overboard." Charlie wasn't surprised they knew he had searched the ship. Whether the doors were locked or unlocked, he still felt powerless. He was pissed at the way Wan was mocking him.

"You've got a lot of guts rat boy." Henry could see Charlie's body start to tense so he stepped between them, in case.

"Easy there, fellow Padawan," said Wan. "Let me explain. You thought I was a local with pull, right? Surprise. And wow, you sure speak good English, for a Chinaman. Right?" Charlie didn't know what to say.

"I came with my family the same as you did—here for a few years while my dad's company does it thing, and then home again."

"But there's more, isn't there?"

"There is," said Wan. "But that's for later. Come on, let's get out of here."

As they headed out Henry stepped between them to make sure things stayed under control. After walking through the maze of narrow, grimy corridors, then up three steep flights of stairs, Charlie began to smell fresh air. Two minutes later they were on the main deck. The river and the green walls of the gorge were a breathtaking contrast to the stink hole where he had spent the last week. Leaning over the rail, Charlie was mesmerized by the swirling black eddies, pushed to the side, as the boat plowed through the water. The river air was soothing but Charlie could not relax. He was still ready to explode.

"No more 'Wan' to you, Charlie my boy. Jerry's the name. Growing up in San Francisco helps a geak to speak English real good, don't you think?" Charlie didn't know what to say. Jerry continued, "Sorry Charlie. I know you're not the typical *laowai, gringo*, ugly American expat. I have to move on as soon as we dock and I have a lot to do before we arrive so, I'm leaving you all alone with Henry. He's driving me nuts with his English lessons. It's too bad you're mixed up in all this. Don't ask Henry or me for information because even we don't know the big picture. I think we can assure you that you and your dad are safe. After so much sacrifice by so many people, nothing can be left to chance. And don't even think of jumping over to escape. Those currents would suck you down to a place you don't want to go." Before Charlie could say another word, Jerry Zhiang was gone.

Chapter 19

Bill Zhiang was not a kid kind of person. He didn't have the time. Over the years, to Jerry's delight, that changed. The transformation started slowly. Jerry became a little human being with possibilities. Other dads could toss around a ball. Bill Zhiang designed computer systems while driving to work.

Jerry understood the implications of some emerging technologies better than some of his dad's employees. At the age of twelve, he asked his dad, "Can I drop out of school if I become a millionaire before I'm a teenager?" After laughing in astonishment, his dad considered the question. "An emphatic no." The scary thing for Bill Zhiang—Jerry was serious. It might be possible. The elder Zhiang could guess where the seed had been planted. As much as he wished to keep himself out of the public eye, the world at times was desperate to know his business. After seeing his father's face on the cover of *Fortune 500* magazine, Jerry better understood his father's fame. Not only did he own seven companies, but Bill Zhiang was thought to be one of the ten richest men in the world.

"Jerry, I haven't done a very good job and the school you attend hasn't done any job at all teaching you the responsibility we all share in using technology. It's not about making money. It's not about technology for technology's sake. I was lucky to go schools where innovation and creativity were everything, but developing a social conscience was not. Do you know what I'm talking about? "

"I'm not sure. Don't you love what you do?"

"Yes, very much."

"Do you think people like what you do?"

"Yes, absolutely."

"Is what you do important?" Bill Zhiang was taken aback at hearing such unexpected insight from his son.

"Yes, Jerry, I think what I do, and what the people I work with do, is extremely important. But what I am saying…" And here Jerry found his dad at a loss for words. They were on a veranda looking out over the city. Minutes passed.

"I may not be the best role model about this subject Jerry. You know we lead a privileged lifestyle – the houses, the jet, the yacht, etc. This is not the way most people live. I always thought money was a well-deserved by-product of a person's hard work and energy.

"The world faces many challenges. I thought what I was doing and what the company was doing—helping people communicate more effectively—was an admirable thing to do."

"But Dad, it is."

"I know it is Jerry. But there is so much more we can do. I was sidetracked for a while, but now, with all the resources I have, with all the energy I can find, I will help bring about positive changes for the Chinese people. Now go back to work, we'll talk later. And stop dreaming about becoming a millionaire." His dad ended this conversation with such finality that Jerry knew it was no use prying any further—at least not now.

Changes in China—what did that mean? Must have to do with business. Jerry tried to remember the few things his dad had shared about growing up in China before coming to the United States. He asked his mother numerous times for more information but she always deflected his questions by telling him to ask his dad. Once, after continual harping, his mother broke down.

"Your dad's family lived through a horrifying time in China. His father died in prison and his whole family was accused of being traitors. All their property was taken—it was a terrible, terrible time. You need to study the Cultural Revolution Jerry—there's lots of information on the Internet. I am sure someday he will tell you the whole story. I hope this is enough for now."

On the day Bill Zhiang asked them how they would feel about moving to Shanghai, Rita Zhiang was ready. She knew from all his recent travels and their discussions that a move was very possible. She loved their previous visits and knew she could easily adapt. But how would Jerry feel about the disruption to their lives? She might have guessed. As long as his dad was there she had nothing to worry about. And maybe now Bill Zhiang would share more about his life with his son.

The job his company was doing for the Chinese government was important and worth billions. They would be gone two years, maybe more, but they would keep their home in the States. One night Jerry overheard his dad tell his mom that the company's work would have an impact far beyond what the government bargained for. What did that mean? The move also held out hope that they would have more time together.

Other than *you stink, hello* or *good-bye,* Jerry knew very few words in Chinese. His dad knew the language. His mom did not. Jerry seldom heard it spoken at home. The Zhiangs thought Shanghai would be a great place for him to learn.

Jerry's initial excitement dimmed in the first few months, before they had packed a single bag. Things were going the wrong way. His dad was gone for longer and more frequent trips. Top-level meetings took him repeatedly to China and to other cities in the States. The only consolation was their nightly teleconference. Having such a high tech father meant a nightly chat with the family on a wall-sized flat screen.

"Hi Honey, how are you? Are you getting enough to eat? Are you sleeping? Do you miss us?" His mom was such a mom. Jerry had other things on his mind.

"What are all the meetings about?"

"Just business." Bill Zhiang knew that wasn't enough for his son.

"Very big, very exciting business." One night, after Jerry's unrelenting pressure, his dad let it slip.

"The Olympics. We are playing a major role in helping China bring the Olympics to the world." That opened the floodgates. The company was positioning itself to become the most important telecommunications presence in all of Asia. At times, the big picture shown so brightly that the details weren't important. Jerry's greatest hope was that he would get to see a lot more of his dad. No worries there, promised the elder Zhiang. For the past half decade, he always kept his son close to the action – if only by high tech means. Jerry always wanted more. His dad promised. Jerry also had high hopes for his new school – another promise. Please, he thought, pleasse let it be a thousand times more challenging than the private, over rated school I'm sleeping walking through now.

Chapter 20

"Don't ask me. I don't know very much about Jerry. I have nothing to tell you." Henry said, expecting Charlie's next question. "I only came for English practice. Do you still want to help me? We will be docking tomorrow and I have big test next week."

"You're in school right now?"

"What, you think Chinese boys just loaf around? Of course I am in school. I am only on this boat trip to help with you."

"With me? What does that mean?"

"You find out later."

Charlie was so full of questions he could barely concentrate. At least the deck of the boat was a whole lot better than being cooped up below.

Charlie put this line of questioning aside for a minute. "Weren't you worried that I might try to escape?"

"You didn't. Why would you do that when you know we are taking you to your father? Where would you go? And what were you looking for the night you snooped around the ship?" No reason not to tell him, Charlie thought. They had probably guessed.

"My dad. Is he on this ship?"

"That is what you were looking for? Sorry Charlie. If you ask, I save you a lot of time." Henry shook his head as he opened a book. Charlie didn't want to believe him, but he did. Now he felt more helpless than ever.

"Hello, my name is Henry. I wish to discuss China's foreign policy. What is your name?" Charlie ground his teeth so hard he could barely make out Henry's words.

"Stop. I'll coach you as much as you like if you tell me one thing."

"I cannot say Charlie, but ask me."

"Why was Jerry in my class?"

“That is easy. He was there to spy on you—or maybe not. They did not tell me. But you not worry about that right now. I do not know for sure the truth. Maybe he was there… just because.

“Just because why? How is he connected? Who is his family? Why is he here?”

"He said he was in China like you and any other expat students. Anything beyond that I do not know and if I did, I would not tell you.” Charlie decided to go for broke. Henry hadn’t stormed away and Charlie knew he wanted to continue practicing his English.

“Last question—are they going to kill me and my dad?”

“You said only one question, but okay. To be truthful, I do not know. I believe what Jerry said. I do not think so. This is all the answers I will tell you, and only because I know the equipment they bought to bug you not working, for now. Cheap stuff they bought at one of the electronics markets. Idiots.”

“You mean I have bugs on me? Listening to what we’re saying?”

“No, no. Like I said, they not working. No worries.” Henry smiled as Charlie started patting himself down, trying to find the bugs.

“You never find them. Not working anyway. Last thing. I know none of us knows everything. To keep us all safe, any person involved only knows what they need to know right now.”

“You've got to be kidding. But...”

“No but. That is all. I told you. No more.” Charlie could see Henry was getting worked up.

“Okay, whatever, let’s practice.” Although his heart wasn’t in it, he worked with Henry for a solid hour. Charlie thought he believed Henry about the bugs, but he couldn’t help searching himself. As Henry began to leave, he looked at Charlie.

“Don’t have to look for bugs. Just kidding. Good one, yes?” Charlie couldn’t help but smile. “Yeah sure, good one.”

“Serious. If you know anything about the Red Spears, it is very important to tell them.”

“You too?” Charlie sighed.

“Yes, me too. You cannot believe how important that we know what you know, if anything. You got three questions. I have one.”

“Okay, one last time. I told Mr. Liu the nitty-gritty, but even with all the details, there’s not much more.”

“What is nitty-gritty?”

"The most important thing, the heart of the matter. You understand?" Henry nodded. In only a half-hearted way, Charlie went through it again.

"Like I told Mr. Liu, I love hero stories. Especially where the heroes are so right and those in power so rotten. The people in this country have suffered through decades of brutal warlords, lying, cheating government officials, and corrupt Party members. It didn't matter who was in charge. There was always someone to make the lives of the people miserable." Charlie was surprised how Henry settled down to listen.

"The Red Spears came from a very poor group of villagers who lived in the mountains and marshlands in central China. They were sick and tired of being treated like dirt. When all the work on the Grand Canal ended there wasn't much for them to do. They had no place they could call home. Like Gypsies, they roamed the land and were hated for their backwardness and nomadic lifestyle.

When they found their calling as bandits, they were not only able to help themselves, but many others as well. It was a time when places like Shanghai were beginning to thrive. Thousands of these people were finding their way to the big city to work as coolies, transport workers, or prostitutes.

"Farmers, shopkeepers, and factory workers, were all threatened at times if they didn't pay protection money. They said it was for taxes or license fees. It was all the same—a way to steal money from the people. If someone couldn't pay, they figured out a way—sometimes a percentage of a farmer's crops, or kidnapping a family member to work off the debt. To make a point, they wouldn't hesitate to cut off a hand, or even a leg—sometimes, much worse. People were in constant fear. Even the police, who were supposed to protect them, were scared into doing the dirty work for these 'officials.'"

Charlie was surprised at the number of times Henry interrupted. "I hate this. People struggle for long time, but so little changes." Charlie wondered if he should stop, but Henry wouldn't let him.

"Please, tell the rest. This sounds like what is still happening today." With such a willing audience, Charlie felt himself just getting warmed up.

"The Red Spears continued to be a thorn in the side of whatever government officials were in power. They robbed the rich and gave back to the people. Over the years, sadly enough, they became corrupt by the power they wielded. By the time Mao was on the rise, the reason for the

Red Spears no longer existed. Many were easily recruited into the Chinese Communist Party." Charlie paused again to see if Henry was satisfied.

"You are good history teacher, Charlie. Like today—too much corruption, too much power. People are still led. No vote, no power." Charlie was surprised to hear this from Henry, especially about matters concerning the government. Truthfully, he had no idea what to expect from this kid.

"Maybe change coming Charlie. Someday the people win. Maybe sooner than later."

Charlie had one more thing to add. "This piece of history wasn't even important to what I was trying to find out. The history and the name were interesting but it was of no use to my report so I dropped it."

Charlie wondered what was going through Henry's mind as he sat quietly for another minute. "Thank you Charlie. Time to go back." Abruptly, without another word, he took the lead in escorting Charlie back to his cabin. Charlie stopped before opening his door.

"Are you locking me in again?"

"No reason. Can you think of a reason?

"I guess not."

"Like Mr. Liu said, you are not prisoner. We are taking you to safety. Same reason you were told not to open any doors—did you?"

"Honestly? I tried, but none opened."

"Good for you they did not. Tomorrow we practice again, that right? Okay. Good night." Charlie was relieved to hear that their lessons would continue—maybe he still had a shot. With so many questions left hanging, it looked like another long, restless, night.

Chapter 21

Ominous words about a plot and the sacrifice of many people added up to what? What had Henry given away in his reaction to Charlie's story about the Red Spears? For a minute, Charlie tried to fit everything into a much bigger picture. Yes, his science project and yes, the river—but why now? The Olympics were fast approaching and the world would soon be at China's doorstep—the river and the Olympics? And all these people organized and working together on what—with no one person knowing the big picture? Why had Henry let that slip?

Charlie was desperate to sleep. He had to stop thinking about it. Lights on, off—it didn't matter. Before he had time to hit the switch, he was out. Hours later, the lights started mysteriously flickering. The boat was slowing down. He could feel docking procedures begin. Five minutes later the engines shut down. Charlie listened nervously to the sound of doors opening and closing. The noise of chaos—people yelling, a million horns blasting—filtered down to his room. They had to be way past Wuhan, and maybe up to Chongqing. Chongqing had a big harbor, but he couldn't remember going through the temporary locks. Was it possible? He couldn't have slept that long. Were they now at the foot of the dam? Charlie prepared himself for the door to fly open. Nothing. After a few minutes he stepped into the passageway and was almost knocked down. Crewmen rushing in either direction sped past. If there was any chance to escape, this was the moment. The only thing that made him stay was the revelation that he was being taken to where his dad was. But what if that was something they intended him to hear? Charlie was beginning to wear himself out thinking of all the possible scenarios.

Leaving his door unlocked still didn't make sense, but he was extremely curious where they were. If these people believed he wouldn't run, then a stroll on deck wouldn't matter. He stepped into the passageway, kept pace with the traffic, then vaulted up the three sets of stairs to the main deck.

The early morning darkness was lifting. The dam was nowhere in sight. From all directions, city lights and lights from far across the river sparkled and danced on the water. The air was warm but not fresh. With no attempt to conceal his movements, Charlie moved around, exploring, like he belonged there. At one point he looked up to the ship's bridge and saw Jerry, Henry, and Mr. Liu looking out. They were sipping something that steamed, and probably having breakfast. I'd sure like something hot, and something good for breakfast, for a change. And I'd sure like to be off this dammed boat and home with my family. What right did these people have, whoever they were, to grab him and his dad?

Keeping an eye on his hosts, he walked toward them until he was almost under the bridge. Why not pay them a surprise visit? Could he get that far? They had left his door unlocked and already knew he'd been searching the ship. No harm now in taking a little walk up to the bridge. Maybe he would overhear something useful. He might even get a cup of something hot to drink.

In the few minutes he had been on deck, the face of the cliffs began to lighten. The beauty of the chiseled stone was breathtaking. The bedlam of the boats and people, in the shadow of this beauty, was China. Charlie had lived in the Middle Kingdom over half his life and scenes like this always had an emotional impact on him. Despite it all—the threatening political climate, and the color of his skin — it always felt like he was home when his family returned to China from their visits to the States.

At the foot of the bridge, Charlie grabbed onto the handrails and quietly climbed the steep stairs. They might have good reason to believe he wouldn't run, so letting him have his freedom was a no brainer—and maybe they would earn some trust. But would the same be true if they suspected his stealth in being able to eavesdrop on a private conversation? He had to be quiet. The door to the bridge said *RESTRICTED, SHIP PERSONNEL ONLY.* He could hear conversation inside. The ship had completed docking and no one was there except Jerry, Henry, and Mr. Liu. He quietly slipped in, held his breath, and kneeled down in a hidden alcove.

Chapter 22

"I think he is telling the truth," Henry said.

"And you Jerry?" Mr. Liu asked.

"Same. Why would he lie? What else can we do?"

"He will be questioned one last time, to make sure. Neither of you will be part of that interrogation." Charlie froze. He tried to control his breathing. He hoped they couldn't hear his heart banging against his chest. The banging grew louder with Mr. Liu's next statement.

"He and his father will not be going back." Before Mr. Liu could elaborate, someone with a death grip picked Charlie up by the neck and asked, "Does this cockroach belong in here?"

"What a resourceful young man you are Charlie," Mr. Liu said.

"You bastard, you lying bastard—all of you. You are going to kill us?" Charlie tried to spin loose of the man's grip but it was clamped on tightly. The more he struggled, the greater the pain.

"Resourceful and dramatic," Jerry said. "I wonder how long he's been there."

Mr. Liu added, "It won't be long Charlie. But now, for your own safety, we must again lock your door." Charlie's struggle lasted only a few seconds. When the pain from the man's grip became unbearable, he collapsed. By the time the seaman got him back to his cabin he was wrung out.

Early the next morning the ship's engines fired back to life. Before his visit to the bridge he was intrigued and wanted to know more about Jerry and Henry. Now he knew all he wanted to know. The disclosure that he and his dad would not be going back and that he was to face another, more frightening interrogation, filled his head with multiple escape plans.

His planning ended abruptly when the cabin door flew open and two sailors entered. Charlie was standing at the toilet.

"Don't you know how to knock?"

"Sorry, sorry, get ready, time to go." Charlie could see smirks, but their amusement gave him the second he needed to pretend he was going along. A quick zip then a lightning knee to the groin of the sailor closest to him. The next move found his elbow in the other man's face and a two-step lead as he ran out the door. A third sailor was waiting in the hallway. He grabbed Charlie in the same spot he had been grabbed the day before and Charlie dropped like a ruptured tire.

"You want some of this again? I can pinch right through if you want." The shoulder muscle was still sore from the day before and this time Charlie nearly passed out from the pain. He could barely whisper. "Let go, please let go. I'll stop."

"I know you will. Now, quiet and no move."

Things wouldn't be the same now with these men. After what he had heard they would certainly consider him a flight risk. Not only were Charlie's hands tied behind his back, but he was blindfolded and gagged as well. After being guided to an exit ramp, he was placed in a wheelbarrow, covered with a tarp, and rolled down a short gang plank into the back of a waiting truck, similar to the one he had endured in Shanghai. This time, there was nothing but silence on a grueling three-hour ride over unpaved roads. Charlie was sure these men wouldn't make the same mistakes his first captors made—no more conversation in a language they knew he understood.

When the truck finally stopped, they continued on foot along a slippery path Charlie found nearly impossible to navigate blindfolded. After several painful falls, the two men lifted and dragged him the rest of the way. When they finally stopped, his blindfold and gag were removed. The relief was immediate, not only to be outside the dungeon environment of the ship, but now, to be overlooking the river from a breathtaking vantage point.

"Undo his hands. He is not going anywhere," an old man instructed them. "When was the last time he ate?"

Charlie answered the man in Chinese. "Not since last night, *Shen shen*." The man turned to Charlie.

"Well then, sit. I will share what I am preparing for dinner." When he walked the men outside Charlie overheard them ask if he could hide the boy for a few days, until final preparations were in place.

"He will not be a problem."

"They wanted us to interrogate him one more time to see if he left anything out, but we did not have time. Will you do it?"

"Not in the way you mean, but I will try."

"Trying will not help. We must know for sure." Charlie could tell from the old man's response that he disagreed with what the men wanted him to do.

"I will do what can be done. I will not say it again." In the few minutes Charlie had to himself, he made a mental note of his surroundings. The old man's hut was precariously set on an avalanche of rocks, hundreds of feet above the river. He had a vague idea where he was but the landscape was unfamiliar. The hut had only one room, no electricity, and the walls were old boards that looked like they'd started life in a dynasty long ago. The one and only window faced the river and was used to vent smoke from the stove. Coal pellets were neatly stacked inside the door and their sulfurous smell permeated the room.

From the day he had arrived in China, the smell of coal had lingered in Charlie's nostrils. It was the primary source of energy for all of China and one of the most often used arguments for erecting the new dam. The sulfuric acid that burning coal emitted helped create seventeen of the twenty most polluted cities in the world—all in China. The dam would help produce cleaner energy.

"They are afraid you will run away." The old man said, as he entered the hut. "You are safe here, so please, do not run. I know treatment by your captors has varied at times but was based on their perception of you as a flight risk."

"*Shen Shen*, that is the second time someone has talked to me about my safety. Can you tell me why I was not safe in Shanghai?"

"I am sorry son. I cannot. Tell me you will not run." The tone in the man's voice was more than a polite suggestion. It had an urgency that Charlie knew he needed to honor. "I will not run, but will you tell me more than the others about why I am here?"

"Probably not. I have rice and a few vegetables and earlier, friends stopped by with some chicken. It will be ready in a few minutes. Sit and tell me how you came to speak Chinese so well."

"What is your name *shen shen*?"

"Call me Wang." Charlie knew that was like being called Smith in America. It was probably disrespectful for him to ask. The old man was as mysterious as the others, but there was a kindness about him that put Charlie at ease. Then he saw the sling on the wall.

"Were you a tracker, Mr. Wang?"

"The man turned from what he was doing and looked at Charlie. "How did you know?"

"The tracker sling on your wall, the scars all over your neck and arms, and your muscles. You were a tracker, one of the river men who did one of the most dangerous jobs on Earth." Charlie said, with great admiration.

"And again young man you surprise me. I think we have much to talk about. Please sit. The food is ready." Wang took two plates and served each of them rice, vegetables, and the chicken he had stirred up in an old, blackened wok.

Charlie started to tell Mr. Wang about his education in Beijing and Shanghai but he was famished. After inhaling the food Mr. Wang had set out he noticed that Mr. Wang had not yet begun to eat. Charlie set his chopsticks down, knowing how rude he had been.

"Do not feel bad Charlie. I know hunger is something you are not used to and you must be very hungry. If you eat each bite slowly, your hunger will stay away longer. This is all I have to offer."

"Thanks Mr. Wang." Charlie then began to balance what he ate with what he had to tell the old man. The small plate of food lasted over an hour. By the time they finished, Charlie had told Mr. Wang about the local and international schools he had attended, and his family's reason for being in China.

"You are a bright young man Charlie and I am grateful to have such interesting company. You are one of the few Western people to ever set foot in my home. I am sorry it has to be under such strained circumstances. Your reserve and insight are most impressive." With this comment, Charlie felt disarmed—he was desperate to know more.

"You have many questions, justifiably, but you have spared me retelling answers you have already heard. Many of us have a role to play in rapidly unfolding events. For our own safety, and for the safety of our families and friends, none of us can know all the parts." With this, Charlie lost some of his reserve.

“My mom…” and that was all Mr. Wang would permit Charlie to say.

“I am not surprised by your inquiry. I have been told about the closeness of your family. Of all the questions you have been forming, this one deserves an answer. She is safe Charlie. All of you are now safe.” Charlie’s mind went off again. Did this mean she had been kidnapped as well?

“I heard them say that me and my dad don’t get to go back. What about my mom? And why can't we go back?" Mr. Wang stopped the stream of questions again by holding up his hand. “You and your family are not in any danger from us. You must believe me.” He said it with such finality that Charlie knew he would get nothing else from Mr. Wang. But what did that mean, *from us*?

“Please tell me about your life as a tracker. We learned a little bit about them in one of my classes but I never thought I’d get to meet one.”

“Yes, Charlie, thank you. Mr. Wang poured them each another cup of tea and then sat back and looked at Charlie. “For generations, the men in my family have hauled boats up river against these rapids. Sometimes a hundred, sometimes as many as two hundred men were assigned to use slings like these to pull ships as heavy as 120 tons up some of the most dangerous parts of the river. Very few of the men married. They knew the life of a tracker was short. Only a few of the fools dared to have children.” Charlie looked at a photo standing on a small table and then looked at Mr. Wang. “Yes, Charlie, I was one of the fools. Those are only three of my five children.”

“I thought, with the one child rule…”

“That law came into effect long after I had had my children. Life as a tracker was hard and destined to die out – children or not—with the building of dams, better transportation to cities upriver, and so on.” Charlie hesitated, but the next question was a logical one.

“Where is your family now?”

“They are all dead Charlie. But we will …” Before he could go on, Mr. Wang hesitated, as if what he was about to say was forbidden.

"Almost all of them died Charlie, all but one—a grandson. No one could believe a tracker would outlive most of his family. No one.” Charlie looked at him and waited.

“As I said, many could see that our way of life was destined to end. My oldest daughter worked hard to get an education in spite of many obstacles. In mid-May, 1989, she and her husband were so excited to tell us of something important happening in Beijing. We were frightened when they left to attend an enormous rally in the capital city. We knew little of democracy or a new government. We did know how the CCP treated troublemakers. She told us this was different, that the government would have to listen. She told us there were a million people in Tiananmen Square. She told us it was filled with students, workers, peasants, and people wishing to practice their religious beliefs. After what was happening in Eastern Europe, the world was watching, and the government would have to listen.

"A month passed and we had no word from her or my son-in-law. One day an official came to tell us to claim their bodies. There were many dead and they tried to tell us they were trying to do what was humane. We knew the truth. There was no way the government could explain such a massive grave to the world without acknowledging that a massacre had occurred. So they said come get the body or it would be burned.

"As we were leaving the building where the bodies were stored a nurse rushed up to us with the most startling news. Outstretched in her hands was a small bundle, a tiny baby wrapped in a heavy wool blanket. My daughter had been many months pregnant and this brave nurse, noticing my daughter's condition, risked her life to deliver the baby. She kept it a secret for weeks, hoping relatives would come to claim the body and the child. After a quick explanation of what had happened she rushed away, crying, trying to avoid any unwanted attention. Before she left she asked one thing.

"Promise me that this life will help give meaning to all this destruction." We never found out her name to thank her. We were told to never discuss what had happened or we would suffer more. And that was all. It went without saying that my grandson's identity would need to stay hidden.

"Do you know of the tragedy at Tiananmen Square Charlie?" Charlie nodded his head.

"It is called the *living lie*."

"Yes, Charlie, that is correct. This is all very sad. Do you wish me to continue?"

"It must be very painful for you Mr. Wang. I would like to know more, but only if you feel up to it. Can you tell me what happened to your grandson? Did you raise him?"

"Again, your father and mother would be proud to know they had raised such a kind hearted son. Yes, I can go on. It is the greatest pain of my life, but it is my life. I would like to pass it on to someone who can take the story outside this village. But of my grandson I cannot speak. All I can tell you is that we kept our promise to that nurse. He has been raised to give meaning to the death of his parents."

When Mr. Wang's story came to an end, having recalled the deaths of his children and wife, Charlie felt his eyes moisten. Mr. Wang reached out to hold Charlie's arms in his leather beaten grip. "No tears, Charlie. We are beyond that. If we succeed in what we have set out to do, they will not have died in vain. Please rest now. I am going for a few supplies." As he left, he turned to look at Charlie.

"I promised. I will not run."

"Thank you son. It is for your own good. Please believe me." Charlie still couldn't help thinking about Mr. Wang's grandson and what had become of him. In Communist China's tightly controlled communal and village systems, there was no way a child could accidentally appear without a reason.

Chapter 23

Charlie strained to see more of the river, but the window was too small. Mr. Wang didn't say he couldn't go outside. After finding a large, flat rock, Charlie made himself comfortable. The view was spectacular. With the sound of the water's roar, and the whirling of a million thoughts, he didn't hear the two men sneak up behind him. Pain ripped through his body after one of them grabbed him by the neck. A spasmodic jolt wrenched him free of the man's grip and sent him reeling. The only thing that kept him from flying into the river was the other man's desperate grab for one of Charlie's arms.

"You were told not to run."

As soon as Charlie planted both feet on the ground, he braced himself in case they tried to grab him again. "I didn't run, I was…" This time Charlie was ready. When one of them ran at him he had no problem landing a smashing kick to the man's face. As the attacker reeled backwards, his buddy rammed Charlie's mid-section, driving them both into the cabin.

"You big ape, let me go. Get off!" Charlie's words were an instant, frightened mix of Chinese and English. Before the man had a chance to recover, Charlie banged the sides of the man's head with the heel of each hand. The man rolled to the side, dazed, giving Charlie time to regain his feet. Before he had a chance to get out and run, the other man dragged himself into the cabin. Again, Charlie tried to plant a foot in the man's face but this time he grabbed Charlie's leg and pulled him close enough to give Charlie a blinding head butt. In that stunned instant, both men grabbed hold, wrestled him down, and tied him to a chair. "Now we start again," one of them said, as Charlie was shuffled to the table.

But Charlie wasn't done.

As soon as he shook the pain out of his head, he stood straight up still lashed to the chair and started swinging it like a weapon. One of the men caught a chair leg to the chest and screamed when he saw blood spurting down his shirt. The other man was now blocking the door and Charlie found himself backed into a corner. He turned sideways with the chair, ready to smash away if the men stepped toward him again. The speed of his big, ugly assailants took him by surprise as they sprang to grab whatever they could of the chair. With unwavering grips, this time they had him, and the chair. As they spun him around, their punches started landing with deadly accuracy. Limp, in more pain than he could ever remember, Charlie barely had the strength to look up. For a second time, they forced him to sit at the table.

"What do you want?" Charlie whispered.

"Shut up. I bet old Wang didn't get any information out of you."

"About the Red Spears?"

"Yes, about the Red Spears," the man said, grabbing a cloth to stop his bleeding chest.

"I told Mr. Liu everything I knew. Do you want me to tell you again?"

"No more lies. You know much more. One last chance – what do you know about the Red Spears?" Charlie's body shuddered with pain as he told them exactly what he had told Mr. Liu. They could see Charlie trying to sit up, get control, but they were in no mood for Charlie Evers. More wicked slaps and Charlie felt like his face was on fire. When he was able to focus, one of the men clenched Charlie's head in his hands and moved within inches of his face. The man's cheeks and nose were badly scarred and his breath reeked. Charlie didn't know what to say next. Then he saw what the men were doing. His left arm was tied behind the chair. His right hand was strapped down on a piece of wood. All fingers were tied together except the pinky, which was isolated, flat, by itself. When the man pulled out a meat cleaver and ran his finger over its edge, Charlie understood perfectly what was happening.

"Don't, please, I told you everything I know. I promise." Charlie began to feel light-headed, nauseous. He thought he was about to lose control of his bladder.

"Brave boy," the man said as he raised the meat cleaver. "One finger, maybe two. Let's see how many it takes." Charlie started to scream. "One last chance boy," the man rasped. Charlie could feel spit hitting his forehead. Even if he had something new to add, he couldn't have said it in time. Moments before the blade was lowered, Charlie heard a war cry. He looked up in time to see Mr. Wang swing a fist that caught both men at once. As the blade flew out of the one man's hand, he stumbled sideways. The other attacker crashed to his back. Mr. Wang reached down to grab each man by an ankle and then drag them outside. Charlie knew Mr. Wang had to be strong but the way he handled these two goons was something else. When he looked out the small window, he could see both men held out over the river, flapping like a couple of mackerel about to be returned to their home. Above the swiftly moving current, Mr. Wang's voice rang out in a fury.

"We are not like them. We will not be like them. Our revolution will never succeed if we stoop to their level."

"What revolution, old man?" one of the men yelled. "If we cannot hide what we are doing, or get information from one teenage boy, how can we hope to succeed?" The other man followed with, "If we don't have the courage to do what is necessary, nothing will change." When Mr. Wang could see his words were not having any effect he reeled them back in. After they were dropped on the rocks next to the hut, he told them to come inside for tea. Charlie thought this was a bizarre show of mercy. Predictably, they ran off, continuing to yell something about what a useless, crazy old man he was.

"Humble apologies, Charlie. It is a good thing they only have minor responsibilities. Both have suffered great losses like many of us. The wisdom of dividing up our roles is again clear." Mr. Wang untied Charlie and let him compose himself. "Breathe deeply. Sit up straight if you can. You are safe. Unfortunately, I have learned that you will have to be moved sooner than expected. Tonight will be your only night with me. I will miss getting to know more about my friend Charlie Evers." After calming down, and not only out of politeness, Charlie replied, "I would have liked that."

"Promise me something Charlie, something an old man can look forward to. Promise me that if we are successful, you will visit me again someday, along with your mother and father. I would like to meet them as well."

"I wish I knew more to be able to keep such a promise. If there is a way, you have my word."

"That is good enough. Tomorrow is an important day." Charlie was on the verge of asking Mr. Wang why, but he didn't. After the sun went down, with his stomach somewhat full, and his wounds looked after, he was content to listen to the sound of the river.

Chapter 24

Morning arrived in the damp river cabin long before Charlie was ready for it. He hadn't bathed in over a week. After catching a whiff of himself, he longed for a hot shower. The itching from the clothes he had worn everyday—and whatever had crawled into them—was nothing compared to the leftover pain from his attackers. Muscles Charlie didn't know he had were cramping with exposure to the early morning chill.

"It is time to go Charlie," Mr. Wang whispered, as he gently rocked Charlie's shoulder. "I have packed you some food in case they forget to feed you again. You are on the last leg of your journey, the one that will reunite you with your father. The two men outside are not the two you encountered yesterday so do not worry. They promise to treat you well." After Mr. Wang handed him a cup of hot tea, Charlie asked for a minute to wake up. He let the cup warm his hands. When Mr. Wang stood, Charlie knew it was time.

"Be well son. Safe journey. And remember your promise. It gives this old man something to look forward to."

"I won't forget Mr. Wang." As Charlie turned before stepping outside, the old man pressed Charlie's hands together in his. The strong, reassuring grip reminded Charlie of a similar protected feeling he had felt once before — from his mom and dad.

After all he had been through in the past week—especially with the beating and near loss of his fingers—Charlie Evers was not the same kid who had relied on the safety of a world he once took for granted. Although the strength of Mr. Wang's grip quickly evaporated in the damp morning air, Charlie felt stronger and ready to face the next leg of his journey.

With no time to waste, he was led down a path to the river. A slightly transformed, aging cabin cruiser was waiting for him. Charlie was amazed with what looked like a rickety old pile of junk, sprang to life on the water. He was almost content to watch the river as the boat sped to the West if only his handcuffs hadn't been clamped on so tightly. With the hum of the engine and the sound of the wind, it was impossible to get either of the men's attention to loosen them. One of them was in the open bow of the boat, and the other, Charlie thought, had to be on the bridge. He would have to deal with the pain.

Refocus. His thoughts drifted back—what could have ripped he and his dad away from their life so suddenly. The research for his class project obviously had something to do with this—the river, the Internet, the Red Spears, the dam… democracy? Ideas, arguments, rants and raves, poured in from around the world. Charlie was spellbound. Bringing down the current government, which sounded ludicrous to Charlie at first, began to sound like a surreal possibility.

At first, the words Mr. Fathom had planted in his head—*endangering state security, spreading rumors, and subverting state security*—scared him to the sidelines. Without a doubt, they would come for him. Watch and read. Stay safe. Research the river. Charlie said these things to himself again and again. Watch and read. Stay safe. Research the river. His mantra started to evolve, and then began to lose strength. He wished Mr. Fathom had still been there. He was a cat and curiosity was his killer.

Over the years, some of the politics he and his dad talked about were vague. Many times a discussion ended with his dad promising more information later. The later was now. Charlie wished his dad had been home to help pull more of it together. The research was becoming a means to a different end. The assignment began to feel more like a mission than a school project. The game at the dinner table—playing the devils advocate—Charlie decided to bring to a larger audience—a much larger audience.

Boldly he had typed, "what would happen if someone blew up the Yangtze dam? Could the dam withstand a major earthquake? What if the turbines became clogged? These kinds of questions were safe at the dinner table, but in the real world? In China? When his questions flashed on the screen, he knew he had stepped in from the sideline.

Chapter 25

It was 2 a.m. when someone started pounding on Jill Evers's front door.

"Charlie," she whispered, as she threw on her robe and ran to the door. Please let it be you and your father." Her face fell when the only people on her front porch were two uniformed PSB. A third waited behind the wheel of a black, unmarked car.

"Do you have word of my husband and son?"

"Yes, you come with us now."

"Do you have them? Do you know where they were taken?"

"You get dressed. Come with us."

"Please answer my questions."

"Too many questions now. You come with us." This isn't right, she said to herself.

"Please wait a minute while I get dressed." She raced back to her bedroom and grabbed a phone next to the bed. They aren't taking me anywhere until I call the American Embassy. Jill Evers kept the number in her cell but as soon as she unlocked the phone, a hand grabbed her arm.

"No time, we must go now." Still holding onto her wrist, the cop handed her a coat he had taken from a closet by the front door. Jill yanked her arm free, planted her feet, and glared at the man. "I'm not going anywhere until I call the American Embassy." The officer grabbed her around the waist, held her on his hip, and started to carry her out. He had not anticipated the screaming and wrestling, flying elbows and weapon like fingernails. He was battered, bloody, and greatly relieved when he was finally able to get her outside and into a police car. As they started to back up, a beat up old taxi pulled behind them. In that split second, Jill ripped free from her captors and jumped out of the car. The driver sprang after her and with one quick lunge, caught her by the ankle. The other policemen were about to jump out, when a dozen hooded men sprang from behind bushes, pointing guns at the stunned policemen.

"Who the hell are you?" she asked. Jill Evers had never seen guns in the hands of anyone except PLA soldiers.

"Face down, all of you, on the ground. Now! Not you Ms. Evers." The PSB were handcuffed, pushed back into their car, then driven away by two of the hooded men.

"Get in Mrs. Evers. We have no time to lose and no time to explain. You are safe, as are both your son and husband."

"Who are you? How do I know I can trust you? Maybe you're the ones who kidnapped my husband and son."

"We are, Mrs. Evers." Before she could speak, one of them handed her a piece of paper with one word written on it—*Homer*. It was an agreed on code between she and her husband. It meant she should trust whatever situation was at hand. At the time John Evers had suggested it, she thought he had read too many spy novels. She grabbed the paper and held it to her chest.

Chapter 26

Henry was not good at waiting. His father still wasn't home—time for another quick stroll past the bathroom? No stopping to spy this time. He told his mom he was going to the market for an ice cream. "Only if you get me one too." She tried to be the stern one in the family, the one who did not endorse unhealthy food, but Henry knew she loved ice cream. "You are a wise guy," she said, meaning not smart, but in a clever way.

On his walk through the village, he suddenly spotted one of them. He didn't recognize the man's face, but from the work suit and the strange piece of machinery, there was no mistake. Henry slowed down, gave the workman some distance, and tried to be inconspicuous. Instead of going to the public toilet, the man wasted little time shuffling down streets that lead out of town, toward the bend in the river. Glancing several times over his shoulder, the man hurried to a forested area. He stopped next to a tree, looked in every direction, and then flipped up what looked like a manhole cover. After lowering himself into the hole, Henry heard a scraping sound as the cover was lowered. When Henry tiptoed to the spot, he could see that it had been painstakingly camouflaged. Although the thought crossed his mind, there was no way was he going to risk a trip down that hole. Not now. Now he had to buy the ice cream he had promised his mother. His father would be home soon and Henry would show him everything.

A few days later, when his mother told him that his dad had been delayed for at least another week, Henry began to imagine other possibilities. Although his courage wavered, his curiosity was making him crazy. On the first moonless night, he was ready.

Flashlight, rope, and a pocketknife—just in case. After scouting the area, he felt safe enough to approach the hidden entrance. He pulled open the iron hatch and was relieved to find a rope ladder already in place. The climb down was easy and the area he entered was not entirely black. Light was coming from a tunnel to his right. To his left, another tunnel looked much less hospitable. Slowly, he crept along the edge of the friendlier looking one, sliding his hands over the slippery rocks to balance himself. Within a hundred yards the light became brighter and the air warmer. Henry could now see his footing and the walls of the tunnel. He was exposed—nowhere to hide. It didn't matter. He wasn't about to return empty handed.

He tried to imagine how proud his father would be after seeing his son's amazing discovery. Although, it struck Henry how strange it would be for this thing to exist without his father's knowledge. If his father did know about the tunnels...a shiver ran through him. Would he be in big trouble? His parents had warned him many times about sticking his nose in where it didn't belong. Too much thinking—he had to concentrate. Quietly, hugging one of the walls like a shadow, he moved closer. Once he discovered what this was, he would figure out the best way to reveal what he had found. His father would be impressed.

Before he had time to take another step, beams of light flooded the tunnel. Voices suddenly echoed off every surface as they raced toward him. More lights ahead. Henry stumbled backwards, caught himself, then ran like he had never run before. Several times he slipped and smashed his knees and hands. Fear exploded in his chest as he cursed himself for being such a nosey idiot. The lights were coming faster and Henry prayed he had enough of a lead to get to the rope ladder before he was caught. He had to stay on his feet. The ladder was now in sight, partially hidden on the darker side of the tunnel. After quickly grabbing on, he noticed the voices had quieted down. The lights were now aiming down the other tunnel. Still sweating, panicked and bruised, he slowed himself down to steady the rope ladder. As he pushed the manhole cover up, he heard the cocking of several guns. A powerful hand lowered and wrapped his forearm in a death grip.

Chapter 27

Henry shut his eyes when he heard the clicks. This is it. But I'm only fifteen, he thought.

"Stop! This intruder may deserve to be shot, but not right now." Henry opened his eyes as the voice of his father rang out.

"You young man are not where you are supposed be. If I had not been here you might have been shot. Gentlemen, return to what you were doing. I will deal with this boy." Still shaking in disbelief, Henry knew to follow and not to talk. Judging from the elder Liu's pace, Henry could tell his father was furious. After they walked a short distance, his father stopped and turned to him. "Is there any chance you were followed?"

"No. I told no one about my discovery. I was waiting for you to come home." Edward Liu stared at his son.

"You will tell me everything when we get home." Henry's mother was amazed to see her husband with son in tow.

"He knows."

"How can that be?"

"He is a boy who thinks he needs to know everything."

"Just like his father."

"Henry, from what you have seen... well, I can only imagine what you are thinking. We are part of an undertaking you must, for now, know nothing about. I want you to swear that you will not reveal any of what you have seen or heard to anyone. Our lives depend on this remaining a secret. Your time will come." Henry couldn't believe what he was hearing—both his parents involved in some dangerous, mysterious project. His father was right—such an amazing thing he could never have imagined. Edward Liu could see his son needed a moment to think, but he did not have a moment to give.

"Henry!"

"I promise father."

"Listen carefully. I will only give you a brief background so you might understand the seriousness of what we are doing. ChinAlive is movement, hundreds strong in China and around the world. Our plan started coming together five years ago, right after the International Olympic Committee announced China would host the 2008 Games. What we are doing is complex, dangerous, and holds great risk for us all." Henry looked at both his parents with continuing disbelief. Their expressions remained somber, unsmiling.

"But how? What is…?" Henry felt himself lost in a jumble of questions he didn't know how to ask.

"The movement is decades old, but only in the past few years have we had the opportunity and the means to effectively organize ourselves."

"What are you doing? Organize yourselves, how? For what? Why are the Olympics important?" Edward Liu could tell the floodgates of Henry's mind had opened.

"When we began, we thought we could keep our families in the background. That turned out to be wishful thinking. From what you have seen and what I have told you, you have a vague notion of what we are doing. I promise in time you will know everything. The whole world will know. For now, no more questions. I have much to do." Before he could say another word, his father was gone. Bewildered, Henry stood staring at the door.

"Are you hungry?" his mother asked.

"Mother, can you…?'

"No, I cannot."

"How did you know what I was going to ask?"

"It's time I made dinner." Henry wasn't hungry but he ate out of habit. He and his mother sat in silence until he went to his room to study. He tried to focus on some notes for an upcoming test, but his mind was too confused to study.

When his father returned later that night, Henry could hear his parents whispering in the next room. They had always talked softly, but now Henry guessed that they would be extra careful to keep things from him. His only consolation was he hadn't promised not to keep his ears open—wide open. It was a small house. They might have thought their voices were low enough, but they had no idea of Henry's stealth.

Sometimes, he wished he hadn't heard what they said. How could pieces of conversation like—"changing the course of history," or "speeding up the timetable for long overdue changes in the government"—go without follow-up questions? How could he possibly strangle off thoughts and ideas like that without wanting to know more? His father had promised to tell him everything. Henry never would have guessed the promise would take two years to keep.

Chapter 28

For a naturally inquisitive kid, Henry's wait was the worst ordeal he had ever endured. Every day he focused on the routines of his life; school, homework, reading, and his job on the river as a tour guide. Even during the busiest time of year, only a few tourists made the trip from Lijiang to his small village, Shigu.

Most of them headed further up river to the Tiger Leaping Gorge, one of the most famous and beautiful places in China. The Gorge was where the Yangtze narrowed to its tightest, most violent passage. From a mile above it sounded like a freight train cutting through the cliffs. The turbulence of the water, the beauty of its green valleys, and the majesty of its towering walls, made the hike a favorite for walkers and back packers. The legend of the leaping tiger and his twenty-five meter jump to escape a hunter's wrath had created the Gorge's mystique.

Henry wondered how long the mystique would endure if the proposed damming of the river in the Gorge became a reality. Although his father was leading a local committee to try and change the mind of government officials, they knew it would be an impossible battle to win.

For most of the tourists, the importance of Shigu had nothing to do with the town itself—it was the mountain next to the town. Cloud Mountain was arguably the most important geological site in China and maybe the world. The story of its origin was a tale Henry and all the children of Shigu loved to believe. Over the centuries, myth and history had become so knotted together that the romantic notion of an emperor and his dragons, battling the forces of nature to save China's most important river, became a legend even adults loved to hear.

To engineers and scientists like Henry's father, it was the scientific matter of tectonics at work. Between the Eocene and Miocene eras, India broke free of Africa and drifted north to Asia. The explosive force of these landmasses colliding gave birth to the Himalayas, and to the little mountain that towered over Henry's village.

Edward Liu had explained to their class on a recent visit, "that the Yangtze in ancestral times flowed to the south, into the valley of what is now the Red River." He made it clear how the Red River eventually lost its biggest tributary, and China gained her greatest river."

Henry and most of his classmates were far more captivated by the story of Da Yu. Their teacher laughed at the tale and insisted they take Mr. Liu's version, the scientific version, to heart. Some of the students asked Mr. Liu about the fabled dragon caves but he laughed as well. "I wish they were real. What a great tourist attraction that would be for our little town." As he looked at the students for questions, Henry caught his father's eye—if they only knew. The caves were indeed real. Were they home to dragons — probably not. Were they headquarters for a group of people trying to change the course of China's history? All Henry could do was trust his father and keep what he knew to himself.

Chapter 29

"Your discovery of our project was the subject of much discussion a couple of years ago." Henry stopped serving himself and looked at his father.

"You have done well in concealing what you saw. You have showed great restraint in keeping your questions to yourself, for the most part."

"Please pass the rice," his mom said. Edward Liu started to eat. Henry waited, dying to know. Was this the conversation he had been waiting to hear for almost two years?

"Tell him Edward. Can't you see he is about to go crazy." The elder Liu smiled. His mother looked more sympathetic.

"Mother is wrong. I have already gone crazy. I will die soon if you don't tell me."

"Henry, I had hoped to keep you and your mother's roles to a minimum. After your discovery there was—there is—no use in it. The time has come. Tonight, you will learn much of what you wish to know, especially after I take you back to the cave. You will not learn all of it, but I will tell you enough to calm your curiosity and enough so that you might help us with an immediate role we wish you to play. You must have faith. What we are asking you to do is important. It will also help your standing in this household in regards to your previous snooping."

"I have faith father and I am ready." Henry's mom smiled at her son's exuberance. After father and son walked out to their garden, the real conversation began.

"Henry, there is an American high school student named Charlie Evers who might have accidentally stumbled onto an important piece of a communication code essential to what we are doing. He is meiguran – an American. A good boy, a smart boy, and coincidentally, the son of one of the most important people in our project—we are relocating him here to keep him safe. The PSB and the Ministry of State Security were about to start looking at him as a person of interest. He cannot be told anything. We must know if he has intentionally, or accidentally, divulged what he knows to anyone. He probably has no idea what he stumbled on but we must find out."

"What can I do?"

"At this moment he is being taken up the Yangtze to our cave. His family will join him there soon. He is frightened, so much so that he cannot help but think we are the enemy. For now, this is good. We…you… need to gain his trust, be his friend, and find out information about some Internet inquiries he has been making. They involve a secret code that is very important to us—Red Spears. You are close in age so we are counting on that to help. As I said, he probably knows nothing that can, or has hurt us. But we need to know for sure. When the boat reaches the docks at Wuhan, you and I will board, along with another boy who is the son of one of our chief project planners. This young man is also playing an important part and is being relocated as well. The two of you will meet soon to discuss plans for the best way to proceed. In this you have my trust and great hope for success. Do you have any questions?"

"Why, if he is the son of one of the project leaders, don't you ask him what he knows? Don't you trust him or his dad?"

"A fair question. I wish it was that simple son. We have many interests to appease and a few trust issues that still need resolving. Any more questions?"

"Yes. Can you show me the cave now?" His dad laughed.

"Oh, you remember that?"

"The place where I almost died?"

"You are most dramatic tonight my son. You think you are ready?"

"You are making a joke. I have been ready for two years." Henry's father put his hand on his son's shoulder and led him to compost shed a few feet from where they were standing. After lifting a latched door that was covered with dirt, weeds, and manure, Edward Liu flipped a hidden switch. A lighted stairway appeared. Henry silently followed his father down to an underground passageway that gave him a strange sense of deja vu.

"How long has this stairway been here?"

"A few years."

"Why have I never seen it?"

"Oh, you did son. You just never looked carefully. All the men who were supposedly planting in this garden, or harvesting corn in adjoining fields, were building entrances to our geologic wonder."

The tunnel they followed looked much like the one he had discovered two years earlier—same height, same slippery rocks. But the light his dad had flipped on made the going much easier. At the intersection of two tunnels, Henry's dad ran his wallet over a hidden RFID sensor. "Bypasses the alarm you tripped son." The lights grew brighter as they approached an arched entranceway. Henry stopped. Before him was the largest cave he could ever have imagined. In their path stood a dried up river bed at least twenty feet wide. After using a bridge to cross, they came to an area that included open-air offices and meeting rooms. In the distance, Henry made out what looked like a television studio. Men and women were moving about in a business like way and took little notice of them. A few of the people Henry recognized as friends of the family. Some he knew worked in the village. A few waved and said hello in an amused way, like they had been expecting him.

"Hi Henry." It was Mr. Xiao, the bakery shop owner. "So, your dad finally decided to let you in on our little secret."

"Back to work lazybones," Mr. Liu replied. "And if you have to know, Mr. Surveillance Genius, he discovered this place all by himself."

"Impossible," Mr. Xiao replied. "Couldn't happen." Mr. Xiao, his dad explained, had been trained by the CIA in surveillance and had only been a baker a short while.

"So that's why all his cookies are taste-free." Henry laughed. "What's that over there? And what is this place? Did you and these men dig this place up? What is all this stuff—the cameras, the offices. And what is that?" he asked, pointing to the huge mechanical doors along a thirty foot section of what looked like a metal wall. Before Mr. Xiao returned to what he had been doing, he looked at Henry's father and said, "You're the big shot engineer geologist." Henry looked at his father while his father stood contemplating, trying to figure out where to start.

"We did not dig this cave son. And don't get some romantic notion that your Da Yu the great earthmover built it either. The story about Master Yu's dragons is true to a point. When the plates of the Miocene era were throwing Cloud Mountain up in the path of the great river, a current of water continued under the mountain. It was a violent thousand years before man walked on the earth. No one discovered the cave because the mountain put down a door that blocked all its entrances. I stumbled on it when I was home one summer from engineering school. A project I was involved in had me hiking every inch of the mountain. I was picking berries from a bush that was recessed into a hole hidden for centuries by weeds and brush. It was on the far side of the mountain where hikers seldom visit. I was hungry. The more I went after the berries, the more the mountain pulled me in. Eventually, I ran out of berries but the path grew wider, darker, and steeper. In the following years, I discovered five more entrances. This cave was the result of thousands of years of glacial carving. Or, depending on what you want to believe, the place where the great Da Yu's dragons peacefully lived until their extinction."

"Why didn't you tell someone? Wouldn't this have been considered an important find?"

"You mean like the Mogao Caves, or even the warriors of Xi'An? Yes, absolutely. But look what happened to those places. They are extremely important finds but with the help of the government, they have become more commercialized than Disneyland. Can you imagine how the tourist industry would have destroyed our village?"

"Did you find bones, or other artifacts?"

"Henry, the wealth of things we have found under this mountain has helped finance our project. Some of the artifacts go to research, some go to museums, and some go to auctioneers in Hong Kong."

"You mean this whole project was funded with relics from in here?"

"Not quite. We do have one very wealthy American benefactor. But one of the greatest ironies of the whole project is our most unexpected funding source – the Chinese government."

"How can that be? Why would they spend money on this?"

"One of the worst displays of corruption in this country is the money that is sent to local government officials for projects that usually have little value, cost a fortune, and enrich party members and their friends. Fortunately, the leader of our fair village is one of us. When he made application to build a four lane highway to our front door, so that tourists could come to our new shopping mall, his request was warmly received."

"What shopping mall? What four lane highway?"

"The government, in their gross ineptitude, gave us $30 million dollars without question, without any oversight, only if their friends could get the contracts. No one has ever checked to see where the money was spent, or if it was spent. As long as the lending institutions made money, and those getting rich were party members, it was money well spent. Close your mouth son, you'll catch flies."

When they were done with Henry's introductory tour, his father again reminded him of the seriousness of his mission—find out what Charlie Evers knows.

"Good thing I've seen some of those American cop shows you won't let me watch."

"You think I don't know?" his father said. "In two days you will leave to join the ship. Your teacher will be told you are ill. You should be back within a week." After two-dozen more questions that his father would not answer, Henry was frustrated, but ready. This was the kind of intrigue he had only read about in books.

Chapter 30

Jerry's dispatch to Shigu had been well planned—with one slight change. He wasn't going back to Shanghai. His dad thought it best not to inform him yet. The permanent move was supposed to happen later but the timetable had to be drastically moved ahead due to the involvement of his classmate, Charlie Evers. They needed to know what Charlie knew and Jerry was in a unique position to help. All the elements were coming together quickly. The elder Zhiang had to move his entire family out of harm's way. Two things made Jerry's involvement indispensable; he had developed one of the programs running their communications network, and, by a fortunate coincidence, was already acquainted with Charlie Evers.

Jerry Zhiang and Henry Liu were the perfect team to find out where Charlie Evers' cyber exploits had taken him. Charlie needed to be brought to safety eventually but his research had drastically changed things. The kidnapping would fool the authorities and keep them on the sidelines for weeks to come.

Travel plans for Jerry's mom and Charlie's mom had also been set in motion. They were heading to Shigu by different routes. Very few of the ChinAlive conspirators knew how all the pieces fit together. It would be a relief for all of them, when and where all their paths would finally cross.

#

Jerry and Henry were only given a day to prepare. How would they find out what Charlie Evers had discovered about the Red Spears? First, they were curious about each other.

"You did not know Charlie Evers when you enrolled at the school in Shanghai?"

"No. I know how strange that sounds. If he had not been in my science class and if he had not talked about the Red Spears, he would never have gained our attention. We are sure that the government is now onto him as well"

"What is Red Spears?" Henry asked.

"I don't know how deep your involvement is Henry, so all I can tell you is that it's part of the ChinAlive communication infrastructure." Probably a lot deeper than yours, Henry smiled to himself.

"Communication infa…what? What does that mean?"

"Sorry Henry. It means the systems we have designed to run – computer, satellite, even ground transport. Okay?"

"Okay, I know. Go on."

"I was asked by my dad to help devise this thing – and it is a simple thing, believe it or not – but I'm not even sure how it fits into the big picture. Who in their right mind would have guessed Charlie Evers would have stumbled onto this piece of the project's communication mechanism? I mean—you know, the way we get information to each other."

"Thanks, I know. How about coincidence – something that happens by chance? Yes?"

"Yes, that's about it. Big word Henry—coincidence. Good one. "

"On my last vocabulary test. Serious. How will we get Charlie Evers telling us the truth about what he knows?"

"If it was by chance, or for some other reason, we need to know why he was looking and what he discovered. Can we agree on that?"

"Yes," Henry replied. Their collaboration then began in earnest and lasted until Henry's dad interrupted, three hours later.

"Time for dinner gentlemen. Have you had success? Plans you can share?"

At the dinner table, they reviewed a four-point plan that met with everyone's approval. Simple, direct, many elements of which they had seen work well on American cop shows.

Chapter 31

It was twilight by the time the boat started slowing down. Charlie had been cramped, uncomfortable, and cold for hours. He couldn't sit, he couldn't stand, and the sound of the engines isolated him behind a wall of noise. As the boat slowed, the engines quieted. Charlie was relieved. He could relax. He was sure they had gone beyond Chongqing, but how far? Tiger Leaping Gorge would still be ahead. They could never have navigated the Gorge's suicidal rapids.

Looking out over the bow, the river flowed at them on its southbound course. A hairpin turn immediately redirected it back to the north. This was the famous first bend in the river. When the boat came to a complete stop at a seawall, Charlie could hear one of the men talking on a cell phone. "Yes, much later, when no one is near. We will wait." The man told Charlie he was off to find them some dinner. In the meantime, the other man unlocked Charlie's cuffs, guided him to a bed inside the cabin and snapped one end of the cuffs to the side of the bed.

Once he found a comfortable position, the quiet, gentle sway of the boat rocked him to sleep. Charlie didn't know how long he had been out when the hum of the engines brought him back to life. This time they did not continue up the river. This time, strangely, they moved a few feet out and turned to face the seawall. The men undid his handcuffs and brought him up on deck. They laughed when his eyes began to widen.

What he saw was like something out of a James Bond movie. He blinked, and blinked again, and again, then looked at the men laughing, then back at the seawall. Was he dreaming? Part of the seawall was slowly rising. The entire 300 feet of seawall was titled toward the water to deflect the waves. A twenty-foot section was now drawing up to a 45 degree angle to a position parallel with the water. Charlie and one of the men were lowered into a small inflatable boat. The other man stayed behind.

With one gigantic slurp, they were sucked into the opening. The trip through the seawall lasted only seconds. When he looked up, Charlie could see that the raft had landed in a narrow riverbed, inside a cavern bigger than a small stadium. Behind him, he heard the seawall close with a quiet hum. The cavern had an eerie glow that at first caused him to squint. After his eyes adjusted, there on the shore was Mr. Liu, without his PSB uniform, and next to Mr. Liu, was his dad.

Chapter 32

After John Evers wrapped his worn out teenager in bear hug, two other familiar faces appeared. Jerry and Henry couldn't help smiling as they watched Charlie try to figure out his new surroundings. They both remembered their own astonishment when they first gazed, bug eyed, out over this underground city—something very much like a misplaced movie set. With the appearance of his dad, Charlie's astonishment was more than a match to theirs. His dad looked healthy. He wasn't cuffed or guarded. Charlie sensed a giant disconnect between what he'd imagined and what he was about to learn. He continued to stare, dumbfounded at his new surroundings.

"Where are we? What is this place?"

"Charlie, you look pooped. After some dinner and a shower I'll show you where you're going to bunk. Tomorrow I have things to share that you will find fascinating."

"Is Mom here?"

"She's on her way. She should be here in the next few days." But that wasn't all Charlie needed to know.

"I'm not waiting for tomorrow, and I'm not waiting for dinner and a shower. What the hell is going on here?" Before they could answer, Charlie started to move away from them. With his dad, Jerry, Henry, and a whole bunch of ChinAlive workers following, he stumbled ahead. John Evers motioned the others to go back.

"Give us some space everyone, I'll take care of him." While the other workers retreated, Jerry and Henry stayed close by. Charlie kept squinting at the unnatural lighting trying, to focus—first on the fifty-foot high walls of the cave, then the temporary office cubicles, the dreamlike nature of his surroundings, and the seemingly ordinary way everyone was going about their business. His last shot of adrenalin was used to take in everything he could possibly see—like his first moments at Disneyland. But this nightmare didn't come with a stuffed Winnie the Pooh or mouse ears. Twisting, turning, paying no attention to his dad, he stumbled, stopped, and ran to make sure no one got in his way. By the time he reached the end of the cave he was completely exhausted.

"Come on Charlie," his dad said, putting an arm around him. Charlie still wasn't ready to go back, but his strength was gone and the steadiness of his dad's arms was a welcome relief. Now he wasn't sure he could even manage a shower or food. When his dad tried to pass him off to Jerry and Henry to show him the way to the showers he wouldn't let go of his dad. It was up to John Evers to guide and get his Charlie ready for bed.

The next morning he and his dad joined Jerry, Henry, their dads, and a roomful of strangers for breakfast.

"Have you been here before?" Charlie asked. Henry nodded yes, Jerry said "no."

Mr. Liu, overhearing Charlie's question, responded, "This must be quite a shock, Charlie." But the shocks weren't over.

"Hello Charlie. Welcome." A familiar voice greeted him from behind. Charlie almost dropped his chopsticks when he turned around.

"Mr. Fathom. How did you…I thought…"

"And you thought this was going to be a boring year." Charlie looked at his dad, the boys, then back to Mr. Fathom.

"Charlie, eat your breakfast. Catch up with your dad and your new friends. You'll be mine soon enough." With a reassuring pat on the shoulder, Mr. Fathom turned to his own breakfast.

"Your teacher of course," said John Evers. "You don't think you're going to hang out and do nothing for the next three months?"

"Three months? We're going to live here?"

"And go to school. You liked Mr. Fathom. And now he's all yours. Your school year will stay the same so you should be finished by mid-June. We then have work for you with ChinAlive."

"Now that's what I call a great teacher student ratio," said Jerry. "Wish I could join you. Might be fun."

"Your wish is my command," said Bill Zhiang. Jerry stared at his dad.

"What do you mean?"

"Jerry, you're here to stay too. You won't be returning to Shanghai." Now it was Charlie's turn to enjoy Jerry's disbelief.

"What about school...and our apartment...and everything? And Mom?"

"She's on her way son. As far as our safety, no worries—everything has been taken care of." Jerry and Charlie looked at their dads, each other, Mr. Fathom, and Henry. Then the questions erupted. Before they spiraled out of control, Mr. Liu stepped in.

"Charlie, I'm Mr. Liu, Henry's father. I've been looking forward to this real introduction. I'd like to apologize as well. Once you know more of the details I think you will appreciate the necessity of what we had to do. Henry and Jerry helped us clear up every last doubt. But now you are here, safe and sound, and we look forward to your help."

"My help?"

"Yes Charlie. Yours, Henry's, and Jerry's."

Jerry's dad spoke next. Reaching across the table to shake hands, he looked about the same age as Charlie's dad.

"I'm Bill Zhiang, Charlie. I hope they weren't too hard on you. Everyone involved with your abduction was told to be careful. I heard at one point, things almost got out of hand. We're relieved to have you here. Jerry and Henry confirmed what most of us already knew—you had no knowledge of the Red Spears as it related to our project. I promise, no more questions."

"So Mr. Liu, you're not PSB, and Mr. Zhiang, you're not PSB..."

"No Charlie, I am definitely not PSB," said Mr. Liu.

"And this safety thing—I can't wait to find out why I am safe now. I am beyond confused. And what's ChinAlive?"

"The name of our project. Much more on that soon."

After a few more minutes of conversation, John Evers led them to where a meeting was getting ready to start. Charlie followed along, again trying to comprehend his new home and the previous week's events; first the abduction, then the tent, the barge, the Yangtze cruise, the shack above the river, the attempted finger removal, the cabin cruiser, and finally, the magic opening that sucked him somewhere inside the earth. Could this get any stranger?

The proof was all around him—a set at Universal Studios, under a mountain, in the middle of nowhere, with a group of people led by his dad, ready to do who knows what. Mr. Fathom said it best—a boring year? Before he had time to scan everything he wanted to see, Charlie found himself in what looked like a classroom. No door, only a sign that read *Classroom 1*.

Charlie's dad took a position at the front and asked a couple of coworkers to hand out headsets to everyone who was not bilingual.

"Listen up. Please set the switch to "2" for English and "1" for Mandarin." Before the meeting began, Charlie looked around and counted—fifty-two with a few stragglers still coming in.

"Welcome to ChinAlive," said John Evers. And then he looked straight at his son. "Charlie, my humble apologies. I know you knew nothing more than the simple facts you learned from your research. But there is a lot at stake. Many people involved in this project don't know me yet. They needed to be sure. As it happened, we were only a few days ahead of the MSS, the Ministry of State Security. The opportunity to bring you to safety gave others a chance to double-check what you knew. Are we square on that? Can you forgive me?"

"Seems pretty extreme Dad. But I'm so happy to see you…I'll probably get over it. I can't wait to find out what this is all about."

"You are not alone Charlie. The timing of your arrival is most opportune. Today we begin a series of short meetings to get everyone on the same page." John Evers turned to face his audience. "To start things off, I'd like Mr. Liu to explain the history of this cave. He was born in Shigu and the cave was his discovery. He is the expert." Charlie watched, speechless, as the man from the ship, Henry's father, stepped forward.

"Thank you Mr. Evers. We have much to do so I will be brief. If all your questions are not answered today, there will be many more opportunities over the next few weeks. Please look around. You are sitting in the middle of a piece of history and lore that dates back thousands of years in geologic time. It was said that the great Emperor Yu lived in such a mythical place with his dragons after taming the floodwaters of China."

Jerry and Charlie were captivated. Henry had heard it before. *The plan, when will we get to the plan?* His father's short speech went on forever. Why was the history such a big deal. *I've waited two years.*

Mr. Liu continued. "With the mountain blocking the river, an eighteen degree hairpin turn to the north was created. The river carved out the Tiger Leaping Gorge, then headed southeast on its present course, emptying into the South China Sea. Without Cloud Mountain, the China we know today would not exist.

"I do not have to tell you the importance of the Yangtze River to China's history and its very existence. The river is the major route by which goods are moved and by which travel and tourism is made possible in China. For as far back as the history is kept, the river has facilitated the growth, manufacture, and transport of goods like rice, silk, tea, and tongue oil." *Yes father, we know this – the plan, what of the plan?*

For Charlie, the history was fascinating. He had studied the river and was excited to revisit so much of what he had learned. What's up with Henry, he thought—he looks almost bored. That ended with Mr. Liu's final remark. "That is why one of the most important pieces of our project is to stop the river from flowing. Or should I say, divert it to meet our needs?"

Henry, Charlie, and Jerry sat straight up. Had they heard correctly? Charlie scanned the faces of others in the room. Mr. Liu purposefully arranged papers on a desk in front of him, let his words settle, and prepared to answer his speechless audience with an explanation.

Chapter 33

After an unnaturally long pause Mr. Liu pulled down a map. "This is the way the river flowed before Cloud Mountain blocked its path. This is the eighteen-degree turn it took afterwards. For centuries, water flowed into the mountain's core. Slowly, inexorably, this glacial carving process formed the cave in which we are sitting. It was not here when the mountain originally thrust upwards. When I first discovered the cave it did not extend to the riverbank. Part of our mission was to join the river by digging a trench."

Mr. Liu pointed to an exterior wall. "On the other side of that wall flows the great Yangtze." He stepped away from the place he was speaking and asked everyone to follow.

"Please focus your attention on the mechanical device imbedded in the wall," he said, as he climbed an open stairway to a platform with a bank of controls. A series of rhythmic noises began, followed by a number of locking and snapping sounds. Part of the wall began to move. When the mechanism stopped, a space one foot high had opened. The great river stretched out before them. The space remained open for only a few moments before Mr. Liu closed it.

"For your eyes only. We don't want any unwanted visitors looking in."

"How can you tell when the coast is clear?" Charlie asked.

"We have a series of cameras and motion sensors stationed around this area."

"But why would you want to divert the river? It means everything to the people of China. And how did you build this without anyone noticing? It must have cost a fortune."

"You will understand in a few minutes—patience, please. ChinAlive is at the point where everyone here must now know the entire plan. All of you hold key positions. The fate of thousands of patriotic men and women rests with your ability to keep them informed. You know that I am not overstating it when I say all of us are risking our lives and the lives of our loved ones to bring democracy to China.

"In fact, we do not wish to stop the river. We only wish to frighten the government into giving us a chance." Stopping for a drink of water, then turning to the whole audience, Mr. Liu continued. "To outline how this will happen, I would like to introduce Mr. John Evers."

Chapter 34

Captain Qi Fan Lee's anger was well hidden under his sharply pressed uniform. He always started out cool, in control, but Group 22, Rong's group, braced itself. The morning tirade was as certain as the sweat that would soon form on the Captain's forehead.

"For months we tried to track this Red Spears movement. Hit and run, no follow up, but still it expands. And expands—first in Shanghai, then Beijing, then all over. This team has been working night and day tracing every lead—chat room references, emails, blogs, everything. Is that right?" They all nodded their agreement. "And finally, we get a solid lead—this Evers man? And his son? And PSB asks us, Ministry of State Security, if we kidnapped the dad. This is crazy. And then the boy disappears? And finally, someone gets the bright idea to grab the mother. While they try to do this simple arrest, men with guns grab her right out from under our noses. So far, the facts are correct?" Again, they all nodded their agreement.

"What is going on here?" The sudden explosion of his voice shook the room. "We did not kidnap them, and PSB says the same. In a very short time the world is coming to our doorstep. All seems to be going well. But then there is this. The United States is concerned that a whole family has disappeared. We are lucky they trust us—or pretend to trust us—to find this family. As you all know, we walk a dangerous line. We want them, but for different reasons." After using his fist like a sledgehammer on the table, no one moved. "Progress report—now."

A member of Rong's team stood nervously. He wished it were someone else about to give the report. "Sir, after months of looking into this, we have concluded that Red Spears is nothing more than a hoax. We are sure that the involvement of the Evers family was coincidental. It was the boy and not his father using his father's computer to do research for a school project. His interest in the Red Spears suggested nothing worth noting. Our biggest concern was the timing. First, the father disappeared as we were about to interrogate him, then his son, and now the mother. John Evers supposedly works for an environmental NGO, which we have long suspected of being a CIA cover. Neither we nor PSB had any intention of questioning the boy or his mother beyond our initial interviews."

"Where does that leave us Cadet?"

"We are doing everything we can to find the family." Rong stared straight ahead, trying to catch a glimpse of the Captain's face out of the corner of his eye.

"And the hoax? Why would such a monumental hoax be carried out at this time? And how did the Evers family get tied into that?"

"Many hoaxes are bred on the Internet, Sir. There are literally thousands of conspiracy theories and threats all the time against the government. We quickly filter the relevant ones out, shut down their places of origin, and deal with those responsible. There were so many hits on the Evers' computer that we had to look at them closely—but it was nothing." The cadet hesitated a minute, realizing what he was about to say would greatly upset the captain.

"Well, go on Cadet."

"Yes Sir. We think this hoax was intended to divert our attention and resources away from a much bigger plot." The captain's eyes began to widen.

"And what would that be Cadet?"

"We don't know Sir." The captain lowered his head and pinched the bridge of his nose. Two men silently joined the group at the back of the room. The cadets could tell these were high-ranking members of one of the other bureaus. Rong's radar started kicking in as he sensed this was more than the usual update they had had in the past. After the men conferred for a few minutes, the cadets were instructed to spend no more time on the Red Spears question. It was time to return to their general surveillance duties. As the men were leaving, Rong heard one of them say something about bringing the most sophisticated intelligence units in to help find the Evers family.

"Not necessary," one of the men said. "We have the mother and an added bonus. Let's go. I will give you the details upstairs."

Was he supposed to have heard that? Rong's mouth went dry. The longer he stayed undercover the more he started second-guessing everything that happened. Did they have Jill Evers or was this a ploy to see if Rong would act on the information? If he reported what he had heard, could the leak be traced back to him? To keep the security agencies continually off balance, the Red Spears campaign was supposed to have lasted much longer. They had counted on Rong to fill in the gaps, but with the heightened security, getting new information out was going to be even more difficult. The stress of having to second-guess himself at every turn was beginning to interfere with one of his most reliable tools – natural instinct.

Chapter 35

The few minutes Charlie had spent with his dad were not enough. From a fairly conventional expat life to this—what was this? Had his whole life been a lie? Who was this man, speaking to all these people, about plans that could have them all arrested and executed? Charlie had spent weeks worrying about his dad. With his own capture and now, being reunited with his dad, in this place, under these circumstances—they needed to talk. But all he could do was listen.

"The Olympics will begin on August 8, 2008. One week prior to the opening ceremony, journalists and people from all over the world will begin pouring into China. Our plan begins on August 1. Mr. Steven Yang, a high-ranking Party member, has invited a large group of journalists on a cruise up the Yangtze. He is also one of us. His influence and reputation have been more than enough to insure a large turnout. Their trip ends once they have cleared the locks. Before they return, each reporter will get a message that something interesting has happened further up the river. Although unscheduled, they will insist on seeing what is going on. Astonishingly, a few miles west of the lake, they will find that the river no longer exists. The government will try to explain that many of the largest rivers have sustained a period of drought. The journalists, a rather skeptical bunch, will inform the world that something strange is going on. The government will hopefully do what they do best—cover things up. This will cast even more suspicion on the event.

"An hour after being stranded at the river's dried-up center, we will have people standing by with plane ride offers back to Chongqing to expedite getting their stories out. The Party will be in a frenzy trying to figure out what has happened. Proof of this event will be evident the following day when water levels at the dam are unbelievably low."

"How do you know that thing will work Dad?" Charlie asked, pointing to the mechanical doors.

"It's been tested twice for short periods. Both times were at night during heavy rains so the tests went unnoticed. Many of the main rivers of China have suffered drought periods. Even if we hadn't been so lucky with the rain, it is highly unlikely that we would have been found out.

"A message saying, 'give us democracy, or the river stops,' will be posted to every listserv, newsgroup, social networking site, and blog possible. Thanks to our talented Internet guru Jerry, this will be as easily spread as the Red Spears hoax." Henry and Charlie turned to Jerry. "Hey, no big deal," Jerry smiled.

Suddenly a new man walked into the room waving his hands. "Gentlemen, distressing news." John Evers motioned the man to approach the front and then took him aside. The boys were close enough to hear the gist of their whispered conversation.

"We just found out from one of our sources that the authorities have figured out what our Red Spears plan was all about. They will now be focusing all their energies on why such an effort was made to distract them and from what. This is no small development." Charlie shot a glance at Henry and Jerry. "Hoax?" They both shrugged their shoulders and whispered to Charlie, "We didn't know." Charlie looked at his dad to see how he would react to the news. John Evers stepped away for a moment and looked to be collecting his thoughts.

"A disturbing development for sure," he said, almost to himself. He then looked to the back of the room and Charlie could tell he was signaling some of the others. "We need to meet as soon as this meeting is over," he said.

"Let's continue everyone—you need to have this information." Charlie watched and wondered, along with many of the others what this meant. His dad then took a deep breath and continued with his speech.

"The media will be in a frenzy but that will be nothing compared to the reaction of the Chinese government as they get ready to stage their biggest propaganda event in history. Every journalist's attention will be temporarily distracted then refocused. The government will probably stop allowing all visits west of the dam at a time when they are bragging about opening up the country."

"Won't the government be able to find the source of the problem?" another worker in the audience asked.

"We sure hope not. The diversion will only go on for an hour before we close the doors and direct it back to its course. After the reporters get the message out, all of China, especially the Chinese people, will once again sense an apocalyptic sign that suggests the government is not capable of either telling the truth, or cannot be trusted to ward off such a monumental disaster. Although the waters will flow back to their present course quickly, the world will know that some group has the power to dry up the greatest river on earth. This is when it gets tricky. We don't want the people to panic and we definitely don't want an overreaction." Charlie's hand shot up.

"What does that mean?"

"If I'm not mistaken, I think that is something Mr. Fathom plans to discuss with you."

"Indeed John." Mr. Fathom agreed. He was sitting a couple rows in front of Charlie. "This is history you will find most fascinating. Class begins soon." Charlie could tell his dad wanted to return to the presentation, but was interrupted by another question.

"But how does this tie in with the Olympics? It's still a week off," a man in the back row asked.

"We are just getting warmed up. Two days later we will divert the river again, this time for two hours. And that's it, the last time. We have carefully estimated that this is all we can do until later. Risk of discovery would be too great."

John Evers continued for a few more minutes, outlining details of the shutdown and what they expected the government's reaction to be. If they predicted correctly, it would take so much time and energy for authorities to find the source of the diversion—while trying to figure out what to tell the Chinese people and the rest of the world—that step two of the plan could easily be carried out.

They waited, but step two was never presented. Charlie's dad was about to introduce the next speaker when Mr. Liu handed him a note. After a brief discussion, he turned to the audience.

"Apologies everyone, at this time we need to take a short break. Sorry for all the interruptions. Hopefully this will only take a few minutes. There's tea and snacks in the cafeteria. Please help yourselves. We will make an announcement when we are ready to continue." Charlie desperately wanted to talk to his dad, but that possibility was looking more and more remote. John Evers was swept away, surrounded by too many people who needed his attention. Charlie joined Jerry and Henry as the others left the room.

Chapter 36

Three teenagers, thrown together because of their dads, in a most bizarre circumstance, didn't have a clue how to begin with each other. They looked around for something to do, somewhere to go. All these other people already had a bond. But these three were the new recruits, and they were bound together, not in a way of their choosing. Jerry was the techno geek with underdeveloped social skills. Henry was at a disadvantage with his developing English skills. It was only natural that Charlie, the most outgoing of the three, should feel the least awkward in breaking the ice.

"Let me understand this," Charlie said, as he looked out where the river would soon flow. "I've known about this ChinAlive business for about a week. And Jerry?"

"Five or six months."

"And you Henry?"

"Two years ago I discovered something going on but my dad would not tell me what it was all about. I had to wait two years before they would tell me more."

"So we have to figure our roles grew in an unplanned, somewhat spontaneous way?"

"I don't think we were part of the big picture to start," said Jerry.

"Me too," agreed Henry.

"Well, I don't know where that gets us, but, not to change the subject...what do you think those dirt bikes are for? And what do you think step two is?"

"First question easy," said Henry. "This is big place. And see how all bikes have attachments to pull small trailers. You ride dirt bike?"

"Yeah, I ride dirt bikes—since I was young. In China you don't really need a license and I don't think there's an age limit. I love to ride. Maybe if we asked nicely..."

"Good luck on that one," said Jerry.

"Okay, we'll see. But what about step two?" Charlie swung a leg over the one of the bikes and was instantly told by a passing adult that the bikes were only for certain people. He backed off but the boys could tell Charlie wasn't happy about being told.

"I hope step two tells why the river needs to be diverted," said Henry. All three nodded their agreement.

"Are you living in the cave Henry?"

"No. We live in Shigu, at the foot of the mountain on top of us. I do not think we will move here, but I don't know for sure."

"This is totally bizarre," said Charlie. "How do you think our dads got together on this?" Charlie asked. "Bringing democracy? Overthrowing the Chinese government? Unbelievable! I don't know about you, but I've read enough to know — this is one of those crimes that means we've all dead meat if we're caught."

"We will be executed," Henry said. Charlie stopped abruptly and looked at Jerry.

"And what about those Red Spears? You said you didn't know anything. What's up with that?"

"I didn't know. My dad asked me to put a disinformation spell out there – a funny worm. Nothing destructive, just a fast spreading piece of information that would hit everywhere with closely watched tags. I was never told why. I love doing stuff like that and my dad knows it. I didn't know what it was for."

"Looks like it worked well enough. Too bad they caught on," said Charlie.

"Yeah, well, it bought the project some breathing room," Jerry said. "Looks like they've been preparing for a long time. Sure hope we're covered. I'd like to know how safe we are here, and more about this place. How long did they say we had before the meeting starts again?"

"I'm sure they'll call us when they're ready. You feel like exploring?" Charlie asked.

"Before we start out, I'd like to apologize, Charlie. We didn't know why they thought you had done something to jeopardize their plans, but they really needed to be sure." Jerry said.

"Me too," said Henry.

"I'm still pissed at the both of you, but at least you didn't try to cut off some of my favorite body parts. I better see some serious love coming my way while we're here, or..."

"I don't know you that well," said Henry.

"Henry," interrupted Jerry." It's an expression. He doesn't expect real love."

Henry looked at his companions, confused.

"He means, like maybe we share an extra piece of dessert with him—treat him extra nice for a while," said Jerry.

"It better be more than a while," laughed Charlie.

"You get it?" asked Jerry.

"I think so. Charlie, would you like a piece of my gum?"

"You gotta love this dude," said Jerry.

"I thought you said..." Henry interrupted.

"He means, we must respect how quickly you understand our strange American ways." All three boys nodded.

"One last thing," said Charlie. "I guess you can see I knew nothing. With all this promised love, I'm willing to forget last week. Why don't we start at the back over there and work our way forward. What do you say?"

"Bit of deja vu for you Charlie. I seem to remember your self-guided tour when you first arrived." All three boys smiled.

"Only problem," Charlie said, "I don't remember much of anything I did that night, except finding my dad."

Jerry conceded, "anyone dropped off in Never-Never-Land, after being kidnapped for no apparent reason, might have felt the same. On with the tour."

Not knowing what to expect, they started by following the path next to where the river would flow. It was only about twenty feet wide and about five feet deep. Before they had gone far, Charlie stopped and pointed. "Does it seem impossible to you that anyone could divert a river as great as the Yangtze into a small channel like this?"

"But it's not only that," said Jerry. "Look at all this stuff." Before them was a maze of open-air workspaces. Overhead, a huge mass of cords and cables zigzagged in every direction. Warehouse sized shelving units filled acres of space on the other side of the riverbed. With a quick glance, Charlie spotted everything from generators, office supplies, spools of wire, computer gear, and much more. The most intriguing area they came across was back in a natural alcove—it was set up like a television studio. Lights were hung on battens, a single camera on a dolly was standing ready in the middle of the makeshift studio, and a fully loaded control booth was outfitted in the back. As they scanned the space, Jerry pointed to what looked like a sliding door in the cave's ceiling.

"Let's see how much each of us knows. Maybe we can guess what's about to happen," Jerry suggested. All three were ready to jump in.

"Happy to go first," Jerry volunteered. "This was my idea and we haven't even heard from my dad yet. You two good with that?"

"Could you both speak more slowly? My English understanding is not for fast talking."

"Sorry Henry," Jerry said. Charlie agreed. "Okay, let's see. You probably don't know much about my dad so I think you need some background." After about twenty minutes, they discovered that none of them knew much more than the others. But what they did know was unique. In the middle of their discussion a voice interrupted, announcing the resumption of the meeting.

"I hope we get to finish this discussion," said Charlie. "Let's go see what they have in mind for us." On their return, Charlie spotted the two men who had almost cut his finger off. They both gave Charlie an ugly stare and one of them pantomimed a gesture as if he were chopping with a knife. Henry and Jerry watched as Charlie stood motionless, glaring back at the men.

"What's the matter Charlie?" Henry asked.

"Do you know those men?"

"They are my uncles," Henry said. Charlie explained what had happened in the hut and how he had almost lost a finger or two. Henry said he was not surprised.

"Hot heads, my dad calls them. They are useful, but you have nothing to fear. They would never have been part of this except for the night they accidentally discovered one of our secret entrances. This one was located at the far end of a landfill where they worked. Who knew? No one ever went near that area. They were lucky my dad was in the cave when they were caught. After that, there was no way we could keep them out of the plan."

"Do you trust them?"

"Yes Charlie, with our lives. They too have suffered greatly under this government. Both of them were prosperous farmers a few years ago and each had a wife and son. When the government created the Open Door Policy in 1978, the whole village was excited to see if foreign investment would make its way here.

A new textile plant was built and many locals were hired. Unfortunately, the wages were terrible and the working conditions dangerous. But the worst part was the chemicals the factory let loose. There were no controls. No one thought of the dangers and how they would affect the village.

My uncles led the first protests to the local council to complain that the ground water was being contaminated. They were told it wasn't so bad and to mind their own business. When some of the people started getting sick, the protests continued and started getting ugly. It would have been easy to build a water treatment facility but that would have cost the owners money.

The town was continually told that economic results were first and foremost. The government would only allow more investment if the plant was profitable. The town knew what that meant – party cadres and wealthy foreigners would get rich. The majority of village residents were never to be included. If they couldn't do it cheaply enough here, the Party was afraid the owners would take their investment elsewhere. With no hope for change, continued low wages, horrible working conditions, and no environmental controls, my uncles were chosen to take the protest to Beijing.

"They sat for days waiting to be seen and were finally told no one had time to see them. When they came home they organized more protests. This time they were arrested as troublemakers. While they were in jail, a torrent of the chemicals was accidentally released into their rice fields.

Both their wives and sons were in the fields and they all died. My uncles weren't told until they got out of jail a week later. They were devastated. If it hadn't been for my dad, no one knows what they might have done. For days and days they sat and rocked on our front porch – crazy in a frightening way. The guilt they suffered, for leaving their families, was agonizing. Every day they talked of killing themselves, or Party officials. Keeping them alive became a full time job for my father.

To make matters worse, many of the villagers thought that the spill was intentional.

"Charlie, their loyalty goes without question. Their sanity is another matter. Even now, my father must keep a close eye on them. Look, people are going back. Let's talk later."

Chapter 37

Most ChinAlive members were already seated when Charlie, Henry, and Jerry walked in. Charlie's dad had not yet returned. Instead, an older woman had been introduced and had started to speak.

"World governments have now entered the most insidious relationships with the Chinese government imaginable. A few short years ago, after the dramatic changes in Europe, we began to think the same kind of change was possible here. Everyone now believes that democracy will inevitably come to China. This is a deceit, a lie, and unfortunately, one that too many people are willing to abide in order to do business here." Even with these apocalyptic words, Charlie's attention was drifting elsewhere. Where was his dad?

"Look behind you," said Jerry. "Our dads are still talking outside."

"Doesn't look like they're coming in," said Charlie. The three boys quietly got up and left the meeting. The fathers were so engrossed in their discussion that they didn't notice their sons approaching. When Charlie and Jerry heard their moms' names mentioned, they didn't hesitate to move closer.

"Why aren't you boys with the others?"

Ignoring his dad, Charlie asked, "What's wrong?" The men looked at each other, searching for the correct, or at least the best way to respond. They hadn't had time to process what they were going to do with the information they had received. Before they had a chance to find an answer, Jerry asked, "Is mom all right?" From their blank stares, Jerry knew he had hit the mark.

"Why did you ask that, son?" Before Jerry could answer, Charlie asked, "And what about my mom?" The men knew they had been talking too loudly. They didn't have time to make up stories.

"Minutes ago we were informed by one of our sources that both of them have been detained."

"What does that mean?" Charlie asked.

"At this point we're not sure," said Charlie's dad. All three men knew that limiting who was to know what would have been impossible at this point.

"Both your mom, Charlie, and Jerry's, were part of two different tour groups. My office had arranged to have them both brought up river to Chongqing. After they arrived, one of our men was going to bring them to Shigu. Your moms have never met. Both knew that they were being brought here to safety, far from the reach of the government's police bureaus. They each were assigned two bodyguards.

The message we received said that they had been separated from their original tour groups and had rejoined another group—this time the same one. They have now been taken to a small river town called Fengdu for interrogation. How they both wound up in the same group is a mystery." Although two of the fathers and their sons remained calm with the news, a piercing look shot between Henry and his dad. Noticing their peculiar reaction, the others asked for enlightenment.

"It is nothing more than superstition," Henry's dad explained. "Fengdu is known as the Ghost City. It has inspired many frightening tales." Speaking quietly, Mr. Liu added, "I wish we could have avoided involving our families."

"We feel the same Mr. Liu," said Bill Zhiang. "We have discussed this many times—it could not be helped. We must concentrate on how best to free them."

"How do we do that?" Jerry asked.

"Have we heard anything else from our informant? Can he tell us how our moms were discovered and why they are being detained?" Charlie asked.

"The message said they will be held until a team from the Ministry of State Security can get there to interview them. They will be coming from Shanghai," said Mr. Liu. "The last message was cut off. That is all the information we have."

Charlie's dad asked, "What is your greatest fear, Mr. Liu?" No one spoke.

"I think you know the answer to that John." The boys did not but could guess.

"The Chinese security apparatus, more than any of their counterparts in this world, have, after centuries of practice, perfected the art of…" but before he could finish his sentence, Charlie finished it for him.

"Torture. I've read what the Chinese authorities can do—even under the Olympic spotlight. They won't let anything get in the way of their multi-billion dollar Olympic investment."

"And if the torture is successful?" asked Jerry.

"Between the two of them, Rita and Jill know enough information to hurt us badly." For a moment the fathers and sons stood in stunned silence. Up to now, it had not been so personal. These were two wives: two mothers. This was as real and frightening as any of them could have imagined.

Mr. Liu broke the silence. "I know people who know the area and can be ready to go immediately. We must get to them before the interrogation experts. At the most, we have a twenty-four hour window. I have spoken to you about my brothers, Liu Bo, and Liu Shen. At this moment, I can think of no two people better for a mission like this. Both have been prisoners there—they know the area well." Mr. Liu stopped to look for agreement but there was some hesitation.

Charlie had to ask, "I was exposed to their anger. Will they act rationally? This is my mom, and Jerry's."

"You are entitled to know, Charlie. They are brave men and completely loyal to this project. You will have to take my word. They are also two of the only men we know who survived Fengdu's torture temple." When Charlie added his agreement to the others the meeting was over. The men had to get going. But the boys remained, motionless.

"Gentlemen." Charlie, Jerry, and Henry knew they were being addressed. "The other presenters have much to share with you. You need to rejoin the meeting while these important preparations are made." The boys slowly walked back to the conference room. They were so caught up in thoughts of their own, not even the outline of a plan to overthrow of the Chinese government could bring back their attention.

Chapter 38

A sharp-eyed patrolman on board a tour boat spotted the Evers woman. He had seen one of the posters and immediately informed his superiors. His orders—take digital photos immediately. He wished he had a better camera. As the patrolman continued to observe her on deck, waiting for a good shot, his curiosity peaked when she started talking to another western looking woman. What he could not have known was that they had never met before. When the patrolman sent in digital photos of the two women together, the heartbeat of the entire security community raced. The photos weren't great but they were good enough.

The response was instantaneous—"wait, do not detain until you get to Fengdu." The other woman was Rita Zhiang, wife of one of the most powerful telecommunications tycoons in the world. Her husband was a key player in helping China with communications for the upcoming Olympics. Panic buttons were pushed everywhere. A team of interrogation specialists was dispatched at once.

#

Rong knew he had to act. He continued to worry that the information he overheard was intended to weed out the department's mole but he wrote the message anyway. All day his finger was poised, ready to send—and finally he sent it. By the end of the day, it was confirmed—the two women identified were persons of great interest in a continuing investigation. The information was real. Rong was safe.

All he could do was warn project headquarters and send confirmation that they were indeed being taken to Fengdu's infamous torture temple. He had heard hair-raising stories in school about the temple. How his superiors had always alluded to the city was frightening. "Take them to Fengdu for answers."

He wondered if the women were given proper instruction and methods for dealing with torture. He wondered if they had the strength and commitment to do what was necessary. At times, he wondered the same about himself. One pill, one hard bite, and whatever information was sought would never be retrieved.

Rong knew that Rita Zhiang and Jill Evers had been on their way to safety—ChinAlive headquarters. He knew the consequences of their capture and interrogation.

Rong always found Fengdu's reputation as the "Ghost City" superstitious nonsense. It had much to do with myths passed down from the Eastern Han Dynasty at a place called Mt. Minshan—now Fengdu. The temple's fame had to do with the surnames—Yin and Wang. Combine the two and it sounded a lot like "King of Hell" in Chinese. From there it was easy for Chinese people to conjure up their own visions of what hell might look like.

Landmarks in the area were given scary names—Ghost Torturing Pass, Last-Glance at Home Tower, Nothing-To-Be-Done Bridge, and River of Blood. Pictures of torture instruments were sold at tourist stands. Rong knew much of this had to do with marketing, a way to attract tourists. Unfortunately, the horrifying reports from the few who survived the torture temple helped solidify the macabre reputation of the Temple on Mt. Minshan—not something attractive to most tourists. And now, into the bowels of this mythical, modern hell, went Ms. Jill Evers Ms. Rita Zhiang, with a bunch of excited local policemen.

Chapter 39

Edward Liu's brothers, Bo and Shen, dutifully accepted the mission. The three of them scrounged through the supply shelves taking whatever they thought necessary. When the elder Liu handed them automatic weapons they both refused.

"You know how ruthless these men are. Neither of you can run fast, neither of you knows martial arts. Please, take the guns." Bo looked at his brothers. He stared hardest at his oldest brother, the educated one.

"We don't know anything about these. We would probably shoot each other. "There," he said, pointing to a couple of sturdy looking knives. "We know how to use those." Their brother pleaded again for them to reconsider but their minds were made up. As they were about to close their backpacks, the elder Liu handed them each a pill. "Bite down hard if necessary. It works immediately. Good luck."

Like small boulders tumbling down a mountainside, the brothers moved quickly out of the hidden tunnel and through the village. An inflatable speedboat was tied up at the seawall outside the cave. The black, sixteen foot craft was faster than anything else on the river and was often referred to by locals as *the mosquito.* With lights off, they raced invisibly over the dark water. Grizzled and tough as the two men were, the thought of Fengdu made them shiver. They had survived the Temple of Death, but the scars, mental and physical, remained. They knew the way, but what they would do when they got there, was still uncertain. Death was not their greatest fear. Torture they could manage with the pill. But the project must have a chance. Bo and Shen would do anything to avenge the loss of their families. Their brother, by placing faith in them, had given them reason to go on.

"What time did brother say the women would be in Fengdu?"

"They are there now. He said MSS would probably arrive from Shanghai by 6 a.m. It is now 11 p.m. We have time." For the next few hours, the men remained silent, listening only to the waves striking the bow, and the roar of the engine. When they pulled up to a small dock north of Fengdu, Bo noticed movement under the tarp they had brought to protect their gear. He looked at his brother, held a finger to his lips, and pointed to the tarp. Together they pulled their knives and held them ready. "Get out, we know you are in the boat." As they were about to stab into the tarp, the front edge slowly lifted and three sets of frightened eyes looked up. Not one of the three could easily uncoil after maintaining a severely cramped position for so many hours. The men quickly realized, as the figures uncurled, who the stowaways were.

"You stupid, stupid maggots!" The boys quivered at the ferocity of the two angry men. Shen grabbed Henry and threw him to the dock like a small sack of potatoes. The others boys scrambled to get out before they were grabbed.

"Now what are we going to do? You can't go back. We can't take you with us. We will be noticed."

"It's not so unusual, Uncle," said Henry. Both of the uncles faked a thrust at him. He recoiled but continued. "You see groups, family members like us, walking around together, all the time."

"Oh sure," one uncle said in disgust. "Two beat up old farmers, one young dumb head, one almost Chinese kid, and an American."

"Hey, I'm not an almost Chinese kid," protested Jerry. "I'm an American with Chinese characteristics." Neither uncle found that funny, and each threw out an air punch to shut him up.

The uncles talked for a minute and agreed. "You will all stay here, under the tarp and protect the boat—if you can do that. If we are not back by early morning, return with the boat and tell them what happened. Do not wait for the sun to come up."

"No," Charlie protested. "We came to help. We can help." Both the men made a move on Charlie. As Bo pretended to lunge, Charlie grabbed his arm, turned, and flipped him then planted a foot on his chest. In the next moment, Bo, now in a rage, raced at Charlie. Charlie deftly swung around and caught him in the chest with his foot. This lightening blow knocked Bo to the ground next to his brother. Both uncles were extremely strong, and easily pushed Charlie's foot aside as they jumped to their feet. Charlie instinctively jumped back to a protective stance. The boys were amazed at Charlie's skill, but the brothers had faced off with Charlie before. This time they didn't have the advantage of surprise. They stopped.

"I told you we can help," Charlie said, barely out of breath.

"Where did you learn to do that?" Jerry asked.

"Bruce Lee movies of course," Charlie answered, without taking his eye off the uncles. "And seven years of Wushu training."

"This is too much," Henry said. "The only white boy here and he's the one who knows the Kung Fu Hustle."

"Not exactly Kung Fu, Henry. Are you sure you have any Chinese in your veins?" The uncles didn't know what to make of these strange young men until Charlie said, "these are our mothers and they're in big trouble. We're going with you. This can help too," Charlie said, as he held up his cell phone. "We can call back to the cave and tell them not to worry – and keep them updated as we go." Jerry grabbed the phone out of Charlie's hand. "No you don't. Local authorities might be able to track the call."

"But I left my dad a note telling him that we'd be checking in."

"Then your dad will know to check for the signal. We can keep it turned on so they can at least trace our movements, but that's all. Does the battery have a full charge?"

"Yes," Charlie said. "But how do you know so much about telephone signals?"

"Spy thrillers of course. And having a father who owns one of the most powerful telecommunications companies in the world. Hey, who do you think developed…?"

"Yeah, yeah, we know, the Red Spears hoax," Henry said.

"Not to mention the communications protocol for the satellite back doors that will allow us to hijack all Olympic communications out of China, smart ass," Jerry said. From the disbelieving looks of his new friends, Jerry remembered that they had left before hearing this part of the plan. "More about that later." By this time, the men were itching to get going.

"No more talk. Do you know about Fengdu?" They knew Henry did. "Doesn't matter, too late to explain. Do you have pills?" But the uncles guessed the answer. "Idiots. If you get caught the whole project will fail."

"They won't get anything out of us," Charlie said.

"Oh, they will. They will. And you will wish you had never been born when they are through with you. We would give you ours but you would not have the guts to follow through. We will do our best to protect you, but you are warned—you have made your decision." The men noted what a good job their accomplices had done preparing themselves to look like locals—dirt-smeared faces, ragged, worn out clothes, and they smelled. No more time to waste.

#

At ChinAlive headquarters, three men stared at a note. "This at least shows some intelligence," Bill Zhiang said to the others when the phone didn't ring. The note Charlie had left said he would call, but Bill Zhiang knew his son must have helped Charlie change his mind. With all fingers crossed they watched a tiny ray of hope appear, blinking steadily on an electronic screen.

Chapter 40

Rita Zhiang and Jill Evers had never met before. It was possible they had seen each other somewhere in the expat community, but ChinAlive planners had made certain that as few members as possible met before it was necessary. Traveling in separate western groups, on different days, had been the plan. When Jill got sick they had to postpone her escape. The boat for one of them had departed ahead of schedule so the change in plan was left up to their bodyguards. It was bad luck when they met up, both attached to the same Chinese tour group.

After a few minutes of polite conversation, the women were stunned to discover each other's identity and immediately agreed to change plans at the next docking. They were steady, a bit frightened, but not amazed when PSB told them they were going to be detained. Both of them took some comfort as they saw their bodyguards mixing, unobserved in the background

"Why are we being detained?" No reply. Neither of them spoke much Chinese. After many angry attempts at communicating, an English speaking Chinese man said, "all he says is he has orders."

"Thank you sir. Would you please ask him where we are getting off? And tell him we demand to be taken to an American Consulate or Diplomatic Mission?"

"He says he does not know and that he is waiting for a call. Maybe you are getting off here, with our group," the man said, pointing to the dock of a small town they were approaching. A few minutes later the ladies found themselves separated out, as the rest of the tour group was escorted off the boat. The man who had translated for them wished them luck, then walked away with the others.

With growing dread Jill and Rita watched when three of their bodyguards were forced to get off as well. The fourth bodyguard, after all the other passengers had left, was dragged out from a back room and thrown into the water, a few yards from the dock. The other bodyguards made an attempt to help but were blocked by a newly arrived contingent of policemen. The women were horrified to think the beaten man was dead, but were relieved to see him get up and make his way to the edge of the dock. Along with the others, he was forced into the back of a police van.

Jill and Rita knew they had passed the place where most tourists ended their tours. They tried to make conversation but neither was in the mood to talk. Both were worried they would be overheard. Their only relief on this hot, humid evening was the breeze off the water as they headed west. The policeman offered both of them tea or coffee, but they refused. He continued to be polite but would not answer any of their questions. It was no use arguing with this man.

Slightly submerged in his own thoughts, he was already counting the extra income from the promotion he was sure to get by finding and bringing these women to the attention of higher authorities. He hoped they were truly the women their bosses were looking for.

When the boat landed, the women had no idea where they were. They saw no signs in English, no tourists, and next to no activity of any kind.

"Where are we?" The policeman from the boat and two others who had joined him did not reply as they pushed the ladies along. Jill and Rita stopped. The two policemen behind them, both shorter, almost collided. For the first time, the policeman from the boat showed some expression—a smile crossing his face.

"Fengdu, ladies." And then, as if he had read their minds, "No American here. No Consulate, no Diplomatic Mission."

"You have no right to detain us. We are not moving until you…" Their growing anger was quickly squashed as they were thrown to the ground. Guns were drawn and pointed.

"Silence. You do as you are told."

Chapter 41

Henry tried to imagine how he would feel if his mother had been captured. He wished he could share more of what he knew—what ChinAlive had planned to tell them at the meeting. At least Jerry and Charlie could have made more sense of what this was all about. For the moment, they needed to stay close to his uncles.

Charlie was lost in his own thoughts, dreading what was happening, or about to happen to his mom. This was too much. What had his dad gotten them into? Wasn't this for the Chinese to decide? All he had wanted to do was explore a few different scenarios concerning the Yangtze for a research project. Would he and his mom have been in this creepy little town if he had kept his curiosity under control—or if his father had been home more?

Charlie snapped back to the present when Jerry tripped in front of him. Charlie spun to the side, trying to balance himself. Jerry grabbed his leg, fell over on his back, then let out a muffled scream. A piece of rusted pipe had reached out and ripped a gash in Jerry's calf. Blood began seeping through his pant leg.

"Damn!" cried Jerry, understanding as well as the others how bad the timing was for this to happen. "Damn, damn, damn!" The amount of blood and the pain were at first frightening.

Shen bent down to take a look. After tearing back the pant leg he said, "Not so bad, but we can't wait." He cut a piece off the bottom of his shirt and said, "Keep this tightly wrapped. Nothing else to be done now."

"No," said Henry. "This metal is dirty and rusted and he is bleeding badly. Jerry, you need to be seen." The uncles deliberated for only a minute. "There is a clinic on our way. We can drop him off but we cannot wait."

"That will work," Henry said. "All these clinics are cheap. This is a straight-forward wound. When you are done, you can wait there for us to return."

"What if you don't return?" Jerry asked.

"Two hours," the uncles said. "If we are not back in two hours you must go to the boat. Wait there. If we are still not back, leave before the sun comes up. Tell them what happened. That is all we can do." After a quick translation, they all agreed—the wound needed to be fixed by a person with medical skills.

When they got to the clinic, Henry walked in with Jerry. At the sight of the bloody leg a nurse on duty showed them quickly into an exam room. Jerry was relieved to have Henry explain how he was a cousin visiting from Taiwan and that his Mandarin was not so good. The group had pooled their money and left him with 400 Yuan – almost $50.00—more than enough to pay the bill, or a bribe, if necessary. Henry looked at Jerry and promised to bring his mom back soon. He wasn't surprised to see the grave, fearful look on his new friend's face.

"Don't worry. That wound must be cleaned and bandaged. You wait." Henry hated to leave but knew they had to get going. He hoped the treatment of Jerry's leg would be routine.

The contrast from the florescent-lit hospital interior to the dirty evening smog was intense—it took Henry's eyes a minute to adjust. He looked to where the others said they would be but there was no one in sight. The panic quickly subsided as he saw the three of them coming out of a tiny market with bottles of water. This was not a town where he wanted to be alone.

"Scared we left you?" Charlie said.

"This is scary place Charlie. You have no idea."

"Is that why there are so few signs of tourism? I don't see anyone trying to sell me authentic Ming Dynasty souvenirs—or even a pair of Air Jordans."

"Not here Charlie. Here is famous for one thing, but not something for post card sending." Charlie didn't get to follow-up as the uncles pressed on. He knew it was late but there was no indication that this place welcomed visitors. The only tourist promotion that might be connected to the temple was a small restaurant called the *We Kill You*

Dead Café—written in English and Mandarin. Menu items scrawled on an outside chalkboard in Mandarin might have meant capitalist roader coffee, confession cereal, and truth serum juice.

The uncles advised the boys to be on the lookout for any kind of three-wheeled bike that could be easily borrowed. They would need it to move the women through the streets without being seen. A blanket or tarp would be useful as well.

In a few minutes they found themselves in front of what looked like a typical Buddhist temple. Of the hundreds Charlie had seen in China, this one looked similar but there was something wrong. He didn't have time to make comparisons but his gut reaction was fear.

A single guard at the door was not what they expected. He looked like all the other twenty million rent-a-cops in China—baggy blue suit, white socks, damaged black vinyl shoes, and strangely tilted, ill-fitting military cap. More than one cigarette had fallen into his lap as a reminder of the times he had fallen asleep sitting up. As they approached, he slowly sat up, trying to look wide-awake. Charlie and Bo waited outside while Shen, pretending to be Henry's father, told the guard that they had a delivery to make to this address.

"Everyone knows we don't take deliveries after 8 p.m. And all deliveries are made around the side." When they looked in the direction he pointed, they saw nothing but a tree covered hill that extended for many meters beyond the edge of the temple's front door. They thanked the guard and said they would take a quick look to make sure they could find the delivery door in the morning. As they walked away, Charlie sensed the guard's distrust. At the moment before they left his sight, Charlie and Bo saw the guard lift a cell phone to his ear.

Chapter 42

Charlie and Bo had a slight lead on the other two when they disappeared through a clump of shrubbery.

"It's them," Charlie whispered—a little too loudly.

"No! Go back!" Jill Evers shouted when she saw them, but it was too late. Charlie and Bo came racing through the thicket and almost ran into Henry and Shen. Both moms were sitting on a temple bench, hands tied behind them. Two black Audis and two marked police cars were parked on either side of them. Lights from all four blinded them in an instant.

"Welcome gentlemen." Came a sleazy sounding, invisible voice.

"Finding these lovely ladies cruising up the river tonight was quite a coup, but now, to be joined by you gentlemen, well, what a surprise. I wonder how you knew their whereabouts."

Another voice followed. "Maybe they will tell us, if we ask nicely." A chorus of laughs rang out. "But it's a little dark and dusty out here. We were getting ready to go inside. Why don't you join us?"

Charlie couldn't see how many men were there, but he was so relieved to see his mom that it didn't matter. After rushing to her side, he was grabbed, thrown to the ground, and told to wait. Before the women started to go in, Rita Zhiang asked, "is Jerry with you?"

"There's another?" One of the cops asked. Rita knew immediately she shouldn't have said anything. Charlie covered expertly.

"He's not with us. Wasn't he going to meet you later this week?"

"Shut up. Stop talking." Charlie was relieved they didn't make any more out of what Rita asked. Before they entered the temple, Charlie caught her eye, winked and mouthed the words, "he's safe." She nodded back apprehensively, not knowing what to think. She didn't know Charlie Evers.

When they were all inside, Charlie counted four uniformed PSB and four men in long, cheap leather coats. He couldn't tell if these were the MSS from Shanghai or locals. It was unlikely the real MSS had arrived so quickly. After they were told to sit on benches in a formal waiting area, the four PSB cops stood close by while their plain-clothes counterparts huddled together in the doorway. From a few bits of muffled conversation, Charlie heard that these were indeed locals who had been ordered to hold the women until the experts from Shanghai arrived. One of cops sounded like he wanted to make a name for himself and was not content to share the glory of this night's capture with the "fools from the big city."

"We must follow orders. They told us to hold them. Nothing else."

"But we do not have to tell them about our new arrivals. We can have a go at them first, yes? It will save time for the experts." They were not all in agreement but some kind of plan was worked out. None of the ChinAlive group could make out what they had finally decided.

Charlie was startled when he felt his cell phone vibrating. Not possible. As desperate as he was to check it out, he thrust his hand into his pocket to squelch the buzz.

"How do you like our splendid little temple? It is a temple, you know. And quite famous."

"What are you going to do with us?" Henry asked.

"In time boy—first things first. I want all of you to understand your circumstances so that all of you fully appreciate what is happening, or is about to happen." He then walked over to where the uncles were sitting. "I don't think I need to remind these muddle headed farmers of what we do here." As he bent down to look menacingly at Shen, Shen spit in his face. After letting out an angry scream and quickly wiping off the spit, the embarrassed man slapped Shen so hard it knocked him off his chair. While struggling to get up, the man stepped on his back and pointed a gun to his head.

"Maybe we don't need this one. Doesn't look like he learned anything from his last visit." Everyone froze.

"Don't, please don't shoot him," Charlie's mom pleaded. Charlie took that moment to take a quick look at the screen in his pocket. It was Jerry.

"No, Mrs. Evers. Of course not," the man assured her. "That's not the way we do things these days. Is it gentlemen? Now get up and sit in this chair." He looked back to Charlie's mom. It had been startling to Charlie to hear this cop say her name.

"We are so pleased to see that you are all right. Word spread across the land that you had been kidnapped. Is that so?" Only the two boys, of all those in the room, could have explained why this scene was the way it was on this night. They both knew the women were baffled—not only at their detainment, but to now meet up with these two teenage boys and two strange farmers as well. The cops couldn't wait to start unraveling the mystery. The one who seemed to be in charge now approached Jill Evers with the same demonic shuffle and smile he had used on the uncles.

Charlie continued to grab glimpses of the tiny blinking screen in his pocket. He hoped his cramped thumb was producing text messages that were readable. He continued to maneuver himself behind the uncles to keep what he was doing private. When Jerry wrote that he was right outside, and what was about to happen, the surprised look on Charlie's face almost gave him away.

"Don't look so worried young man," one of the cops said, mistaking the fear in Charlie's face. "You should all be on your way soon. If you have nothing to hide and wish to answer a few questions, this will be easy. First, the tour," he said, motioning with a sweeping arm to the cavernous waiting room where they were gathered.

"The local people here have done well to build on the myths of the past. Ghost City as we are called, has a reputation for strange and evil happenings." The men in the leather coats were smiling. "We of the security watch have piggy-backed on this reputation to create an underground fright zone known mostly to locals. Although, I think our fame is spreading. We needed a place away from the public eye where we could find out anything we wished to know—with a high degree of success."

"You mean like a torture chamber," Charlie said. "Like part of the Gulag you've told the world you don't have?"

"Oh, you mean like your Guantanamo Bay?" the place your country imprisons people with no trial, after none of your hypocritical 'rule of law' has been administered, so they can be tortured out of the public view?"

"Yes and no." said Jill Evers, sharply. "We make mistakes, but at least they get uncovered and brought to the light of day."

"Enough. We are not here for a civics lesson. Our *Temple of Doom,* as some of the locals affectionately call it, could be a movie set, don't you think?" Except in horror movies, Charlie thought, he had never felt this freaked out.

"Most of China thinks this place is a myth passed down by the ancients. Seems that recent visitors—the ones who survived—have spread the word that the myth lives and is quite real. Whatever the reason for our fame, it certainly facilitates the extraction of any information we seek. Pretty scary, don't you think? Or maybe you don't think so, yet. Let's keep going. As your guides, we wish to welcome you to Fengdu's most infamous, ancient chamber."

Charlie was beginning to wonder if he was going to have time to clue the others in about Jerry's plan. If Jerry had time to get things into place, if Charlie was able to do his part, the plan might work. They would all have to react and react quickly. Charlie hoped that these men only had the power to bluff until the real interrogators arrived. This could get much worse fast.

"Please look this way." The man pointed to the wall in front of them. At the push of a button, the rock surface opened to reveal an even larger cavernous space. The sliding doors were twenty feet tall. When the doors opened, a screeching, metallic sound hurt their ears.

"Please, step in."

What they saw made all of them shiver. In the middle of a circular space at least a hundred feet in diameter, were two shiny metal gurneys and two chairs with leather straps. Behind the gurneys were rolling chests full of tools. Many looked as if they had survived the Middle Ages. Strange electrical appliances were located close to the center, as were a number of newer medical instruments. Rounding out the fearsome array of tools was a catalog the man held up in his hand. With a laugh, he showed them the catalog and said, "www.do-it-to-them.com. I love the Internet." His men followed with a deep, almost rehearsed laughter they might have heard in an old horror movie.

"We call this the 'fun room.' But that's for later." He pressed another button and the doors began to close. It was amazing to all how perfectly the doors were disguised and how precisely they fit together. Charlie wondered if this had been one of those local multi-million dollar expenditures awarded to high-ranking cadres under the guise of a public works project. Was there a swimming pool and sauna close by—a place to relax after a hard day of torturing?

"Now, I think we can safely say you have all been apprised of your situation. Maybe you can show us some courtesy by telling me and my men what circumstances have brought all of you together on this night." But before the questioning could begin, a small door in the back opened and a woman wheeled in a teacart with snacks.

"You see everyone, we are not savages. A bit of nourishment before we begin." The PSB cop waited, and then noticed that none of his prisoners were about to enjoy his offer.

"Come, come, nothing here has been poisoned, or even laced with truth sermon. We will show you." At that he signaled his men to take part. As they gathered round the teacart—a shiny metal hospital gurney—Charlie quickly informed the others about Jerry's plan. No one spoke. They all nodded that they understood. Charlie was thankful for the men's loud enjoyment of their food.

"So, are you sure that you won't join us? All right, more for my men."

When the men finished, the prisoners were each asked to sit in a seat that had been separated from the group. Jerry texted again. He wanted more time. Charlie needed to get his mom's attention and Rita Zhiang's. In the blink of an eye, he showed them the cell phone in the palm of his hand and whispered, "stall." Not knowing what else to do, and desperately holding onto this one ray of hope, both moms followed Charlie's instructions. They began by demanding their right to go to an American Consulate or at least talk to Consulate officials. They could tell when the leader was about to run out of patience so they brought up another grievance. This time, Jill Evers scolded them for not being able to find her husband and son and how she finally decided to take matters into her own hands. Rita Zhiang, taking a cue from Charlie, reminded them how she was on holiday and was to meet up with her husband and son in Lijiang.

"But where was your boy then?"

"At school, as Charlie said. But he is now with his father, waiting for me as we had planned. Why don't you release us and we can go find out?"

"But why are two of you on same boat?"

"*Were*, and *the*."

"What?"

"*Were*. You said *are*. It is past tense, what you said. You need to say *were* if you use the past tense. And you need to use the article *the* in front of words like *two* and *boat*. It would be best to say, *why were the two of you on the same boat*."

"What you talking about?" he said, flabbergasted at her gall but relieved that his men could not understand. Jill could see he was taking a deep breath, trying to figure out how to answer, and in which language.

"You cannot provoke me Mrs. Zhiang. I am not here for English lessons. Answer my questions now or we can ask them in much different way—your choice."

"What is your name sir?" Jill asked.

"Colonel Lee."

"Colonel Lee, haven't you ever heard of a coincidence? Ms. Zhiang and I had never met before this evening." Now the Colonel was really getting confused. He and his men had been told who these women were and about their suspicious movements and how each of their husbands were now persons of high interest to the government—but it was all so strange. These boys and these farmers had appeared out of nowhere. He decided to let the women rest and start in on the boys and men.

Charlie got up to take a seat in the interrogation chair. He paused, looked at the moms, uncles, and Henry. Hoping the cops couldn't hear what he was about to say, told the captives to get ready to drop to the floor. In the same instant he showed them the cell in the palm of his hand—it was time. In a loud but calm voice he said, "now." Suddenly, the lights went out, and the sound of a furious gun battle exploded outside the door. In a few seconds the lights came back on as the doors screeched open. The sound of firecrackers continued to go off at the edge of the entrance, and there, unbelievably, was Jerry. Along with Henry and Charlie and their moms, they gathered behind the uncles. Bo and Shin each had a knife at the throat of a plain clothes cop. Jerry grabbed the door remote to the "fun room" and told all the cops to stay where they were.

The men hesitated until both uncles drew blood from the throats they were squeezing. Colonel Lee screamed the order to follow the boy's instructions. When all the cops were as far back in the room as possible, the ChinAlive group slowly backed out into the waiting room. Bo and Shen still had the two cops, knives at their throats. Jerry pushed the remote. The cops could see what was happening and began to tense—ready to try and break free. They instantly stopped as the pressure of the knives cut deeper. When the doors were almost shut, the uncles threw them into the room to join their comrades. The doors sealed tightly with a loud thud.

Chapter 43

Two steps out the door and Rita Zhiang grabbed for her son. "Where does a computer nerd like you learn to behave like Jackie Chan?" Jerry couldn't believe the tears in his mom's eyes. Together they turned and raced down the street.

"So, you liked the way I handled that one?" he asked.

"Not too shabby," said Charlie. Jerry's mom couldn't believe how casual these young men pretended to be. But she could see—all three were shaking with relief.

"Stop," yelled Bo. Without a second's hesitation he cut a chain to borrow a three-wheeled bike parked at the end of a deserted alleyway. He told the ladies they had to hide under a tarp he had stolen from another bike. As soon as they were covered, the boys promised to explain everything when they got to Shigu. Shen pedaled the bike while Bo and the boys walked briskly behind.

"Oh no," Jerry said, stopping suddenly.

"You can't go back," Charlie whispered.

"I have to go back. No time to explain. I'll catch up as soon as I can. Don't worry." When Bo saw Jerry leave the group, he shook his head. When Henry shook his head as well, the uncle knew there was nothing to do but move on.

"We can't wait long," Shen said.

"I know," Henry answered, wondering what he would say to Jerry's mom when she found out. With no further problems, they safely arrived at the boat.

"Where's Jerry?" his mom asked. "Where's my son?"

"He said he had something important to do. He promised he'd catch up," Charlie told her. The longer they waited, the greater their sense of dread. After an hour, a shrill siren sounded, followed within minutes by a second siren. The sound was heading their way.

"We go," Bo said, as he started the motor.

"No," Jerry's mom protested. "We have to wait."

"We go now," Bo said again.

"Then I have to stay." As she made a move to get off, Bo wrapped his arms around her and shouted to his brother to take off.

"Let go of me you ape." Bo had not expected such ferocity. The second after she broke free, she was ready to jump in the water. With split second reflexes, Charlie and his mom each grabbed one of her arms and held on. After a few minutes, she was exhausted, collapsed on a seat, and started to cry. Charlie felt rotten but was thankful his mom was there. Jill Evers wrapped an arm around her new friend.

"You couldn't do anything Rita."

"He is extremely resourceful and he will be all right." Henry said. "How else could he have rescued us?" How else indeed, they all wondered.

"No, no, no," Rita Zhiang said. "He barely speaks Chinese. His only exercise is in front of a computer, and he has a terrible sense of direction. How's he going to be all right? Let's get to my husband as soon as possible—he'll know what to do." Jill Evers knew she would feel exactly the same.

With no running lights the uncles had to concentrate on the river. When they were safely away from the Ghost City, Bo turned to Charlie and asked, "Where do you think your friend got a cell phone? Weren't you the only one who had one when we started out?" Charlie shrugged. "I thought so too." The uncles looked at Charlie with tolerable admiration and then returned to the problem of navigating their boat on a black, moonless night.

"I guess we won't know about the other phone until he gets back," said Henry.

"Why don't we text him back to see what he's doing?" said Charlie.

"Didn't Jerry say that could be dangerous? Maybe we should not take a chance."

"Maybe you're right," agreed Charlie. Other than Rita Zhiang's urging Charlie to check for messages from Jerry ever few minutes, no one spoke until the mechanical doors in the seawall quietly swallowed them up.

Chapter 44

No two people were more relieved the next morning than Bill Zhiang and John Evers, even though their relief was short lived. As everyone headed toward breakfast and a debriefing session, no one was surprised to see both men hang back with their wives. So, the stories about Fengdu are true?" John Evers asked his wife. "You must have thought the world was upside down when Charlie showed up with Henry—at least one boy neither of you knew. And poor Rita, she didn't know either of the boys."

"And no Jerry, but two strange farmers, and all those crazy policemen?" said Rita. "And with Jill Evers—someone I had never met, with as many questions and fears as I had."

"You can't believe how worried we were Rita." As all four finished catching up the focus of the debriefing session changed quickly—where was Jerry Zhiang? It didn't take long to realize that they had no safe way to track him.

Two days went by. No word.

"If he has a phone why doesn't he call—or text?" Rita Zhiang asked her husband.

"Because he's smart, Rita. He doesn't want to take a chance on the signal being tracked. We don't know where he got the phone or what kind of signal the phone is putting out. After what that kid did, getting the rest of you out safely—his abilities should not be underestimated."

Mr. Liu added, "The authorities now know something is going on. They might even guess who some of the major players are."

"Where could that boy be?" said Bill Zhiang. "As if his disappearance isn't enough, I'm now worried about my standing with the government. What will they do if they think the work we have done will somehow compromise the Games?" In the original plan, Jerry and his mom were to meet up in Lijiang for a few days of holiday before fooling the government into thinking they were flying home for good. A long silence fell upon the room before Rita spoke.

"You want me to go back to Shanghai, don't you?"

"As much as I hate to say it Rita, it's the only way. It would be best to have Jerry go with you, but if he doesn't show up in the next day or so, we can work out your pretend return without him."

"How will you do that?"

"From here you will go directly to Shanghai. Once we contact the Consulate, you will volunteer to answer any questions, but only at the Consulate. They can't touch you inside an American compound. You only have to tell them the exact same things you told those over-achieving cops in Fengdu. If they want to know where Jerry is, you tell them he became sick and we wanted to get him home as soon as possible. I'll have the ticket receipts and his documentation in order. There won't be any question. After they leave we'll get you to a private runway at the city airport and you will be out of China within an hour."

"Back here." she said.

"No Honey, back to the States."

"But that's not the plan. I was to be here until this thing played out."

"The plan has changed."

"No it hasn't. Not enough. You, Mr. Big Shot, can dam well sneak me back here while pretending publicly to send me to the States. I am not leaving this country without my son. Or at least not until I know he is safe." Everyone could tell this was now a private matter and politely tried to mind their own business.

"I want to be here when Jerry gets back. Today, or when I get back from Shanghai, he will want me to be here." Bill Zhiang knew he would not win this one, especially after Jill Evers stepped in.

"I'm with you Rita. I'd say the same thing." Somewhat beaten, Bill Zhiang gave in. He looked to see if anyone was on his side. It was obvious—Rita Zhaing would rejoin them in the cave. She would be there until the end.

"But what happens when he shows up?" Charlie asked.

Mr. Zhiang restated what had been agreed upon in previous meetings. "The plan was always for him to stay here after fooling the government into thinking he had gone home with his mom. We need his genius to run the programs he wrote for the satellites. Rita was going to remain with us, safe, out of the reach of the government. Now, she has to prove she is on her way home. It would be impossible, especially with such a concentrated spotlight on me, not to send her home—or at least pretend to do so.

"We will need to keep her and Jerry's whereabouts shrouded in case the Party tries to track them in the States, which they certainly will do."

"What will she tell them when they ask her about my mom, me, Henry, Bo and Shen?" Charlie asked.

"How about this," offered Charlie's dad. "Rita was heading up, like Bill said, to meet with her family for a few days before leaving for the States. Meeting up with Jill was purely coincidental. Jill, having barely escaped capture by some police bureau—which should embarrass them greatly – was heading up the river on a tip to find her family who none of the authorities had been able to find. As far as Henry and his uncles, I would say you had no idea who they were or how they got there. Period. Let them try to figure that one out. Agreed?"

"Sounds good to me John. All right Rita?" Bill Zhiang asked his wife. She nodded in agreement. "But not until Jerry gets back."

Mr. Liu then posed the question everyone was avoiding: "What do we do if they have him?" No one could find the words to speak.

Bill Zhiang looked at his wife, then at everyone else. "I have every resource possible looking and listening. If they have him, we would know. Let's wait for a few days before we send Rita to Shanghai. If he shows up, you both go and answer their questions. If he doesn't show, you go and come back." He said it with such certainty, that everyone was willing to believe it was a good plan. He only wished he could believe it himself.

Chapter 45

"Imbeciles." The Shanghai experts shouted at the men as the giant metal doors parted. "You let them escape." With their own anger, the local PSB responded, "You never told us there were others, but we had them as well."

"Had them, fools, had them. Where did they come from? How did they know where to find the women?" How indeed, he said to himself, as an important follow-up thought crossed his mind.

"Where could they possibly hope to escape? Thanks to your bungling we have wasted precious time."

"Not exactly Captain," the local men smiled. "Before the others arrived we bugged the women. They both have tracking devices in their clothes and shoes. Let's go out to our cars. I will show you the technology we have to start reeling them in." When they got to the parking lot, the fury of the local PSB outdid that of their comrades from the big city. All their tires had been flattened and the car with the tracking equipment was gone. After an hour, using all the local police to help, their car was found abandoned on a road heading up to the mountains. When they found that the tracking equipment had been taken, the atmosphere changed once again from mild anticipation to renewed anger. The incompetence of their country bumpkin counterparts would not go unreported.

"But it will still work," the locals reassured their city comrades. "We know the frequency. All we have to do is find another receiver." The police from the city were relieved but not yet willing to see their hopes flattened once again. They followed the local men to central police headquarters—an old crumbling concrete bunker that did not inspire much confidence.

#

Two boys quietly emerged from the back room of a tiny computer shop after the police cars passed.

"That was close," Jerry said. The boy who had traded Jerry for the phone looked excited.

"This kind of stuff not happen around here. Never. And usually, anyone who go in the temple, do not come out walking," the boy said. Jerry had to be careful what he told his new friend—at least something to gain his trust and maybe his help.

"Trouble makers," said Jerry. "People the government doesn't want anywhere near Beijing when the Olympics start." That was all the boy needed to know.

"Name is Ralph."

"Ralph?" Jerry questioned. "Ralph?"

"Not Chinese name. When meiguoren—Americans—came to stay and teach English last year, we all choose English name. I was reading book about mouse name Ralph and I like mouse. Remind me of me—clever, fast. Ralph here to help mine new friend. What your name?"

"I'm Jerry. Pleased to meet you, Ralph."

"How come your friends go, you stay, PSB come, they go, you stay? Wazzzzuppppppp?" Ralph smiled, and then asked, "That the way it said, the big question, right?"

"Where did you hear that?" Jerry laughed.

"Our teacher told us. He said part of a beer commercial once. Cool, yes?" Jerry smiled, rolled his eyes a little, and agreed. "Way cool."

"You teach me more cool stuff? No, guess not now. You have to get out of here. Escape. Yes? Maybe later?"

"Yes, absolutely. But you're right, I have to get out of here and join up with my friends as soon as possible. If everything works out, I'd love to talk more." Jerry admired the boy Ralph. It was at his father's shop where he had made a deal for the phone. Ralph was sleeping in the back room when Jerry walked in and started looking at the cell phones.

"Help you?" Ralph said, as he rolled out to the front.

"Yes. I have a problem. I need a cheap phone but I have no money. And I don't speak Chinese."

"Problem? No problem. Problem? Yeah man, problem. You see, I speak English a little. But no money? Problem."

"Would you be willing to trade for something?"

"Maybe. What?"

"Show me your cell." When Jerry had it in his hand he continued. "If you give me a cheap phone, I can show you how to get free, unlimited, worldwide usage on your phone forever."

"Not possible. You show me, you can have any of these in front of you." Jerry popped the back off the phone, played with it for a few minutes, then handed it back.

"There you go. Try it."

"I try friend at university in Beijing. Here goes." Five minutes later he hung up and looked at Jerry with a big smile. "Cool. Thank you." Jerry then picked out a phone.

"Do you have a local sim card?"

"Yes."

"Great, thanks. I've gotta go." Before he was a hundred yards down the street, Jerry stopped, turned, and ran back.

"Do you know anything about the temple? I need to know the layout."

"You got it man." Ralph sketched a quick layout. Two minutes later Jerry was on his way. He now had a greatly enhanced cellphone but no idea what he was going to do. When he returned an hour later, in a black Audi police sedan, Ralph's eyes bugged out.

"I need to take this on a road heading out of town and leave it. I want them to think I headed in a different direction. Can you show me?"

"Yaaa man." Ralph agreed. Jerry could tell that the picture of Bob Marley on Ralph's tee shirt was not only a good deal at a local market, but a source of inspiration. After running the car into a ditch, the boys returned on foot, sure that no one had seen them. The windows were covered with a darkened film so their identities were safe. Before they ditched the car Jerry grabbed what looked like some interesting equipment from the back seat. When they returned to the shop he was overjoyed to discover what it was.

"This is…?" Ralph asked.

"This is tracking equipment. I bet they put bugs on my friends. See these bugs? They're probably set for the same frequency. Too bad we have these bugs and the tracking gear. We could really have thrown them off."

"But still we can. They know the frequency, so they can track with other equipment. Yes?"

"Yes, if they have other equipment," Jerry agreed, wondering where his brain had gone. "How do you know about this kind of stuff?"

"I play around, learn by myself." At that moment they realized they were thinking the same thing.

Jerry said, "First we send them north, while at the same time we send them west." Ralph smiled and led them to a local truck stop. When no one was looking, they planted a couple of bugs on one of the trucks. A half-mile away they came to the river, and this time planted three more bugs on a boat heading east.

"I'm guessing, if sending your trackers both east and north, you are either heading south or west. But it's probably better if I not know, right?"

"Right Ralph. But I don't dare go in a straight line to my destination. I've got to make it difficult for them—just in case."

"Let's go back to my father's shop. I have a map for you and we can plan the best way." As they returned, the town was slowly waking up. Food was being cooked and sold on the streets. Ralph offered to make Jerry tea when they got back. Ralph's room was a tiny space with posters of Bob Marley and Bill Gates covering the walls. Jerry had many questions to ask his new friend but he knew ChinAlive members—especially his mom and dad—would be worried.

Ralph was right about being able to track the bugs with a different device. Jerry had to get back to warn them. He was sure that the walls of the cave would block any signal. He also knew that the proximity to where the signal left off would give the authorities a starting place they had never had before. Jerry's biggest concern was how to make contact with someone once he got back. He had no idea how to get to the cave and he didn't know anyone in Shigu.

"Here, you can have old backpack. I put some food in it for you. Sorry, can't help you with money."

"I'll figure something out. Thanks for the pack and the food."

"If you go to Lijiang, maybe get you close. Rides easy to find—lots of tourists go there. Lijiang big market for farmers. They always travel back roads – keep you out of sight." Jerry's biggest challenge would be traveling with no money. As if he had read Jerry's mind Ralph sprang into action. "Be right back." A minute later he appeared out of a back room with a handful of junky looking electronic parts. "Take these. You never know what is tradable." Jerry doubted their value but thanked Ralph.

“I walk you to road where your trip needs to start—on my way to school. I am sure I can find someone I know can help you.”

Chapter 46

Ralph kept his word and found Jerry a driver—a friend of his dad. There wasn't much room in the small van. A couple of heroic shoves and Jerry found himself squeezed in with a bunch of unwashed vegetables. For six of the worst hours of his life he felt like he was being tossed in a salad. The road was no more than a cow trail but it didn't slow the driver down. Jerry wondered if Ralph had told the man speed was important, or if he usually drove with a death wish.

The first part of the journey was over by the middle of the afternoon. Jerry guessed it was too late to sell anything so he helped the man set up for the next day. The farmer motioned Jerry to get in the truck while he went out to do errands. When he came back, he handed Jerry a tin of cooked vegetables with some rice. After sharing the same space with the same veggies for hours, Jerry almost gagged. But he was hungry. The food was filling and he was grateful.

"You hide, night come." The farmer said in broken English. As much as he hated to get back in, at least he had the truck all to himself. He had no idea what time it was when he heard a voice whisper, "Now. Come now." It was too dark to read his watch. When Jerry stepped out, another beat up old truck was idling next to them. The first farmer signaled to Jerry to show the new driver the map. With only the glow of a cigarette lighter, it took a few minutes to make clear where he wanted to go. The route Ralph had suggested was a long, roundabout mess. Ralph was at a disadvantage because Jerry didn't want to tell him his final destination – only the vicinity. The last leg would be the killer, but it would get him close enough. After thanking the first farmer, the man pointed to Jerry's knapsack. Ralph must have told him that Jerry had brought some form of payment. After dumping it out, both farmers selected a couple of items.

Jerry's new ride looked like a tin box on three wheels. He had seen these contraptions before but never imagined himself as cargo. He wasn't sure he could survive another long, pounding ride. Most of this man's produce had been sold so there was no cushion for this leg of the journey. Jerry hesitated. The man understood and offered him a heavy bunch of burlap bags to use as buffers. They worked well for a while, but the roughness of the bags eventually pricked and poked Jerry like he was traveling on an anthill.

After bumping along for three days, with three different farmers, Jerry was sure he could endure anything—if he survived. When his stamina was almost gone, when he was sure that some PSB search team would discover him, or that the farmer—in desperate need of money—would turn him in, he heard a gravelly voice whisper, "Shigu."

"This is Shigu?" Jerry was surprised. He had not told Ralph this was his final destination. Must be a coincidence, he thought. *Careful, Jerry.*

"Shigu, yes." Jerry waited until the man positioned his cart alongside a number of others. It was early evening, almost dark. Jerry helped the man unload his produce. When they saw two teams of PSB patrolling on foot, stopping to ask questions along the way, he knew the farmer wouldn't want any part of the trouble he was in. Holding a finger to his lips, he let Jerry know he would say nothing, but he needed Jerry to leave—now. He thanked the man, left all his remaining electronic parts behind, and jumped behind a group of buildings at the edge of where the produce sellers had set up.

In this unfamiliar setting he had to find a way to blend in. He started to walk—casual like. No cops in front, none behind. He was in the clear. After checking both sides of the street, he hurried down five or six blocks to the center of town. The steps to an abandoned business looked like a good place to sit and make plans. He prayed someone he recognized from the cave would walk by soon.

Chapter 47

Rong watched his crew as they stood mesmerized, staring at red lights flashing on a wall-mounted electronic map of China. Although it was an honor to be asked to sit in on the unfolding of such an important case, all he could feel was sweat rolling down his back and perspiration building up under his arms. His mouth was dry as sandpaper. The high-ranking officials with them watched closely, hoping the bugs planted by the Fengdu group would lead them to something worth all the time they had spent on this case.

Despite his efforts to the contrary, Rong's men had done well in unraveling the Red Spears hoax. He was still uncertain why, of all the groups, his had been accorded this honor. The Ministry of State Security desperately needed to know the reason such an enormous effort had been made in creating and spreading the Red Spears hoax.

With the unexpected appearance of these two American women, and the bizarre appearance of their sons—along with two Shigu farmers—it was impossible to guess what any of this meant. The local authorities were poised to respond to any instructions sent by the higher command in Shanghai.

Rong was hoping their inclusion in tracking the bugs was indeed an acknowledgment of his group's professional efforts, but he couldn't shake the nagging feeling it might be something more. How these boys and farmers knew where to look for Jill Evers and Rita Zhiang, in the middle of a country as big as China, baffled everyone. What if he had been discovered? What if his inclusion was the best way to see if he would slip up and reveal himself in some other way? He desperately needed to contact ChinAlive headquarters to warn them. More than anything else, he needed to be calm, cool headed, and trust that he was still in the clear. The time was getting close The danger was growing.

Then, like a miracle, the blinking lights stopped.

"Where did they go? Where are they? Get on the phone. Rush our men there to the last coordinate and tell those country cops if they screw this up the only police work they do again will be digging their own graves." When the highest ranking official in the room finished screaming out orders, it looked like he was ready to hit someone.

As a contingent of MSS headed to the vicinity of where the signal disappeared, Rong knew he had to make contact soon. His prediction that the walls of the cave would block the signal had come true. ChinAlive was safe, for now. The downside was that the authorities now knew something suspicious was going on in that area.

Under the direction of the Ministry of State Security, policemen from every local town and village descended on Shigu. The local PSB knew that Bo and Shen were from around this area so when the signals left off in the same vicinity, the MSS team knew they on to something. But when they arrived, they could find nothing. No trace—no Bo or Shen, and no sign of anything out of the ordinary. For two days the cops canvassed the area asking every person, every household, and every traveler if they had seen the farmers, women, boys, or any unusual visitors in the past few days or weeks. After the villagers had been questioned with disappointing results, the MSS set up an interrogation office in the lobby of an old, deserted hotel. While teams of PSB continued to scour local villages and surrounding countryside, the MSS started a much tougher round of questioning. Life became miserable for the villagers and they began to wonder what they had done to deserve this.

ChinAlive headquarters monitored as much of the movement as they could around the area and finally figured out that bugs must have been planted on the women's clothing. A search of their clothes turned up no less than five of the tiny devices. When an angry Rita Zhiang crushed them under her foot, Bill Zhiang winced. His last minute idea to send the bugs further up the river had been destroyed.

"They led the authorities here, they could have lead them away," he told her.

What Bill Zhiang didn't know was how his son, using other bugs, had already tricked the authorities with the same idea. They were much less likely to be fooled again, but it would have been worth a try.

Chapter 48

During the long hours on his ride to Shigu, Jerry couldn't help thinking about Ms. Wu's speech—*insidious relationship with the world, democracy coming to China, terrible deceits and lies.* This, coupled with the unfinished conversation he had had with his dad about bringing great change to China, the Red Spears hoax, his teamwork with Henry in getting information from Charlie, the clandestine movie set under the mountain, and the rescue from Fengdu—he was between the pages of an action thriller that had yet to make any sense. He had to find his way back to fill in the pieces.

As the lights of the village grew dim, and the townspeople headed for home, Jerry noticed a man at a bakery across the road. The man was cleaning up and getting ready to close.

Careful Jerry, the baker said to himself. *Careful.* He knew Jerry had no idea he was sitting on steps of the new MSS interrogation office across the street from his bakery. Is it my imagination, or is that man staring at me? Jerry thought. Every time he looked, the man looked back but quickly turned away, returning to his cleaning chores. Jerry stayed still when he heard men talking behind him. They had left the building for a smoke. Suddenly, a strong kick to his lower back knocked him forward onto the street. An angry sounding command followed. With a quick glance over his shoulder, he saw the uniforms. Jerry was terrified; clueless what the man had said. Praying he was following the man's orders, he stood up and started slowly moving away when the man at the bakery suddenly started screaming at him.

"You lazy loaf, do I pay you to sit around? Get over here and make this last delivery." Jerry didn't know what the baker was saying either but understood the beckoning motion the man was making. As he got closer and out of range of the men behind him, the baker whispered in English, "Jerry, you're safe. Peddle this three wheeled cart to the end of that road. Someone will meet you. Don't look back. You were sitting on the doorstep of an MSS office." The baker was relieved that Jerry looked so filthy, unkept, and alone. If the MSS sensed anything unusual about the boy—his skin tone, association with any other strangers, there might have been big trouble.

Jerry never felt so relieved. After peddling the bakery cart for a quarter of a mile, he found himself at the edge of a cornfield. "Pssst, over here." Jerry stopped to see where the sound was coming from—Henry. Henry was waving to him from inside one of the rows of corn. "Don't forget the bread, we need it. Leave the cart out of sight. Hurry."

"Am I ever happy to see you," said Jerry.

"Same," replied Henry. He knew this was not time, but the question burst out. "Where did you go?"

"What?" Jerry said. "Shouldn't we get going?"

"Sure, sure. Sorry. But we were greatly worried. Your story better be good. Follow me." At the end of the cornrow, they came to what looked like a potting shed. When they stepped inside, Henry pushed pots and tools aside to reveal a steep stairway.

"You first," Henry said.

"This is huge," said Jerry as he scanned the tunnel. "We didn't explore much earlier, did we? Can we look around later?"

"Maybe, if they don't chain you to a computer terminal for safe keeping. Turn around now, wave to the camera." As they hustled down a long, narrow tunnel, Henry remembered the same amazement he had once felt.

"No wonder you don't have guards everywhere. Jerry looked at a tiny camera embedded in the wall of the cave, waved and smiled. And then felt stupid, but it didn't matter. He knew he must have had an audience. In the next instant a tidal wave of people came running through the cave to meet him, headed up by his mom and dad. The dirt on his face, now mixed with his mom's tears went unnoticed. He was safe.

With everyone's excitement at Jerry's return, Henry knew he would have to wait for the story. He couldn't believe this non-Chinese speaking city boy from the States could possibly survive abandonment in a strange village, in a strange country, and find his way back—and so quickly. And what precautions did he take to make sure he wasn't followed? Hurry up,

Henry thought selfishly to himself, as he watched Jerry's parents celebrate their son's triumphant return. When the immediate celebration was over, Jerry was turned over to Henry and Charlie to help him get ready for dinner.

"You stink man," Charlie laughed.

"Did you ride in with a bunch of pigs?" Henry asked.

"Just show me the shower and I'll give you the whole story at dinner."

After a well-deserved rest, Jerry was seated at the head of a long table. Ordinarily, such a debriefing would have taken place in private, but they all knew he must be starving, so no one minded an alternate protocol. When Jerry almost fell asleep in his soup, everyone knew they would have to wait until morning.

Chapter 49

At breakfast, Jerry's story kept everyone, especially his mom and dad, riveted.

"I had a feeling," he said, "that they would leave the keys in their cars. When I found the bugs, I knew some of them had been used but figured the cave would hide the signal." Jerry told everyone how he had pointed the cops in the wrong direction with the car, and then planted the bugs to send them in opposite directions to gain even more time. Bill and Rita Zhiang's breakfast grew cold as they listened, mesmerized.

"Do you think they picked up your trail at any point?" his dad asked.

"I don't think so. The boy who helped me in Fengdu assured me that the locals would be happy to help if it meant fooling the PSB. I didn't tell anyone my final destination. For all the last driver knew, I could be halfway to Vietnam by now."

"Jerry, we are all so relieved to have you back. And thankful for your help—Henry's and Charlie's as well." Mr. Liu said in English, then Chinese. He reached over to take his brothers' hands. Bo and Shen smiled and nodded at the boys, "Brave sons, very brave sons." After Henry translated for Jerry, all three boys quietly accepted the compliment with gratitude.

"But the problem is," continued Mr. Liu, "the authorities now know something is going on in this area. Knowing that I was Bo and Shen's brother, they came to me looking for information. I told them I had not seen them since they were released from the temple in Fengdu the first time, two years ago. Other than their little outing to interrogate Charlie, they've been living in the cave ever since. Authorities have followed the bugs this far and have flooded the area with police. Fortunately, few people in Shigu know anything about what we are doing and no one else has seen Bo or Shen. We need to be extremely cautious. Phase one of ChinAlive begins soon.

"Why don't we activate more of the bugs I brought back?"

"You brought some with you?" Jerry's dad asked.

"I figured we might have some use for them. If we activated the same number you found, and send them up river on a boat, wouldn't that lead the police away from us?"

"Chip off the old block," said his mom, much relieved after she had destroyed the other bugs. After a quickly agreed upon plan, they decided to put the bugs on a small boat later that night. Henry's uncles volunteered to take the boat as close as possible to the most dangerous water, jump out at the last minute, and let the rapids take over.

"You can call friends in Chenzhou to meet you." Mr. Liu suggested to his brothers.

"Yes, we will call." As Mr. Liu walked away, he thought he saw a strangely solemn look pass between his brothers. When he was gone Bo whispered to his other brother.

"We will make sure they think we are dead."

The search along that part of the river would take a fair amount of time and hopefully, divert the attention of authorities long enough to give ChinAlive time to safely put the next part of their plan into action.

#

When the bugs mysteriously reappeared on the security-tracking screen in Shanghai's MSS headquarters, authorities were excited and confused. The bugs appeared at least a quarter-mile upriver from where they had stopped before, and were now rapidly heading toward Tiger Leaping Gorge.

"If we take them here," Captain Xiang said, pointing to the small town of Qiotao on a map, "we can at least interrogate them. But if we do not stop them, and they are heading toward a more important location… maybe it would better to wait."

"What if we lose them again? Then what?" It was not unanimous, but an agreement was reached to let them continue while keeping close track of the bugs. Everyone at the meeting knew that darkness was a problem but tracking crews would be close by to intercept at a moment's notice. It was a risk the majority was willing to take.

At midnight the uncles silently drifted into the current. Mr. Evers attached five of the bugs to simulate the five they had found. As the uncles passed Qiaotou—the village at the entrance to the Gorge—the current began picking up speed. As they approached a dock at Chenzhou, friends who were waiting for them watched in amazement, then horror. The men were not coming ashore. Ignoring the screams and the pleas for them to stop, they calmly looked ahead to the wild rapids.

"Brother did not trust us. He must have made the call." Bo said.

"He should not have. If we had wanted people on the docks to help pull us to safety we would have called. I think he guessed, but it was our decision."

#

Their bodies, along with the clothes they had taken from the two women and boys, were recovered the next day. The focus of the search shifted upriver. Their plan had worked. When the phone call came, Mr. Liu felt a sickness in his heart. Somehow he knew. The others were stunned. These were their first casualties and a vivid reminder that there were many dangers to come. After accepting condolences, Mr. Liu and Henry quietly left the cave and walked home.

Chapter 50

John Evers called a meeting the next morning. If Charlie hadn't noticed the effects of his dad's grinding regimen before, he did now. His father's eyes were lined with dark circles and his face looked fallen. The sturdy, upright way he always held himself had given way. After a sip of coffee, some deep breaths, and a few stretching exercises, Charlie was relieved to see his strength return. There was still power in his voice.

"Their deaths will not be in vain. The calculated sacrifice these men made, they made to save this project. They were loved and they will be missed." Only the hum of the cave's generators could be heard in the distance. Everyone sat quietly. For Charlie and all those present, this was a chilling reminder. The moment ended when John Evers brought the room back to the reality at hand.

"New business?" A few items were presented, and then the meeting was adjourned.

"Hold on." Charlie's dad caught Charlie and Jerry as they were about to leave. Mr. Fathom stayed behind as well.

"I know how strange this is going to sound, but you've have missed a lot of school." Charlie and Jerry stopped and looked at Mr. Fathom.

"Your education is only one of my assignments. The Evers and the Zhiangs want you to finish up. One of our members is still at the school you left and guarantees that if you complete the coursework required, with me, the school will give you the credit you need to move ahead with your grade—in China or wherever you land next. I plan to tweak the work to your circumstances, but what I have planned will be more than enough to keep you riveted—and busy."

"No disrespect Mr. Fathom, but...are you serious?" said Charlie." You're worried we might fall behind in school while everyone around us is plotting to overthrow the Chinese government? Jerry?" Charlie turned to his new friend, "What do you think—on my believability scale, one to ten?"

"One for sure," replied Jerry.

Mr. Fathom responded. "I know that after all you have been through, school might sound a bit mundane. But I assure you, what you are about to learn is something most people on this planet will never know. I plan to stretch what you will learn over three different subject areas."

"Okay, said Jerry, we get it, I think. But why don't you have me take the duties already assigned and get Charlie going as well. Save us all a lot of time—don't you think?"

"I hear you," said Mr. Fathom. The truth?"

"That would be nice," said Charlie.

"I don't think your dads ever intended to get you or your mom's involved. They know how hard this is and I think they are trying keep your lives as normal—if there is such a thing—as possible. I also promised them that the things we would be studying would be so riveting that you'd forget, at least for a while, how weird this truly is. So come on, give me a break, it's my job." The boys looked at him skeptically.

"Plus, you wouldn't want to have to repeat 10th grade now, would you?"

"What about Henry?" Charlie asked.

"Don't worry about Henry. His father is rapidly bringing him up to speed at home. He needs to finish his regular schooling as well."

"Great," said Charlie.

"Can't wait," said Jerry. "But this better be good Mr. Fathom." Charlie and Jerry followed him a few doors down from *Classroom 1*, where he handed them an outline of what they would be doing for the next month.

"I thought this was going to be all ChinAlive stuff," Charlie said.

"Much of it is Charlie. But if you want to finish school, there are a few other things. Once you have completed what's in front of you, you won't have any trouble staying up with other kids at your level."

"If we're still alive," said Jerry.

"Well yes, there is that," smiled Mr. Fathom. "But let's be optimistic.

"Guest speakers to include our dads?" asked Jerry.

"Indeed. And you are right Charlie, it will be interesting." They both rolled their eyes but wouldn't admit how much they looked forward to having access to their dads in a way they hadn't for a long, long time.

"So does this mean we get to find out how all of this came together?" asked Charlie.

"That's exactly what it means gentlemen. And a whole lot more."

During the next month the challenge and excitement would grow—as would the fear and the uncertainty. A front row seat to a rapidly changing history didn't happen every day for most high school students. Criminal, fugitive, terrorist, freedom fighter, high school student—who on earth had those credentials, all at the same time, at the age of fifteen? One month of schooling and then full-fledged membership in ChinAlive.

Chapter 51

At 3 p.m. the following day Mr. Fathom had a surprise for them.

"Next door gentlemen. A new group arrived last night so this presentation—your first class—is for everyone." When they all had taken a seat, John Evers stepped up to the front. Jerry's dad and a woman they had briefly seen before were sitting behind him.

"Ladies and gentlemen, this is Mr. Bill Zhiang and Ms. Grace Wu. Mr. Zhiang is, at any given minute, one of the ten richest people in the world. He and his company have been recruited by the Chinese government to help prepare the telecommunication networks for the Olympics. Ms. Wu should be known to many of you because of her environmental work and the television show she produces on environmental issues here. Without their help ChinAlive would have remained a dream. Their presentations will outline the roles they have played and continue to play. First, Mr. Zhiang."

"Good afternoon. As you all know, China is one of the largest countries in the world, so communications is one of our greatest challenges. We must be able to act in unison as our plan unfolds. It is incredibly fortunate that the government's needs have been a mirror of our own, but for much different reasons.

"At the invitation of the Chinese government, our company has helped place a new primary and secondary satellite in orbit to make sure China has all the communication power necessary to broadcast the Olympics to a worldwide audience. Within these two satellites, we have placed backdoors that we control." He paused for a second as he walked a few yards to an open stairway at the edge of the area where he was standing and pointed up—"from that platform." He waited a minute for the group to grasp the meaning of what he said. Charlie looked at Jerry.

"What?" Jerry asked.

"What do you mean what?" said Charlie. You know about all this?"

"Not all of it. But most of it, I guess."

"Most of it? You guess?"

"Well, sure. How else could I write the codes for the satellites if I didn't know most of the plan? Listen up. Here comes the part James Bond would love."

"During the opening ceremonies, the largest projection screen ever built will be used to show those in attendance – and the rest of the world—a welcoming bit of propaganda. We plan to hijack the opening ceremony. While the whole world watches, the Chinese people will be offered their first nationwide election, in a way no one on this planet has ever dreamed. Instead of the multimedia extravaganza the Communist Party has planned, this is what they will see." Mr. Zhiang stepped back and to the side of a large flat screen TV and pressed a remote.

The video began with Ms. Grace Wu, standing in front of a mural of the Great Wall, calmly addressing the world. "Welcome to the Olympics my friends." Mr. Zhiang paused the image. "Questions so far?" he asked, as he tried to subdue a smile at their collective amazement. Everyone was too shocked to say anything. "If I hear no objections, let's play some more of the tape."

"Wait," one man said. "Where will the government be when this happens? They won't let this go on for more than five seconds."

Mr. Zhiang smiled, and responded. "They can do their best, but they have no way to stop it, short of knocking down the screen, or shooting all the people. And even then the same tape will be rolling on every CCTV channel broadcasting to every corner of this world. We have complete control," he said again, pointing to the control booth above his head. "But the best part is coming."

At this point no one was willing to stop him. For the next ten minutes Bill Zhiang let the tape role. Ms. Wu spoke of the hopes and dreams of the Chinese people and how they were entitled to decide their own future. She spoke of the broken promises made by the government and collusion with the West in their hope for riches. She talked about the myth that the Chinese people were different from the rest of the world and how they couldn't handle living in a democracy.

"But no one has ever asked us, have they?" she said. "All the dire predictions by our government, as the world will see, are false. Their goal of pursuing enforced harmony and stability is only a degrading propaganda tool to keep us down and under their thumb.

"My fellow countrymen, now is our time. We do not want our country to fall into anarchy and chaos, but we cannot live any longer without being able to control our own destiny. The Chinese people need to be free to vote for the people we wish to lead us, and prosper as the rest of the world prospers. Time has run out. We are not heavy-handedly telling you to throw out the corrupt leaders in power.

In front of the world, we wish to give you the opportunity to participate in the first national referendum on democracy. The government says we don't want it. Those who do business here say we can't handle it. The millions who are prospering in this country say we should wait. Why—because they are happy with the status quo and see no reason for change? The government says they know what you think, but have they ever asked you? Have they ever held more than the sham elections at the village level to ask any of us if we wanted democracy? Now you will have a chance." She paused, took a sip of water, and held up a cell phone.

"With these. We wish we could offer every one of you a vote but that is not possible at this time. However, over eight hundred million of you own cell phones and every cell phone owner will now have a chance to vote. It is not perfect but it is a start. In the United States, if any election gets fifty percent of the voters to the polls, they are lucky. Here, we have a chance to register a far greater percentage."

At that moment, the screen split and the vote options were clear. "We have two choices for you. Democracy: yes or no. Improving on the technology that has been used in so many interactive television shows around the world, we now have the ability to limit every cell phone to one vote. For those who cry foul at our efforts, these people," and now the screen split again as photographs of a dozen of the most respected technology gurus around the world appeared on the screen, "have testimony to give." When she clicked on one of their images, a recorded testimonial was given by that person on how the technology was sound and how it had been thoroughly tested.

Mr. Zhiang then paused the picture again. "We estimate that the maximum number of votes will occur within the first six hours. This is enough time to reveal to the world the hearts and minds of the Chinese people."

Mr. Zhiang continued: "At the end of the tape Ms. Wu will remind the government of our group's power to stop the river. They must not interfere or the consequences will be on their heads. As Mr. Evers said earlier, Ms.Wu is known to millions of viewers here in China from the weekly television show she produced for CCTV. Her work has always highlighted the importance of the media as a source of information and as a foundation for future environmental NGO activism. I could go on and on, but you need to meet this wonderful woman. Ladies and gentlemen, Ms. Grace Wu."

"Thank you Mr. Zhiang. Isn't what he and his company have done marvelous?" Like a proud grandmother, Ms. Wu's words immediately endeared herself to those gathered as she had done for years with a much larger television audience. Charlie had seen her show. In person she was the same as she was on TV—short grey hair, no makeup. She wore contemporary wire rim glasses and a tailored silk jacket reminiscent of an old Mao coat, stylishly updated. All five feet of her stood with friendly confidence. It was as if she was at an afternoon tea, sharing a most pressing problem with family and friends.

Charlie listened intently as Ms. Wu outlined her background and role in ChinAlive. When she was finished she thanked everyone and said, "I'm feeling a little tired now. I think it's time to answer some questions." Jerry, Henry, and Charlie didn't feel so alone this time as the questions sprang up from every corner of the room and continued until a dinner bell finally ended the session. As they walked out, Mr. Fathom fell in step with the boys.

He had been true to his word. Nothing boring so far, thought Charlie. But so what, neither is a bullfight and I sure wouldn't go to one of those—or a public execution.

Chapter 52

"Are you awake?" asked Charlie.

"I guess. But I wish I were dead to the world. Interesting as this is, it's starting to get to me," Jerry replied.

"Me too. Despite what I told my dad, I wish when I wake up tomorrow, this would all be over," said Charlie.

"Did you hear about the suicides?" asked Jerry.

"Really? Where? What suicides?"

"I overheard some of the workers talking. I'm sure they don't want us to know—three pills, three dead ChinAlive members, in different parts of the country. Must seem pretty weird to government officials. "

"I admire Mr. Fathom… my dad, your dad, and all these people—slugging it out for the good of the world. But I'm beginning to wish they had put me in a boarding school."

Both boys stayed silent for a while, thinking, remembering their first rush of excitement. "Tell you the truth," said Jerry. "I'm sick of toilets that don't flush."

"And I'm sick of that gross tasting green stuff they serve at almost every meal."

"You mean the bok choy? That stuff makes for the stinkiest farts in the world?"

Jerry rolled to one side. "You mean like this."

"You pig," Charlie said. "Just wait brain boy. I feel something happening that's going to melt part of that way too big brain."

"Have at it sport, give it your best shot."

"You asked for it."

"Whoeee, you win. Ease up dude and get me a gas mask. Can we change the subject? When does Henry arrive for good?"

"After his school ends, I think. Not too long from now. I bet he's getting tired of coming after school and then having to leave. At least it will be nice to have someone else to talk to," said Charlie

"Going to miss me?"

"Yeah, I might, if the air ever clears. But for now, let's shut up and get some sleep. I don't want to think about this anymore."

"Me neither. Good night Charlie."

"One more thing."

"What?"

"Did you hear about the engineer here who contacted his family in Bangkok?"

"How did he do that?"

"Don't know, but I heard they were ready to throw him out, or even put him in our makeshift jail. It's way too risky to contact anyone on the outside right now. He must have known. Have you thought about contacting friends?" asked Charlie.

"Every day. This is the part that really sucks. I said I don't want to think about this anymore. Go to sleep."

They stopped talking but neither was able to shut down. While Jerry was fine-tuning a computer program in his head, Charlie was replaying a chronology of events that he still couldn't comprehend.

Chapter 53

The end of their cave studies was timed to end with their school year in Shanghai. The Evers and the Zhiangs wanted to extend whatever degree of normalcy they could for their sons. That time was now at an end. Jerry and Charlie learned where the democracy movement began, how it grew, and how ChinAlive was using every modern tech tool they could to shape China's future. The final phase of ChinAlive was now ready to begin, activity in the cave was mushrooming, and jobs for the boys had already been assigned. The day after their final exams they joined a group of workers assembled to discuss their assignments.

'Well, looks who's here," said Charlie.

"Has Henry finally moved in?" asked Jerry.

"Yes, Henry is here for good." Henry said. "You cannot have all the fun by yourself."

"All the fun by yourself? Dig this guy," said Charlie. "He's really picking up the language." Henry sat down with a big smile. His school had ended, he was ready.

"Excuse me gentlemen, I hate to interrupt," said Mr. Fathom.

"Sorry," apologized Henry. "Please go right ahead."

"Thank you Henry. I appreciate it." But before Mr. Fathom was ten minutes into his briefing, Bill Zhiang interrupted and asked Jerry to come with him. No one was surprised when he didn't return.

In the next hour Mr. Fathom gave all those assembled detailed instructions. Thousands of ChinAlive members would be counting on their daily updates. China Democratic Party members, laborers, students, farmers, factory workers—everyone who had a role needed to be kept up to date on the resources available to them and what was happening. The logistics of meeting everyone's needs was demanding. Trying to keep the movement of goods and people hidden from authorities was one of the project's biggest challenges and greatest concerns.

At the end of the briefing, the group was escorted to a room filled with cubicles. Each worker was assigned a space with a computer terminal, passwords, and working hours—twelve-hour shifts for everyone. In the twelve hours they had off, they rested, read, played board games, talked of their dreams and fears, but none were allowed to communicate with the outside world.

Even under the intense gaze of the police, the boys were surprised to see the continual arrival and departure of workers. Who were these people? How were they able to come and go without being noticed? Where were they recruited? Did they have families? Would they ever be able to go back to their normal lives? Between them, the boys could have written enough questions to fill a book. They had been told over and over again how ChinAlive had been compartmentalized, with only a few people knowing all the details. They both wished they knew more.

Jerry didn't return on the day his dad came to get him, or any day thereafter. He slept in the same area but Charlie or Henry only caught sight of him briefly. Sometimes their shifts overlapped and in one short lived conversation he told them what he was doing. It was difficult to believe someone their age could be so unbelievably smart. To invent and then deploy a computer program that would help change the face of China was mind-boggling. He said he didn't like the way he had to be isolated. They said they missed him.

Charlie continued to wonder where ChinAlive's invisible infrastructure had first taken root. Mr. Fathom didn't have time to cover everything. Dozens of messages entered his mailbox every hour and every one of them needed a response and follow-up. He tried to stay focused, but many unanswered questions buzzed through his mind.

Equally distracted and sitting close by was another teenager with a head full of questions. Henry knew more about ChinAlive, and yet, trying to focus on details rather than the big picture was becoming difficult for him as well. Neither boy could understand how all this communication could take place under the nose of a government that had its own state of the art communications network. It didn't take long for Charlie's curiosity to peak. The Internet. Answers in a hurry, no one would notice. Within a matter of minutes he had a visitor.

"Are we a bit off the beaten path son?" John Evers asked, as he dropped to one knee next to Charlie's chair.

"Wait a minute. Are you monitoring our computers?"

"Charlie, you can't believe the security measures we have in place. Be assured, in this, everyone is equal. I probably wouldn't have stopped by, but we haven't had much time to talk so I took this as an excuse to visit. Weird, I know—hope you're not mad at me."

"Sorry Dad, not mad, but some of this is driving me nuts."

"So, it's a communication question you have, and let's see, your search terms include, oh, very good guess—extremely low frequency (ELF)." By this time Henry noticed Mr. Evers leaning over Charlie's terminal and decided to see what was up.

"Oh no, now it's a stampede." Henry walked over.

"Dad," said Charlie, "it's almost time for our shift change. Maybe you could answer a few questions."

"You have got to get some sleep so this can't take long. Thank goodness we have Jerry locked away." But as the words rolled off his lips...

"Did someone mention my name?"

"Well look who's here? I stand corrected. I'll make you a deal, take it or leave it. Three questions. One from each of you and that's all. We've got a lot of work to do and you know it. Let's go have dinner so we can let your shift replacements sit down."

After they collected their dinners, John Evers asked who wanted to go first?

"I do," said Charlie. "How did the three of you get together? I've never heard you mention Mr. Liu or Jerry's dad. All three of us have a general knowledge of ChinAlive now, but I'd like to know, as I'm sure Jerry and Henry would, how and when you first hooked up."

"Okay, fair enough. And Henry, your question?"

"How can you keep this computer network going, all over China and the world, without being detected?

"Good question, and you Jerry?

"How do you move all these people in and out of here without being noticed? Who are they? Where will everyone go after the vote is taken?"

"Gentlemen, I could take all night, but we don't have all night, so I promise to do my best to answer your questions in the time we have. Eat your dinners while I talk.

"Let's start with Jerry's question, about getting our people in and out and where they will go when this is over—more than one question but they're closely tied in. As you know by now, there are six entry points into the cave, plus the river gate. All of these access points are monitored so we can safely bring people in and out. Safe houses in town are used to shelter our workers if they're from outside the area. As these folks have come and gone you might have guessed how this works. What you don't know about is our big back door."

"Where the water must go when the gate is opened?" asked Jerry.

"Yes Jerry. It has to go somewhere. The opening is only a few feet high and well-disguised on the outside. Next to the opening is another hidden doorway—more like an airplane hangar—fifteen feet wide and twenty feet high. It's through this doorway that we've been able to bring in the heavy machinery that has helped carve this cave into a workable space. When we're done, powerful explosives will do what tectonics failed to do eons ago. We cannot take a chance that this great river, accidentally or intentionally, will ever leave China. That doorway is also the way we brought in the Blackhawk, or as it's now called, the Sikorsky MH-53E Sea Dragon—the Western world's largest helicopter."

"Is that what that covered mountain is over there?" Jerry asked. John Evers smiled. He knew this would get the boys excited, but he wasn't expecting them to rush over to have a closer look. As he caught up to them, Jerry asked, "Isn't this the one the Navy uses for mine sweeping?"

"And mine detection on land. We were lucky to have this one stationed in Cambodia. From this staging area the US military has been using it all over Asia in their search for land mines. Big, isn't it?" After letting them have a look under the tarp they all headed back to the cafeteria.

"How many people can fit in there?" Charlie asked.

"We're not sure exactly, but at least fifty-five people."

"Is that our escape?" asked Jerry.

"That's the plan."

"But I didn't think a helicopter could go that far," said Jerry.

"About 500 nautical miles with a 10 ton load. But our load will be much, much lighter. We've equipped the copter with a special auxiliary tank that should easily get us through. The tanks will be fueled immediately before we take off."

"I don't see any guns Dad."

"This machine wasn't meant for battle son, but believe me, we have plenty of fire power on board. At about 200 mph it should take about six or seven hours. Once there, we'll wait to see what's happening in China before continuing on. I can't tell you where we'll be going after that because I don't know. The local people will have ways to melt back into the countryside. The ones brought in without papers, as well as Jerry's family, Mr. Liu's and ours, will be on a shuttle run to northern Vietnam. I think that about covers the movement of people in out, and the final exit for many of us. Does that help Jerry?" John Evers sensed a great uneasiness in all of them.

"Remember, I told you we only had a few minutes. You can only imagine how many more details there are to an operation this size. Have faith. Let's get to Henry's question—the most technical one." They each nodded their approval, grudgingly.

"Henry, you must know that what Jerry and his dad's company have done—first, the text message voting scheme, and second, taking over the airways—are two of the most technologically stunning achievements for the advancement of peace in many decades." Jerry tried to be cool but Mr. Evers and the boys watched as he visibly started straightening up in his chair with pride.

"Thanks Mr. Evers, no big deal."

"Yeah, right," said Charlie.

"But check this out Henry, I'm not sure even Jerry knows what's involved in our day to day communications platform. I looked over Charlie's shoulder earlier and I could see he was checking on a system called ELF—extremely low frequency. Do you know anything about that Jerry?"

"Yes, a little. But I can't believe it works here. Where could you build an antenna big enough and how would you keep it hidden?"

"Wait a minute," Henry protested. "I asked the question and I don't know what you're talking about."

"Your question was about communications Henry. I found Charlie looking for information about ELF, a system the United States uses to communicate with deeply submerged submarines. You read some of my Nelson DeMille books, didn't you Charlie? Sorry, good guess, but that's not it. Actually it's a lot simpler. Well, not exactly simple. When we first started out we weren't sure if it would work, not knowing how sophisticated the MSS or PSB had become, but, so far so good. One of our members on the inside tells us that none of the agencies has a clue.

"A few years ago one of the engineers who works for your dad, Jerry, developed an email encryption software package that could have made millions. They decided to wait to release it and see how helpful it would be in facilitating the success of ChinAlive. The software is not only text based, but works with voice as well.

When this is all over Jerry's dad and his company will certainly look for the best way to use the program to promote democracy in other countries. Henry, the beauty of this is that we use the conventional electronic structures already in place. It's the encryption software that allows us to send a simple message or even a photograph with a sneaky something extra attached. Unless the receiving party knows where and when to look—and has the code—these undetectable emails can hide a two hundred-page document or even a video or audio message.

Now, does that answer enough of that question?" Henry and Charlie were content but they could tell from Jerry's questioning stare, that he was surprised not to have known this part of the technology plan.

"My turn," said Charlie.

"This is the easiest question son," his dad responded, "but could take the longest—but it won't. You want to know how we met and how our involvement came to be? Okay.

"In the year 2000, to celebrate the millennium, the Chinese government invited CEO's of Fortune 500 companies to a gathering in Shanghai. This is where the three of us first met. All of these corporate executives had been invited to collaborate on ways to start the new millennium. This gathering was supposed to lead the way for us to forge agreements that would continue to open trade opportunities benefiting both our countries. That was when our current dealings with China started taking root.

"My affiliation with an environmental NGO was good enough to get me in and Mr. Liu was an important, high ranking government engineer. We also had friends in high places. The hope we all shared was that once strong business ties were established, and a strong market economy began to take hold, the Chinese government would start to let their people take a greater and greater role in governing and determining their own future.

America's top 500 corporations had a chance to help persuade the ruling officials to start making changes, but that turned out to be nothing but a false promise. Cynical as it sounds, making money was the only shared goal of our corporations and governments.

"Henry, you must know that your dad's involvement goes back many years compared to mine and Bill Zhiang's. When we look back, our coming together was like an unavoidable destiny. We next met at a conference in the US concerning environmental issues. I was already working in an area slightly different than the one recorded on my visa."

"And all those years you kept telling me you weren't a spy."

"Did I say that? Can't remember. Before your dad arrived Henry, Jerry's dad made an appointment to visit with him after the conference. He didn't want to make the mistakes so many corporations had made in dealing with the Chinese. An hour meeting turned into three days." At that moment, Bill Zhiang walked in and pulled up a seat.

"Couldn't help overhearing what John was talking about. That was some meeting I had with your dad, Henry. I walked away a changed man. Wish I could have been at the beginning of this conversation, but sounds like John here is doing a pretty good job. I barely touched on this once with Jerry, but, bottom line: I have a chance to do something more important with my wealth than I had ever dreamed. This project, in various forms, has grown for many years, threading itself in an accelerated way over the Internet. The key piece that had been missing was the communications link—the best way to bring everyone together."

"After that," said John Evers, "it was easy to locate remnants of the old democracy movement. We've been able to gain ground with groups not only from Taipei, Hong Kong, and India, but even from the halls of the United States Congress. Of course there were dozens more meetings and planning sessions, not to mention the dangers and risk… but I think that gives you the big picture."

"Good for me, for now," said Charlie. The others agreed.

"If you do come up with other pressing questions, we'll be around," said Mr. Zhiang.

"We want you to feel, for all the sacrifices we've asked you to make, that this will all be worth it."

After glancing at his watch, John Evers realized an hour had passed and he was anxious to get back to work. The boys were thankful for the information but dead tired and knew they needed to be sharp for their next shift.

"Wait, one more quick question so I understand about the tech stuff," Charlie said. "There are three issues, yes?" His dad looked at him. "Go ahead."

"I mean, one, taking over the television images people will see, two, giving the Chinese people a way to vote using new cell phone technology, and three, creating a communications network based on an encryption method new to the world. That about right?"

"That's about right Charlie."

"And you did all this?"

"Yes. Jerry and his dad, and his dad's company, along with some of the smartest computer engineers on this earth—they did this. Amazing what human beings can do."

The boys sat quietly. "What a strange life we're living," Jerry said, as they headed back to their bunks.

"I guess I could be at school doing homework, and wondering what the weekend would bring," said Charlie.

"I guess I would be doing about the same thing," Henry said. They smiled at each other and then, in unison said, "boring." After listening to the last few moments of their conversation, John Evers couldn't help wonder if they would soon be praying for the boring life they had already left behind.

Chapter 54

As much as it was the Liu brothers' wish to draw the authorities away from Shigu, their plan worked, but only to a point. The distance the police were drawn off helped free up the movement of ChinAlive workers, but they still had to be extremely careful. Close proximity to nearby towns meant ChinAlive workers—departures and arrivals—were within easy reach of the authorities. The Olympics were rapidly approaching and the police were not about to let up on their surveillance. Although the bodies of the uncles and the pieces of clothing of the others turned up a day later, the area surrounding Cloud Mountain held too much mystery – officials sensed something was wrong. Most troubling—why had the signals disappeared for a period of time and then suddenly reappeared? The focus returned to Shigu. PSB and MSS were not about to leave the area.

Roving policemen systematically combed the streets of Shigu and all traffic on the outer roads was stopped. Identity cards were scrutinized. Everyone was questioned. Any person who had had a brush with the law in the past was pulled in for interrogation. Party cadres were promised sizeable rewards for information leading to whatever plot or secret organization they uncovered.

An emergency meeting of the planning committee of ChinAlive was called to explore new ways to again deflect the intense pressure the town was under. After two hours their whiteboard was covered with ideas, but there was no consensus—not even close. The river gate would be going up soon. With so many police close by, the chance of discovery was frighteningly real. After a lull in the discussion, a man from Xinjiang province suggested a disturbance.

"A very big disturbance," he said. "One that would take place all over Xinjiang Province. A disturbance the government could not ignore, and one they would have to send in reinforcements to quell."

"Let's talk about that," said Mr. Liu "Wouldn't they already have enough troops in Xinjiang to take care of any disturbance? It has been a hot spot for some time now."

"Yes, true," the man agreed. "But I'm proposing something bigger, something that has never been staged before. It could involve Urumqi, Kashkar, Tapan, and any other cities that tourists are likely to visit before the Olympics."

"I don't like it," said Jerry's father. "I'm sorry, but both Tibet and Xinjiang are the two regions we have worried about the most. It wouldn't take much to lose control to revenge-seeking minorities. We can't give them any excuses right now." As the debate continued, three uninvited guests listened intently from a pathway next to the room.

Jerry whispered, "Why is that?" to his buddies.

"No idea," said Charlie.

"We shouldn't be listening, we should be sleeping, and it doesn't matter why. We should go," said Henry.

"It does matter and I'm not sleepy and maybe we can help." Jerry said, as Charlie and Henry both rolled their eyes. Jerry looked at Charlie and said, "We already know a lot about the situation in Tibet."

"'Ethnic cleansing lite,' as Mr. Fathom put it," Charlie said. "Maybe we can skip to the situation in Xinjiang. I don't recall reading or hearing much about that except the police being called in to quell numerous terrorist uprisings. What do you know Henry? Any insights?"

"Terrorist uprisings," Henry said, as if he had swallowed a bitter melon, and then said something in Chinese both his friends knew was swearing but didn't know exactly what.

"Another of the government's biggest lies." Although Henry had promised a quick history lesson, the boys could see his fire building. Now it was Charlie and Jerry's turn to try and understand blistering speech in another language. Henry did his best to switch whenever he could to English, but it was obvious, to say what he needed to say, he had to speak Chinese. Both English language natives were mesmerized as they watched the mild mannered Henry go revolutionary on them.

"Exactly like what they are doing to the people of Tibet, the Chinese government is destroying the identity of the Uighur Muslims. They have been living there peacefully for hundreds of years. Without going into great detail, Islam came to this area a long time ago. The people who lived there had, at times, been able to set up an independent republic. My dad told me that they were a proud and independent people whose ethnicity was Turkic, not Chinese, and that they had every right to have their own country." Henry continued to fascinate his friends with yet another ugly chapter of China's brutal desire for control. When Henry finally stopped to take a breath, Charlie expressed both his and Jerry's gut reaction.

"Unbelievable."

"You could say that," said John Evers, as he unexpectedly confronted the eaves dropping boys. Charlie and Jerry had been concentrating so hard on what Henry was saying that they hadn't realized the sound of Henry's voice had escalated in proportion to the outrage he felt while retelling the history.

When they were escorted into the room where their voices had been clearly overheard, the young spies were embarrassed to be the object of many icy stares. After they were made to stand quietly to explain themselves, all three apologized for listening in on a meeting to which they were not invited. As they were about to be dismissed back to bed, Mr. Liu spoke up.

"I do not wish in any way to condone these boys' behavior but I think what we have heard demonstrates a respectable degree of historical perspective and appreciation. Maybe their understanding of our circumstances could be exploited. Instead of sending them off to their well-deserved bedtime gulag, we could let them experience what it is like to make decisions that could determine the future of this country."

"And maybe they have some ideas," another member of the panel suggested.

"What do you say Mr. Liu? Gentlemen?" another member asked the boy's fathers. With many affirmative nods, the fathers of the three young men, not wishing to hold up the meeting further, and knowing private conversations with their sons would happen soon enough, agreed.

The looks they gave Charlie, Jerry, and Henry were those unmistakable ones fathers use to put fear in the souls of wrongdoing teens. But the looks the boys returned, devoid of fear, lacked intimidation. Each of the boy's fathers could not help but notice something different in their sons. The boys sat quietly, doing as they were told, but were undaunted.

Over the next hour a variety of solutions continued to surface but again, no consensus. The mood became more and more somber as the number of suggestions stopped flowing. They needed something simple and effective that could be implemented within a narrow time frame. When it seemed that there would be no resolution everyone was curious to see Henry's arm in the air. At first his father tried to ignore his son, but Henry's persistence would not go unnoticed.

"Yes Henry," said Mr. Liu.

"What if they all showed up in Shanghai—Ms. Evers, Ms. Zhiang, Jerry and Charlie?"

John Evers replied. "Something like that was discussed earlier, before Jerry got back. We thought by sending those bugs up the river we would buy ourselves more time."

"But it didn't buy enough time John," Bill Zhiang replied. "Could sending the boys with their mothers now work like we had thought?"

"I think sending them now would be too great a risk," Mr. Liu said. Henry leaned over to whisper something to Jerry—Jerry instantly understood.

"But what if we send them...without sending them?" Jerry said. Everyone paused.

"What?" said Charlie.

"*Mission Impossible*," said Jerry. And again, everyone looked nonplused.

"But do we have the expertise, and do we have the time?" Charlie continued. Now everyone looked confused. Had these boys met up on some magical wavelength no one else could access?

"What are you boys talking about?" Mr. Liu asked.

"Latex," the boys all said at once.

"I am remembering *Mission Impossible*," said Henry. "Whenever they needed to disguise someone to look like someone else, they created a latex mask that looked exactly like that person."

"Wouldn't it completely take away their steam if they spotted our group in Shanghai?" asked Charlie. The telepathic brainstorming continued.

"Do we have any theater or movie people in ChinAlive? That's the key," said Henry. "The latex technology must be getting better and makeup people here must know how to make such a mask." Some of the committee members were beginning to catch on.

"Yes, I believe we do—in Beijing and in Shanghai. Can you boys be more specific in your thinking, please? We are common men, and have not yet mastered the art of reading each other's minds." For the first time since the meeting started, laughter broke out.

"Just spit-ballin' here," Jerry said.

"Spit-ballin? That means what?" Henry asked.

"You know, thinking out loud. Brainstorming. We could take digital pics of the four of us, send them to whoever is going to make the masks, then find actors about the right size to wear the masks for each of us."

"And then?" asked John Evers.

"And then, and then..." mumbled Henry, not having it all thought out.

"And then," said Bill Zhiang, "we could arrange to have them spotted leaving the US Consulate in Shanghai. We would sneak them in so authorities wouldn't have time to grab them on their way out. But when they leave, security cameras will record their departure. A prearranged taxi will be waiting with darkened windows. By the time they are recognized, the actors will be long gone."

"But wouldn't that seem strange after the outpouring of grief when it was reported that we were swallowed up by the rapids?" asked Charlie

"That's the clincher Charlie. No one informed anyone we knew about your tragic death by rapids so the cops must still be wondering if the people they thought had drowned were really our families."

"So if we all show up at the Consulate in Shanghai...?" continued Charlie.

"Like I was about to say," said Bill Zhiang, "it's monitored around the clock by the Chinese government. Everyone, especially now, is being photographed going in and out and I know the government has photo recognition software. They would definitely make the ID later. This idea has possibilities." The teens watched as the men, in the only unanimous moment of agreement, started the wheels in motion—first, a call to Shanghai. No immediate answer and then, the waiting. As they waited, all attention was again focused on Charlie, Henry, and Jerry.

"Gentlemen," Mr. Liu began. "If this works, I think I would offer a motion of clemency in your behalf." Before he could continue, the phone rang for Mr. Zhiang. After more of the details were ironed out, the most striking words anyone heard him say were, “Make damn sure they are not caught.”

“Henry, Charlie, Jerry—all we can do is wait. Maybe by the time you wake up, we’ll have good news. For now, good night.” After Jerry and Charlie posed for the digital pictures, all three thanked the men, apologized again, and let the exhaustion of a long, tension filled-day guide them to bed and beyond.

Chapter 55

Now that ChinAlive and the Olympics were coming to a crossroads, the pressure on Rong was exhausting. Layers of surveillance monitored every computer, every cell phone, and every movement of Rong's security group. Whether it was software that recorded keystrokes, office cameras, audio feeds, or even an office mole, the MSS, PLA, or PSB were right there. Even under these circumstances, as difficult as it was, Rong knew his updates to ChinAlive were vital.

The Red Spears hoax had authorities chasing a thousand false leads. While pretending to check on these, Rong used the sites he visited to send and receive coded messages. The email encryption software worked well for the rest of the project, but Rong was transmitting from one of the most protected underground bunkers in China. After authorities uncovered the Red Spears fraud, returning to some of the same blogs, listservs, or social networking sites, was taking a huge, calculated risk.

"Why are you still entering this blog," Rong's immediate supervisor asked, in a surprise visit.

"Red Spears may no longer be a target Sir, but it does not mean that these sites are not main arteries for subversive activities." Rong felt beads of sweat beginning to roll down his back.

"Stand up." Rong got up and watched as his supervisor's fingers flew across his keyboard, accessing a program Rong had never seen come up on his screen. He was sure he had left no trail that would incriminate him. Agonizing minutes passed until the man finally stood up.

"Spread out. Look as many places as you can. Take the leads we give you in the areas now under surveillance."

"Yes sir." At least a few of the sites the Captain had mentioned for follow-up were sites already agreed upon by ChinAlive as places that were still safe. Why, if keystroke capture software had been installed in all their computers didn't the Captain check on him from the server side? Why had he come to Rong's computer? Was it a warning—a way to gauge his reaction?

Rong was too nervous to trace where the Captain had been without attracting more attention. He hoped his safe cyber havens would remain safe. On a late Monday afternoon, a message had been placed for him about the attempt to trick Shanghai authorities into believing that Jill and Charlie Evers, Rita and Jerry Zhiang were again in Shanghai. What they needed from Rong was confirmation that the trick had worked.

Rong's loneliness and fear haunted him on his way to the barracks that night. Did he still have their trust? The touch of the pill, sewn into his pocket, made him shiver. They told him one hard bite and he wouldn't feel a thing. Crushed between his molars, the potassium cyanide would quickly release, causing almost instant brain death. His heart would stop a few minutes later. Even with the fake identity he had lived under since childhood, there was no guarantee the authorities would not be able to find his adopted family and loved ones. Failure was not an option.

A plan to disperse the police near ChinAlive headquarters came as no surprise to Rong, but the use of latex masks sounded like a long shot. He wondered if alternatives had been discussed. With time running out, and with so much to lose, he trusted that they had weighed all the options. All he could do was wait and be ready to report.

As he prepared for bed, he noticed that his bunk area was not exactly as he left it. His pillow was slightly turned and the blankets were not as tight. Alarm bells rang when he looked around to see other cadets staring at him.

"Does anyone know how this happened?" Everyone slowly turned away. Rong was friendly with the cadet across from him and waited until the lights were out to ask if he had seen anything.

"Other cadets playing around. No need to worry." Rong's heart started to race. He spent the rest of the night in a black cloud, wondering if he had done something stupid. He prayed for sleep but the second-guessing was making him crazy—he couldn't turn it off. The cadet said others were only playing around. Rong might still be in the clear. For now there was nothing he could do. If everything worked out, his next post would still be in Beijing, openly working for ChinAlive. If he was caught, his next post would be in the cemetery.

#

Two days later, four actors emerged from the United States Consulate in Shanghai. Appearing relaxed, with no agenda other than flagging a taxi, they left from the front gate and disappeared into Shanghai's congested traffic.

When authorities routinely examined the day's surveillance tapes, all the hours of close scrutiny looked like they were about to pay off. Experts were called in. The tapes were played again and again. The consensus—these four were who they appeared to be. The new focus would now be Shanghai and finding Mrs. Evers, Mrs. Zhiang, and their sons. Although officials were still deeply concerned, agreement was reached that there was now no reason to station so many men in the Shigu area, especially with the mounting need for their services elsewhere. These four would still be sought for questioning and finding them would still be a top priority. However, there was one angry and perplexed dissenter.

"Too many unanswered questions," Colonel Chen told them. "How are they connected? Why, if the boy and his mother were kidnapped, were they leaving the US Consulate? And why were they with Bill Zhiang's wife and son? And why have we not been able to bring Mr. Zhiang in if he is so important to our Olympics? And if we thought they died in the rapids, how could they be here?" Colonel Chen was known for his tenacity but with so many other urgent matters exploding, and so little understanding of where all his questions might lead, the higher command overrode his objections. Out of respect for his opinion, they allowed him one request.

Twenty-four hours later, word came from villagers that trucks had arrived to carry away all extra personnel from the Shigu area. When project members found out, silent cheers went up throughout the cave. At dinner that night, instead of the bok choy, eel, and rice the others were served, the boys were treated to their own freshly baked pizza—with Chinese characteristics. They smiled, thanked the cook, and then noticed the approving smiles of everyone there. It was an excellent night—better than any since their arrival. Although they had much to be thankful for, project managers were more than a little worried. No word had come from Rong. They had not found out about the success of their trick until the troops started to leave. All messages placed for him had gone unanswered and there was no safe way to check on his status. Little did they know that while Rong was still safe, the cause for their greatest concern should be the one man, disguised as a laborer, who had jumped from the last troop carrier as it rolled out of Shigu.

Chapter 56

The Money Man, as his comrades called him, felt less and less comfortable reporting back to headquarters. He had found nothing of interest. They called him the Money Man out of respect for his super human skills. When no one else could find what the Ministry needed, he delivered. Cheng Weng Ji—Wushu master, expert calligrapher, renowned for his knowledge of the West, and graduate of Princeton University—was the best example of HUMINT (human intelligence gathering) the Ministry had ever had. He was, in the purest sense, a spy—someone who moved among the people, ear to the ground, unnoticed. He had always helped the Chinese government in the past, but the Money Man was beginning to think that whatever information had led his superiors to Shigu, was false.

The miraculous way in which ChinAlive had avoided detection was a combination of brilliant planning and a little luck. Only those with the utmost knowledge of the Chinese security agencies could ever fully appreciate this miracle. Unknown to the best informed ChinAlive sources, was the way intelligence agencies in China were always in flux—changing names, changing missions, and constantly infighting about each other's roles.

More than anything else, these changes slowed the government's reaction time and now weakened their power to uncover the most serious threat the current government had ever faced. In addition to avoiding detection by the PSB (Public Security Bureau), the PAP (Peoples Armed Police), the MSS (Ministry of State Security) and its dozen or so bureaus, ChinAlive was about to defeat the Money Man—the most highly decorated operative in the Immediate Action Unit (IAU). The Sixth Bureau of the MSS—the Counterintelligence Bureau—never had much faith in the new IAU unit. The Money Man's boss would be extremely disappointed if his best operative turned up empty handed.

Dirty, disheveled, and strapped to the same kind of woven plastic bag every peasant used to carry what worldly items they owned, he easily blended into the street life of Shigu. After a week with nothing to show, the Money Man sipped hot tea at a local food vendor, further evaluating all the mental notes he had taken. By now he should have something to report. Had an internal power struggle set IAU up to fail? What a waste of time if the idiots in charge were playing games.

A passing bakery delivery stirred his appetite and redirected his thoughts. He had counted on a few unclaimed vegetables and discarded baked goods to satisfy his daily needs. The bakery cart was making its way to the edge of town. Strange, he thought, how overloaded it appeared. And where was there left to make a delivery—the cart was already at the edge of town? A smile crept around the Money Man's face.

Chapter 57

"This is it, ChinAlive junior members," said Jerry. "Only a week left. Last dinner before it all begins."

"We know," Henry replied. "No one in, no one out."

"Good thing I got here on time." Henry looked up, relieved to see his mom finally join the cave dwellers. She had stayed behind until the last minute. Of the three moms, she alone knew her family's immediate future. They would not be returning to their home, or to their village, for a long time.

"The river doors go up tomorrow," John Evers added, as he and the other fathers sat down with their families. "One more time in the middle of the week, and then, in a few more days, it all begins." Everyone was well aware of the timeline and the solemn reminder. There was no turning back. No one started to eat.

"Any questions?" John Evers asked.

"What if the doors don't close, Dad?" Charlie asked, always ready to play the devil's advocate.

"And what if PLA soldiers are waiting at the cave's exit once farmers on the other side report a surge in water to their lands?" Jerry asked.

"And what if the MSS has a way to override our uplink to the satellites?" Henry joined in.

"And what if you don't want that ice cream bar?" Jerry's mom asked, as she reached for her son's dessert. With too few moments to share any light heartedness, this move produced welcome laughter, especially when Jerry started fighting his mom for the ice cream. When Henry and Charlie held Jerry back, he knew he would have to go to the kitchen to get another one.

"Traitors," he said. It was now the perfect time to introduce a plan Jill Evers and Rita Zhiang had kept under wraps for weeks.

"Now then, we—meaning all three of us moms—have worked out a mental health break for all three of our families and anyone else who is interested. For the next hour, every soul in this bizarre space has been instructed to chill out, relax, and get ready for the rest of their lives. Our group, please follow me." On a flat, dry spot in the middle of where the mighty Yangtze would soon flow, the ladies set up an expanded game of *Twister* so as many who wished could play. Even the guards were drawn away from their posts to see what was happening.

For the next hour, howls of laughter filled the area. Members of ChinAlive, for the first time, in a variety of ways, were able to relax and enjoy each other's company. Much to their delight and embarrassment, the moms' chosen venue for their strategy session was in such a public place, that within minutes, the entire cave's population was there, watching a side of their serious leaders and coworkers they had never seen before.

As the merriment spread throughout the cave, an intruder flipped open his cellphone. Damn, he thought. The walls were too thick. No matter. Something was going on that was distracting everyone's attention away from him.

After the three families had gone a few rounds, other members jumped down to give it a go. The Money Man did not know what to make of it.

Not possible, one of the guards said aloud when he returned to his post. The red warning light was blinking—must be a mistake. But when he rewound the tape, his worst fear was confirmed. An intruder had entered the cave minutes before. The guard punched the alarm and rewound the tape again. After the ChinAlive leadership watched it over and over, they were dumbfounded. Could the vagabond they were looking at be some unsuspecting homeless person looking for shelter? Could he have found another natural entrance? They all knew at once that they didn't have time to weigh these questions. They had to find him.

Within minutes Bill Zhiang's voice rang out over the PA system: "Ladies and gentlemen, we have an intruder. Please assemble immediately in the emergency staging area." When everyone was there he continued.

"By letting our guard down for one minute, we have put our mission and ourselves in danger. A destitute looking man was caught by one of our cameras sneaking down tunnel number three. He looks like a street person but that is highly unlikely. While our guards hunt for this person all of you must stay here. Two armed guards will be stationed in this area while the rest of us search for the man. Our compound isn't that big so we should find him quickly. Please don't panic. We are not ready to change any of our plans." The staging area was filled with chairs and dining tables and as they all sat down, coffee, cold drinks, and leftover bakery goods were set out. The boys found each other quickly as did their moms.

"I think we should help look," Charlie said.

The mothers' reaction to this bit of manliness rose up like an angry storm. "Don't you even think it," said Rita Zhiang. "I know I speak for all of us when I promise that we will sit on each of you if we have to. Is that clear?" The boys all nodded their agreement, but with a degree of hesitation the moms could not help but notice. After an hour they were all relieved when the searchers safely returned, but disheartened to learn the intruder had not been found.

"What if he found his way back out Dad?" Jerry asked.

"One of the cameras would have picked him up Jerry. He was not clever enough to disable the cameras or sensors so he might be a low level local op who got lucky. If he carried a cell with him, he now knows it won't work in here. We can't let him get away. Two guards are posted at each exit. The exits are dark and each of the guards has night vision goggles. He won't get out."

Good information, the Money Man thought, as he listened from a hiding place close by. With enough food to last a few days, the discovery of this fantastic place would enable him to settle in for a guarded night's sleep. He knew no one else in this encampment was going to get much rest. How delighted his superiors would be when he informed them of his discovery.

"Until we find this man," John Evers said, "we don't want anyone to be by themselves at any time. We will find him, but let's stay safe until that happens. Sleep the best you can, we only have a week left."

That caught the Money Man's attention. Whatever they were planning, was happening in a week. As the lights were turned down, he knew he'd have to wait—too little sleep, no chance to look around, and too much at stake.

Chapter 58

Restless energy filled the bunks where Jerry, Henry, and Charlie were supposed to be sleeping. In less than twenty four hours the river gates were going up. The Olympics would begin in a week—showtime. But now, an intruder was in the cave, and Charlie had a theory no one believed.

"I know where he's hiding," Charlie whispered.

"Well? Are you going to share or keep it to yourself? "Jerry asked.

"What are you talking about?" Henry followed up.

"Charlie thinks he knows where he's hiding but he won't tell me."

"I didn't say that. I think we should go check it out."

"You're not talking about the helicopter again are you?" asked Jerry. "Didn't your dad tell you hours ago they had it thoroughly checked out?"

"Yeah, but they didn't take the tarp completely off. It's huge and there are many places he could have found to squeeze into. He's got to be there. There aren't any other places he could hide."

"I think we should try to sleep," said Henry. Jerry was silent.

"Come on, you know we're not going to sleep tonight."

"How do you plan to get past the guards?" asked Jerry. "You know our moms have warned them to be on the lookout."

"By the time the guards intercept us, we'll be half way to the cafeteria—which is a lot closer to the helicopter. It shouldn't be too hard for them to believe all we want is a cup of hot chocolate, to help us sleep. They can watch us the rest of the way."

"And then what? How do we get to the helicopter after that?" asked Henry.

"I'm not sure." From their questions, Charlie could sense both of them beginning to thaw. "Let's go, get dressed. We can figure this out."

It didn't take them long. Charlie's mom wasn't surprised to see the boys stumble into the cafeteria.

"So, how did you clever boys get past the guards?" Charlie pointed back in their direction and gave a little wave—the guards waved back.

"Well, pull up a seat me buckos. Big week coming up so don't plan on spending too much time in here."

"Charlie knows where the intruder is." Jerry blurted out. Henry laughed while Charlie shot both his buddies an irritated look.

"That wouldn't be the helicopter, would it?"

"That's exactly where," Jerry said. "You Evers people really connect on a different level." Jill Evers looked wearily at her son. "Didn't your dad already tell you they looked in there? And didn't he tell you they found no trace of him? What's different now Charlie?"

"The size of the thing is so darn huge. After thinking of all the places he could hide, no other place makes sense, unless he got back out. And Dad said that was next to impossible."

"Do you believe Charlie?" Both Henry and Jerry stared straight ahead.

"He has a good point," said Jerry, finally.

"And Charlie is smart," Henry agreed. "It does make sense, if only it had not been already searched," Henry conceded. Charlie could tell their support was half-hearted and he knew his mom sensed it as well.

"What would it hurt if we took one last look Mom?"

"It would mean you weren't in bed trying to get some sleep. It would mean you went against your dad's wishes, and it would mean you couldn't follow simple instructions. Now gentlemen, finish your drinks. Your next assignment—get Charlie Evers and yourselves safely back to bed. Got it?"

"Got it."

Halfway across the small bridge that spanned the dry riverbed, they noticed Charlie doing a slow shuffle. He stopped to scan the end of the cave where the helicopter was covered. For a moment, they were content to stand and watch with him, wondering what he had on his mind.

"Look at that. Did you see that?"

"What are you talking about Charlie?"

"Look closely at the helicopter. There. See that, there's movement. The tarp is moving slightly at the side door." All three boys stared as hard as they could. By the time either of them could focus in on what Charlie was talking about, he was ready to act.

"Then we better get closer for another look."

Jerry suggested, "two of us could sneak down the river bed while one of us stands watch." Henry didn't like the idea.

"Why don't all three of us stay here for a little longer to see if we can see what Charlie saw," said Henry. While they were still debating, Charlie, completely focused, saw the tarp move again.

"No time." Before they could do anything, Charlie jumped down to the riverbed and began running, staying low, zigzagging, to keep from being seen. Within twenty yards two men dressed in camouflage suits jumped down, grabbed him by either elbow and practically threw him out to two other guards. The next few moments unraveled in slow motion. Armed commandos instantly appeared everywhere, as if on some prearranged cue. Two-dozen automatic weapons were all pointed at the helicopter.

In the next split second, the tarp Charlie thought he saw move was ripped to the side by an M16 mm machine gun. As the weapon started to take aim, a voice on the cave's PA system boomed, "Drop the weapon and slide out from under the tarp." Whoever was holding the gun ignored the warning and began spraying bullets. As everyone ran for cover, a guard who had been hit screamed out in agony. There was a pause. The shooting stopped.

To everyone's relief, the weapon was thrown out. The shooter calmly placed his hands behind his head and surrendered. Everyone close to the helicopter quickly moved toward the man, but in the next frightening second, a muffled explosion inside the helicopter sent out a shock wave that knocked those closest to the helicopter off their feet. When they were able to stand, surprisingly, the intruder hadn't moved.

As the wounded guard was helped up, everyone waited and watched to see if he was alone. Guards quickly knocked him to the ground, scanned the area, then tied his hands behind his back. When they were sure there were no others he was led away. In the next instant, ChinAlive members came running with a fire hose but the flames and intense heat were too much. The firefighters quickly realized their primary mission was now to keep the blaze from spreading. Fortunately, the hose was close by, the water pressure strong, and the fire was contained within minutes. They would have to wait to see how badly the helicopter was damaged.

"Planning committee members, please meet in the strategy room at once," John Evers's voice boomed over the PA system. On his way to the meeting he passed the boys, checked to make sure they were all right, and told Charlie he was to attend the meeting as well. Jerry and Henry were sent to their bunks. They were relieved to see the guard who had been wounded, able to walk to the infirmary with minor help. Charlie was more than a little shaken but confident of a slap on the back. It was his persistence that had uncovered the intruder's hiding place. He wondered where the man had been taken.

Everyone summoned arrived within minutes. When Charlie entered, John Evers grabbed his son by the arm and forcefully sat him down in the back. "Because you couldn't follow simple instructions one of our men was almost killed, many of our people were exposed to a dangerous situation, and our main means of escape has probably been destroyed." Charlie was shocked but had no time to defend himself.

One of the workers came racing in to tell the committee to come look at something immediately. A few seconds later they were all shaken to see that a stray bullet had hit one of the water gate's hydraulic hoses and water was beginning to seep out. After many minutes of consultation, committee members were told that it would be at least a couple of hours before the mechanics would know enough to make a recommendation. Worn out from the evening's events, committee members reassembled in the strategy room. John Evers got back first to finish the chat with his son.

Charlie jumped in first. "Dad, I discovered the man in there after you missed him. If it hadn't been for me…" His dad angrily interrupted him.

"If it hadn't been for you, that hydraulic lifter wouldn't be damaged. Charlie, a key piece of our plan might have to be cancelled because of you." John Evers waited a second for this message to sink in.

"I don't understand," Charlie said

"I know you don't," his father replied, "because you couldn't do as you were told. We knew he was hiding in the helicopter but we didn't want to spook him, taking a chance on a dangerous confrontation—at least one in which we didn't have control. And now you can see that our worst fears have come true; the helicopter has been badly damaged, one of our men shot, a gate lifter damaged, and if this intruder is as good as we think he is, we probably won't get any information out of him—there's not enough time."

Charlie could barely whisper an apology. The horrendous consequences of what he had done burned in his gut like a knife. As he got up to leave, he sensed no let-up in his father's anger. A crowd had gathered outside the strategy room. Facing his mom, his friends, or anyone, made him feel numb. Henry and Jerry told him not to worry about it, that he had no way of knowing. But he knew. He knew how recklessly he had acted. Everyone knew. Minutes later, back in the bunkroom, after the lights had gone down, Charlie looked up to find his mom sitting on the edge of his bed.

"Charlie, we are all under unimaginable stress. Your dad knows what he and the others have asked you boys to do is way beyond what the founders of this project had ever imagined. You're only fifteen. Believe me, older men, men of greater wisdom, have made much bigger mistakes. Try to get some sleep. We love you."

"But what about the hydraulic lifter mom? If that can't be fixed…"

"Let's worry about that when we know for sure. Until then, get some rest." She left him with his eyes wide open. The anxiety and shame would keep him awake long into the night.

Chapter 59

Forty-seven journalists from some of the largest news organizations around the world waited contentedly for their ship to emerge from the last lock on the Three Gorges Dam. They were all woken up several hours ahead of the time stated on the original itinerary and some were still worn out from the overload of activities CTS (China Travel Service) had planned for every one of their waking hours.

The trip had been carefully laid out months in advance to assure positive press coverage on a number of fronts. Several journalists had been invited to take the new high-speed train from Beijing to Tibet. Numerous other junkets had been planned with great care to bring a highly favorable focus on the Peoples Republic. Every corner of the Middle Kingdom was to be visited.

After an hour waiting for the water to rise, bringing them to the river's new lake above the dam, some of the reporters began to wonder why it was taking so long. At each inquiry, their host deflected questions by offering more food—champagne, lobster. It had been a dazzling buffet but the journalists were getting full, and many were still recovering from a lack of sleep and jet lag. After two hours, some of the reporters started getting restless and began demanding that the trip proceed or they be taken off the ship. The director of the locks, as well as the crew, knew the emergency procedures they were going to have to follow. It would be an embarrassing moment, but keeping their guests on board any longer would be worse. As the reporters started climbing up the ladders that had been lowered, the crew—as well as all of their guests—was stunned at the sight before them. When they reached the top of the dam, they stared in silent disbelief. After many seconds of confusion one reporter asked, "Where's the water?"

When the news started getting out, ChinAlive members listened and watched with great relief. Henry's dad couldn't scan the channels fast enough. The news had spread around the world. All the workers in the cave were incredulous how successfully their plan was working. Reporters, scientists, politicians—nobody knew what to make of it. Nobody had answers and the more the government tried to explain away what had happened, the more skeptical every news report became.

On the heels of this bizarre incident, a message, exactly like the one that had been sent twice before, started appearing all over the Internet: *Give us democracy, or the river stops for good.* On every blog, in every news headline, electronic or print, and on every social networking site, messages and video of a dried up river were broadcast and shared around the world.

The plea for democracy in China was a startling and provocative demand, especially at this time—a time when the Chinese Communist Party was looking forward to its most glorious moment in modern history. Much to the relief of government officials, the river levels returned to normal an hour later.

In a hastily called meeting to inform ChinAlive members of their success, John Evers congratulated everyone in attendance. Charlie's hand shot up. "So the damage to the hydraulics must have not been so bad?"

"Yes and no Charlie. The damage wasn't that bad. We could have repaired it completely if we had had time to bring in new parts. Instead, we worked all night to find a way to lower the wall, and then, without using hydraulics, a way to get the wall back up."

"But it's going to be okay?" Jerry asked.

"Not exactly," his father replied. "We've had to support the wall using other means. Do you see those timbers and screw jacks? Believe me, those are temporary and we are praying that they hold before we arm the explosives that will seal this place up forever."

"But the worst thing," Mr. Liu added, "is that we can't back up our threat to stop the river during or after the voting. Our wall cannot work again when we want it to work. Without the risk of letting the river go and never getting it back, we must hope that our final demonstration will be a sufficient threat."

"Mr. Liu, I don't get something else," said Charlie. "All the stories say the journalists were stuck in the locks. I thought you were going to time the river diversion so they had cleared the locks."

"That was the plan Charlie, but we couldn't be sure if our intruder had communicated his findings. If there were others out there, discovery of the diversion would have been much easier in the daytime. Darkness provided a much better cover. It actually worked to our advantage. You can see by the anger of the reporters that they were more frightened by being trapped in the locks. I am sure it was like being trapped in a huge concrete tomb."

Jerry's dad then took the floor. "In one week the Games begin. This is all the time we have to double check our systems, make sure every contact is in place, monitor this mountain to make sure no one uncovers our headquarters, and get any information we can from our intruder."

"But what are we going to do about the helicopter?" one of the workers asked.

"That's a tough one I'm afraid," John Evers responded. "We have a team assessing the damage, which was considerable. If it can't be fixed, we'll figure out another way. Stay tuned and cross your fingers." On that note, the meeting ended and Charlie was relieved when his dad came over and put a hand on his shoulder.

"We were lucky Charlie. Don't worry about it. Concentrate on doing your job this week. With a little luck, you might be able to tell my grandkids someday how you helped change the course of history."

Chapter 60

During the final week, the length of the Yangtze, from Chongqing to the Tiger Leaping Gorge, swarmed with every law enforcement official the government could spare. Within their closely monitored dragnet, the radio bugs had vanished, twice; the river had stopped; the foreign journalist fiasco had happened; and now, no word from the Money Man in over a week. Something was terribly wrong. In a rare moment of unanimity, all security agencies agreed to tighten the noose. With enough pressure, something had to give.

Inside the cave, all video monitors, motion sensors, and audio pickups were manned twenty four hours a day. ChinAlive headquarters was locked down. Most of the soldiers and police dispatched to the area searched in and around every town, village, and hamlet. Highways, roads, cow trails—any place where tire tread or footprints landed, authorities landed as well.

"I wish I knew what we were looking for," one bored soldier confided to a comrade.

"I asked. Captain says, 'keep looking.' I don't think he knows."

"I do not want to miss all of our Olympics.

"So far they look at us like we are stupid. Not only with anger, but with disrespect—like we are bumbling police. Next person who looks at me like that…they will wish they had not."

"Does no good. Others have tried. Either there is nothing to know or it makes them more determined."

"I don't care. They should at least respect the uniform."

Many of the troops climbed Cloud Mountain, but none had reached the top. With no clues to what they were looking for, no one could imagine what reward the top of the mountain could hold. With nothing to show for their interrogation and threats, a few of the troops started offering bribes—free trips to the Olympics, cash, livestock—anything they could think of to pry loose whatever information the local people might be hiding.

"There is nothing here. Who would be so stupid? With thousands and thousands of local and national security forces, this country is locked up tight. I think our leaders are becoming paranoid." With mild amusement, their conversation was being listened to from a place they would never dream existed.

"Listen to these idiots," one of the security people said to Charlie and Henry, as he held out his headset. They were on their way to the cafeteria but this was way better than food. Both of them held one side of the headset to enjoy the laugh. Jerry was right behind and when the headset was handed to him. He smiled and handed it back.

"You know I can't understand them. Keep listening, but you better translate everything." Henry was delighted to share the soldiers' few remaining moments of blissful ignorance.

"I am glad big shots are starting to ease up. We want to enjoy the Olympics too. Where did they get their information?" Asked one of the skeptical soldiers.

"Where indeed?" Jerry laughed.

"This is getting better," said the security guard, holding out another headset.

"Don't you love that summer breeze?" said one of the soldiers.

"This is a momentous time," said another.

"We need to find a TV. We need to be part of this history. The whole world is about to take notice."

"You are so right," Henry said. "For more reasons than you could ever imagine.

#

The Money Man laughed to himself after each of their puny attempts at interrogation. He had been trained by the toughest, most ruthless experts in torture imaginable. These people had no idea nor the willpower needed to extract information. He had no doubt that once left alone he could easily escape. Even with two guards stationed around the clock, the room was not a jail.

The start of the Olympics was only a week away. He overheard them say something was happening in a week. How could anything they have planned have any effect on China's great Olympic Games? To make sure, he would find out what it was, and escape in time to warn the government.

Chapter 61

On the morning of the eighth day of August 2008, the world anxiously awaited the start of the 24th Olympic Games. In the small Chinese river town of Shigu, hundreds of police, military, and secret service personnel abandoned their search—they had found nothing. They were not about to miss this historic moment — their Olympic Games. After an exhaustive hunt, the only TVs the invaders found were at a few street restaurants. Coat hanger antennas boosted the signals to the small color sets but the reception was still poor.

Although the locals were content with the fuzzy images, the new crowd was not. Unfortunately, there was nothing they could do. The uninvited guests hurried to stake out positions in small, flimsy folding chairs. Beer and food was ordered. An excited buzz spread among the soldiers but it wasn't from the alcohol. Stories were passed around of how someone knew one of the athletes, or had come from the same town. None of the locals were impressed. The Olympics were as remote an ideal for them as it was for many millions of their countrymen.

By 7 p.m. the glare from the setting sun made the TV screens, no matter how they were turned, difficult to watch. China was the only country in the world to keep the same time zone throughout its 3,600-mile length. The darkness in Beijing would not get to Shigu for three more hours.

At precisely 8:00 p.m., in the middle of great fanfare, laser lights, fireworks, and an arena filled with thousands of athletes, spectators, and volunteers, China's Olympic committee chairman stood nervously waiting until the final torchbearer was lifted to the platform to light the Olympic caldron. After a short welcoming speech, he was to stand aside while a fifteen-minute video of dignitaries from around the world presented their best wishes and congratulations.

In the control room, the director flipped the switch he had flipped on many practice runs. In the same instant, a switch was flipped in a cave thousands of miles away—the director's signal was immediately overridden. Along with the rest of the world, he was about to receive a mind blowing television first—and the greatest shock of his life.

"Ladies and gentlemen, honored athletes, and guests from around the world, welcome to the 24th Olympiad. We are honored to host this auspicious event," Ms. Wu said to the audience, in her modest, quiet way. As she spoke, her words were subtitled in English.

At first Mr. Tien, the director, leaned forward and rubbed his eyes.

"What the hell is happening? Who is that? Where is our signal?" Sweat started pouring from his forehead as he used his hands to squeeze from his temples a sight that had to be a bad dream. In seconds his voice intensified to an explosive level. Everyone in the control room scanned every switch, connection, and face in the room. Within minutes officials of every rank came bursting in, followed by armed PSB and MSS.

On the big screen, Ms. Wu continued. "Before we begin this year's Olympic Games, myself and the ChinAlive Project would like to invite all of you to join us in an unprecedented appeal—first to all my countrymen, and secondly to our Olympic audience. We are a patriotic group, thousands strong, who wish to improve the lives of all our Chinese countrymen."

In the following seconds it became clear to authorities and viewers around the world that this was not part of the well-rehearsed Chinese government's program. Ms. Wu's demeanor was dignified, her delivery spellbinding, and the worldwide audience, though startled, was captivated and willing to listen. As the disruption continued, those in the stadium as well as those glued to their screens, began to sense their participation in an historical event without precedent.

The law enforcers in Shigu sat frozen. The locals who had shown such a lack of interest now sat spellbound, along with their unwelcome guests.

"With four billion of you watching, including one billion of my countrymen and over half a million visitors, we thought it would be a splendid time to make our appeal."

As Ms. Wu continued, all eyes of the ChinAlive crew were locked in on her. Two thirds of the people on earth were watching. She had to remain calm, using the energy of her friends and comrades in the cave.

Everyone looked from her to the two large TV monitors on her left and right. It was happening. After all the planning, all the hard work over so many years, it was happening. Steadfast as always, Ms.Wu delivered the same folksy performance she had done on her weekly show on the environmental issues of China. Charlie glanced at the cameraman and the tech crew. They weren't just doing a show—they were broadcasting history. Everywhere Charlie looked, the same intensity, the same focus. They all knew their lives would never be the same when Ms. Wu was finished.

In the distance, Charlie saw how precisely the surveillance equipment was being monitored. How close were the authorities? Bill Zhiang looked at Jerry and others in his crew and nodded his approval for the success so far. But he could sense the fear and feel their anxiety.

"There is no way," he whispered, "they could have predicted something like this. It will take them hours to get a high tech search going. Even then, the way we have the signal bouncing from satellite to satellite, they'd need a miracle. Watch this, here comes the part that's going to blow their minds." Just as if she had hit the pause button for a bathroom break, Ms. Wu stopped talking and stepped away from the camera—but her performance continued. After she drank some water and rested a minute, she returned to her position and waited for a cue. Without skipping a beat, the broadcast returned, live.

"What was that?" Charlie asked.

"Another little something we cooked up to keep the authorities guessing. The broadcast is live only from this cave. Parts of it were recorded. The spliced pieces are being sent from three other sites. It is perfectly timed to look like it is coming from one spot. It should be driving the authorities nuts by now. Like it?"

"Love it," Charlie said.

"Sweet," said Jerry.

"Yes, that is very clever," Henry smiled.

As the list of Ms. Wu's grievances grew—from the millions of displaced workers, to the horrendous impact of environmental degradation, and the ethnic cleansing going on in Tibet and Xinjiang provinces—her demeanor never wavered. She was a calm, resolute grandmother, forcefully reprimanding those in power, and urging the bullies to start making things right.

"We never could have dreamed of a better worldwide venue and audience to propose our plan." Everyone in the cave had heard the speech before but it didn't matter—they were all transfixed.

"From the highest offices of governments around the world we hear—without too much examination—that China will soon be adopting democratic institutions. Why? Why would they have to do that if everyone is so happy with the way things are? This is the worst fantasy the Chinese people have had to choke down since the promises of Mao."

Taking a moment to sip some tea, Ms. Wu took a deep breath—and then her demeanor changed. Everyone in the cave could see she had transcended her small, dirt-covered stage. The worldwide audience was no longer some remote abstraction through a small, round camera lens. From her heart, she was speaking to each individual soul, and she was beginning to lose her grandmotherly cool.

"You gave us the right to trade with you and most of us hoped that would lead the way and open the door to a freer, more responsive government. It has not. You have made a devil's pact to do one thing and one thing only—make money. All of you can fool yourselves into believing that democracy is coming to China but that is the worst lie of all. As long as so many of my countrymen are prospering along with the rest of those on our doorstep, why would they wish to change?"

When she saw John Evers trying to get her attention, she knew she had moved further and further away from her planned speech. ChinAlive translators were frantically trying to update changes in the English subtitles. They had all agreed on a time limit. She could see the time in a corner of the teleprompter and immediately caught up with where she needed to be. John Evers saw her holding down two fingers to her side and nodded his approval for two more minutes. Her grandmotherly tone did not return.

As Ms. Wu headed into her tenth minute, the frenzy among the Beijing Olympic organizers caused the deputy secretary to have a heart attack. A crisis meeting in the control room with several branches of the military and the Olympic organizers was called.

Many of them were so caught up in trying to figure out what to do that they almost missed the part about "diverting the Yangtze River forever." At that moment a PSB captain grabbed the microphone and made an announcement: "Ladies and gentlemen, our humblest apologies for this disruption, but we think it best if everyone quickly cleared the stadium." And with that he had the person in charge of the public address system turn on an ear shattering sound that had everyone in the stadium covering their ears.

"Idiot, who authorized this?" The head of the Beijing Olympic Committee yelled. As he faced off with the PSB captain he ran over to the audio control and flipped the screeching off. But that wasn't all the captain had planned; many uniformed PSB began backing athletes and people away from the big screen as ropes and chains were used to pull the screen down as fast as possible.

Again, the chairman of the Chinese Olympic Committee was outraged and demanded that the highest-ranking officials in the room tell PLA members to stop the destruction of the screen immediately. As one group of military or another began running in different directions, the thousands of people who filled the stadium began to get more and more nervous, realizing that no one was in charge and no one had any idea how to resolve this. As soon as the screeching sound ended, their attention was again focused on Ms. Wu. "What did she say about the river?" Once again they turned to the big screen and to their monitors.

"We simply wish to give our countrymen a vote on how their lives are to be run. We don't believe all the lies that democracy is a Western thing. We want our freedom—freedom from persecution, freedom from torture, freedom to think and pray if we wish. Chinese, as well as Americans, and Russians, and people around the world—all of us as human beings share a common desire. This is not merely a Western notion. To give our people a chance at this kind of freedom we are here to offer a unique opportunity for all our voices to be heard."

In one quick moment, all those running and all those bickering in the control booth snapped to attention. "No one has ever asked us what we want, the people of China. No one has ever given us the chance or even provided the question. No one. Tonight, in front of this historic audience, we will be given that chance. We are not offering a specific political party or preconceived agenda. No candidates, no new constitution—not yet. Yes or no—do you want democracy, or not? It's that simple."

To millions of people, Ms. Wu might have been part of an elaborate hoax, or a new reality show, or someone selling something. But she was a bright, articulate, woman, well known and highly respected in her own country, delivering a message from somewhere in television land—and she could not be shut off. Every TV set turned to the Olympics—four billion of them—could not dismiss or end what she wanted to say.

Jerry, Henry, and Charlie were on the edge of their seats, wishing they were there to see the faces of the huge crowd, especially the faces of Party members and Olympic organizers. Jerry said, "the heck with them. I'd love to see the expressions on the faces of the ordinary man or woman in the street."

"How about the farmer in a field whose wife comes racing to tell him the news?" said Henry.

"Or shoppers at a department store getting the news on a bank of a hundred TV sets all tuned to the same station," added Charlie. Although Charlie and many of the ChinAlive workers were watching a repeat of the tape Mr. Zhiang had showed them before, it didn't matter. This was not a trial run – this was it. This was going out to the whole world.

"After all these years..." mused John Evers.

"No John," Henry's dad interrupted, in a whispered voice. "Never. Never in their lifetime would they have permitted themselves to dream that an opportunity like this would ever come their way. And especially not like this."

"I feel lucky to know you, my good friends." Henry said, as he turned to Jerry and Charlie.

"Hey, don't say it like this is the end," Jerry said. "This is the beginning. Keep watching. We'll know soon enough if anybody is catching on to us."

As Ms. Wu continued, members of the military and police in Shigu sat bewildered, paralyzed, without a clue what to do. Superiors began yelling at each other to do something, so they all jumped up—and then what? They continued to stare at the screen. When Ms. Wu started talking about cell phone voting people held on to their cell phones as if they had turned to gold. When every military person who had a phone held out their own, their superiors screamed to put them away and arrest anyone seen trying to use one. A look passed between each officer and his men. The same disbelieving look passed between citizens everywhere in China. Between PSB members, between PSB and ordinary citizens, between farmers and their wives, sales clerks at Ikea and their customers, coffee drinkers at McDonalds and Starbucks, and between people who swept the streets in every corner of China. Citizens in buses, taxis, and private cars, pulled over to listen incredulously at what they were hearing, and to make sure they understood the instructions clearly.

If people didn't have first-hand knowledge of what was going on, the vast majority quickly became informed. Newly empowered voters who sensed that authorities would treat cell phone users the same way they treated criminals were perceptive in their fear. In some places the first right to vote met a tragic end. Those in authority, blindly acting on frenzied orders, shot Chinese citizens holding a cell phone. Reports of this response came in not only from the countryside, but from big cities as well. Fortunately, these desperate acts were the exception, not the rule. Millions rushed home or to a secluded place to text their vote.

As Ms. Wu's speech continued, preparations for escape began in earnest. ChinAlive workers wished they could watch every historic minute to the end, but they knew there was much to do to get ready. The speech was being broadcast everywhere within the cave and there would be recordings to watch later.

Greatly adding to their preparation time was the loss the helicopter. It could not be fixed, so in the days that were left, a quickly formed team put together an alternative plan—an underground network to move everyone safely to the Vietnamese border. Instead of a six or seven hour journey, the escape would now take at least two days or more—if everything went according to plan.

"My countrymen, brothers and sisters; from Hong Kong to Taiwan, Tibet to Malaysia, Canada and the United States, and everywhere peaceful, freedom loving people live, stand with us. As certain as we are of the effectiveness of this new technology, there is one piece of our plan that we cannot control—the efficiency of the authorities in discovering a way to turn our efforts off.

I have been advised that the optimum time we have is six hours. As you can see, our vote tabulation will be directly recorded using this screen for the world to see." The screen to which Ms. Wu referred was now divided in to two halves. She was on one side and a second location appeared next to her—the United Nations building in New York City.

"We would have loved to use this sanctuary to promote our freedom, but the reality is, the Chinese government has so many friends whose vested interest is in keeping the status quo, that we dared not count on help from the UN." The next half image on the screen was from the inside of what looked like a well-fortified, deeply hidden room somewhere in the world. The camera scanned a number of men and women who were all at work preparing for the vote as it came in. Faces of some of most recognizable and trusted public figures filled the screen. Former presidents, legislators, Nobel Prize winners, entertainers, and business leaders each gave a wave as the camera recorded their presence.

Charlie turned to his dad, as did many others in the room. "Did you…how did…when…how…?"

John Evers responded to their amazement; "Wasn't easy, but I had a lot of help. You'd be surprised how many thousands of people around this world wanted to work with us. Not everyone has been fooled."

"Make no mistake gentlemen of the Standing Committee, the Politburo, and the entire Chinese Communist Party—if you plead a case to the UN, if you try to shut us down, the redirection of the Great River will be on your heads. There has been no assistance from any foreign government, this is not a violent overthrow, and this is not a movement to send our country back to the Dark Ages. In every village, in every city, we have patriots in place, ready and able to start making a peaceful transition. Of course we will stand aside if the vote goes against us—it will be broadcast as the results come in."

Chapter 62

As the broadcast continued, Rong Choi and his unit listened, on edge, ready to take orders—but no orders were issued. ChinAlive had predicted a period of uncertainty, a window of opportunity to move many of their members into positions where they were needed. Rong knew it was too early to reveal himself to his men, but he needed to get out of the underground bunker that housed his unit. In anticipation of a favorable vote, a team of ChinAlive negotiators had been selected, positioned, and were standing by. Rong was to be part of a small contingent accompanying this group to wherever negotiations were to be held. It was left to him and others on his team to break free of the men with whom he served.

"We cannot stay here." Rong stood up and shouted to the men and women in his unit.

"What do you mean?" One of the others asked.

"We cannot hide out in the safety of this place. No one yet knows what to do but we have to be ready."

"He is right," another cadet responded.

"But shouldn't we wait for orders?"

"And who put him in charge?"

"What orders?" said Rong. "Where have our officers gone? They too are as much in the dark as we are. At least if we are in a position to help, we will be commended, instead of waiting around." The men and women hesitated for many moments. When Rong headed for the security door, swiped his ID card, and boldly made his way out, most of his unit was up and ready to follow.

#

On the edge of the Great River, in a small hut near Chongqing, Rong's grandfather felt a well of pride for the efforts of all the people who deeply loved their country. He had no phone, not a cell or a landline, only a battery operated radio he had been given to listen to the events of a day that would live in history. Not wishing to be alone, he walked into the local village to see if there was more information about what was happening.

To his horror he came upon many bodies lying in the street. As he bent down to retrieve a cell phone in the hand of one dead man, he heard a shout to leave it alone. Mr. Wong could see on the screen a number had been typed in. In this man's last moment of life, Mr. Wong was proud to know that this man had voted "yes."

The extent of the bloodshed they had predicted was impossible to determine. Mr. Wong had worried about his grandson for over two decades—the worry never let up. And now he worried even more, and wondered if Chong Roi was safe, and able to move into the important role he had been groomed play.

Final preparations to leave the cave were in full swing. Only an essential crew was to remain to finish the broadcast, but Ms. Wu's final words brought everyone to a stand-still — everyone except Charlie Evers.

With ChinAlive members focused on Ms. Wu, they didn't see what he hoped was another alarmist figment of his imagination. Behind him, in the riverbed that had been part of their ultimate threat, a stream of water began to flow. Trying not to bring attention to himself, Charlie grabbed one of the dirt bikes and raced for the mechanical doors. He needed to keep his discovery under wraps until he was certain—he'd already exhausted everyone's trust and patience once before.

"I must go now my brothers and sisters," Ms. Wu continued. "But I would like to leave you with the words of a kindly gentlemen I once met. His name was Václav Havel and he was a poet and a playwright—and the former President of Czechoslovakia. He spoke eloquently about the lives we wish to live and the lives our oppressors want us to live.

Not too many years ago our esteemed President told us 'censorship in China was necessary because otherwise the press, and now the Internet, would disseminate falsehoods and confuse people's minds.'

Mr. Confucius—you all know him—said about the same thing when advocating an authoritarian approach for those who should rule and those who should be ruled. I think their time has come and gone. Mr. Havel went on to say that any ruling strong men, along with their cronies, 'become captive to their own lies. In so doing they must falsify everything. They falsify the past. They falsify the present and they falsify the future. They falsify statistics. They pretend not to possess an omnipotent and unprincipled police apparatus. They pretend to respect human rights. They pretend to persecute no one. They pretend to fear nothing. They pretend to pretend nothing.'

"I have seen reports by some Western journalists who quote tourists who recently visited our country. After listening to taxi drivers tell of their anger with the government, the tourists thought it was most insightful to say how much freedom we now have. But they never wonder if these same taxi drivers would ever stand up on a street corner and broadcast their anger in public.

All those who lost loved ones at the Tiananmen massacre had to endure Prime Minister Zhu Rongi's description of those days as 'a minor incident he forgot not too long after it happened.' We all were told not to discuss it and we were all told to pretend it didn't happen.

As Mr. Havel put it, 'by living in a lie, individuals confirm the system, fulfill the system, make the system, are the system.' Tonight my countrymen, we no longer have to endure the lies. Tonight we take back our country. Tonight we change the system. Thank you and good night."

Chapter 63

As everyone started to applaud the final portion of Ms. Wu's speech, Charlie, panting, out of breath, tugged on his dad's shoulder. "Dad, I think we have a big problem." It took John Evers a second to realize how serious his son was in light of what appeared to be ChinAlive's amazing success.

"What's up Charlie?"

"Look behind you," Charlie said, pointing to the riverbed.

"Oh no. That can't be." John Evers dropped what he was doing, grabbed one the nearby dirt bikes and joined his son on a sprint to the front of the cave. Along the way he yelled for a few others to follow. When they got to the mechanical doors, they were all dumbfounded. A steady leak from the river had found its way in. The hydraulic jacks, supported by heavy wooden beams, were starting to sink under the pressure of the river.

"We've got to get out of here and I mean right now. If we lose the river, we lose everything we've worked for and the Chinese people lose a lot more," As John Evers and a growing entourage started moving to the exits to warn the others, exploding bullets bounced off the path in front of them. After slamming to a stop, they turned, horrified to see the Money Man standing above them on the control platform, aiming an automatic weapon.

"Sorry to spoil your gathering, but I have some serious people in Beijing who wish to know what is going here. Please tell me who is in charge?"

John Evers stepped forward. "We will explain everything but please, if we don't blow this cave up right now and make our escape, the Yangtze River will break that door down and forever leave China." Evers quickly realized, to someone who had no idea of what this was all about, his plea would sound ludicrous.

"Sir, I am not an idiot. I see controls in front of me that must have something to do with that mechanical door. I wonder, if I used these controls, maybe I can let in some of the hundreds of police waiting nearby. Perhaps that is what you are worried about. I think that would even things out between us, yes?" But before he moved any of the controls, he swung around, sensing someone behind him. With a resounding crack, Charlie went down, ducking just enough to lessen the blow. Before the Money Man could swing his weapon around, Charlie landed two feet in the man's midsection. The Money Man barely flinched, but the gun flew out of his hands and off the platform. He knew his only play left was to get the doors open while keeping the boy at bay.

John Evers, frightened to see his son battling this well trained operative, yelled out, "run everyone, get out, leave. We will take care of this man." Charlie's dad and a few of the ChinAlive guards began to race up the platform stairs but stopped when they saw Charlie being held with a knife to his throat. The men backed off but not far or fast enough for the Money Man. Only when they saw a trickle of blood from a deepening knife wound did they know how serious the man was.

"Everyone, leave, go, get out." John Evers yelled again, as he motioned those who had stayed behind to do the same.

He turned to face the Money Man. "Don't do this. The river is on the other side of that door and if it comes crashing through, no one will ever be able to divert it back. Our plan was always to blow this space up to block the river's path permanently. You must believe me." In the split second it took the agent to consider what was said to him, two hammer wielding arms reached through the lower part of the platform's scaffolding and smashed away at the Money Man—one blow to his shins and the other to his left foot. The painful distraction was all Charlie needed. Using all his strength, he pushed the man off the platform. Two smiling faces appeared.

"Dudes, nice move. Thanks." said Charlie.

"He never saw it coming," said Henry.

"Thanks goes double for me," said John Evers, as they all raced for the exit. Looking down to see what had become of the agent, Charlie's momentary pause made him the last one down. When he looked back under the stairs he saw a couple of ChinAlive guards making sure the intruder couldn't stop them again.

"We have to go," he yelled at the men. "We have to get out now." Both guards stopped immediately, tied the man to the staircase, and ran to join Charlie in retreat.

A few minutes later Jerry and Henry anxiously stood by the cave's rear door, waiting for Charlie. Fortunately, nothing had to be shut down, hidden, stored, or disassembled. A timer had been set to blow the cave after everyone had cleared the area. John Evers stayed close to the project's munitions expert as the man grabbed the timer and changed the mechanism to enable a cell phone signal to detonate the explosives.

Multiple charges had been placed in strategic locations to insure completion of a job nature began thousands of years before. The munitions experts on their team joked many times how the amount of explosives planted were enough to level Beijing. With one push of a button no record of ChinAlive's headquarters would ever be found and the river would stay securely flowing within China's borders.

"I can't believe we have to leave all this stuff behind," Jerry said; "state of the art equipment about to be buried forever." A small amount of computing gear had been staged at the exit but with the uncertainty of escape, John Evers thought it best to leave it all behind. Henry thought he could see a tear in his friend's eye as he sadly stroked a keyboard.

"Go ahead," said Henry. "I will wait if you wish to kiss your computer good bye." Jerry waved a mouse menacingly at his friend. Henry laughed about Jerry's computer relationship.

"And where the heck is Charlie?"

"I thought he was right behind you." The boys did a quick survey of the area while the others were hurriedly assembled for the last time. Henry's dad was the first to offer his thanks. "I am speechless," Mr. Liu said, as he paused to look over his shoulder at the giant electronic board showing the final, overwhelming vote for democracy. I do not think we will cross paths again. Many of you will go into hiding."

"Wait a minute. Has anyone seen Charlie?" Jerry yelled. Everyone stopped.

"Go ahead Mr. Liu," said Charlie's dad, as he took the boys aside. Sensing John Evers growing concern for Charlie, Mr. Liu continued, hesitantly.

“We have taken great care to help those in immediate danger. Many of you will return to the safety of your home countries. All of us might be hunted, but for how long there is no way to know.” As he spoke he couldn't help but turn his attention to what John Evers and the boys were increasingly panicked about.

“We have set in motion what we wished would happen. How well we set the infrastructure to follow will determine how our efforts will be rewarded.” He had more to say but someone shouted that the small stream of water had now turned into a larger, quickly flowing stream.

“John, where’s Charlie,” Jill Evers shouted.

“Too many good-byes,” Mr. Zhiang said. “We have to get out of here now or our remains will be here for someone else to dig up in the next millennium.” They all knew that once the cave was blown, the authorities would be all over the mountain and its proximity. The original detonation had been planned to give them a good head start—that head start looked like it was about to vanish. Fortunately for the escaping ChinAlive members, the search was still focused on the side of the mountain facing the river. None of the police had been able to imagine a small escape path from under the mountain, out through the Red River valley, on a straight line to the Gulf of Tonkin.

After every ChinAlive member came running out, desperate to clear the mountain's danger zone, John Evers raced back in. The moment he crossed the cave's threshold, he heard it—a deep volcanic rumble. The river had broken loose. In his hand he held the fate of the most powerful river on earth—and the fate of his son. With his heart pounding, he jumped on a motorbike. It wouldn't start.

"Come on, he screamed at the bike. He tried again—nothing.

"You lousy, cheap, local piece of junk." He stomped the kick-starter several times – nothing. "Charlie, where are you?" Tears started burning in his eyes. He only had an instant to make the most agonizing decision of his life. Deep in his gut he knew, he prayed, that somehow Charlie had gotten out. For now, he had no choice. He threw the bike down and ran for his life. The wall of sound from the river's rampaging escape muted every other sound so well that John Evers couldn't hear the smaller rumble of an overtaking motorcycle.

"Dad, beside you. Get in."

"What the hell?"

"Jump in, this isn't a movie." In three decades as a spy John Evers thought he had seen it all.

"Indiana Jones Evers, at your service." After he his dad flopped into the trailer he found himself next to a wounded ChinAlive guard. The trailer was shaking so hard that neither man could keep from banging into the other. A hundred yards out from the cave's exit, using every bit of strength he had left, John Evers pulled himself up to the front edge of the trailer.

"Stop Charlie," he shouted. "Stop. We're out of time. The water is coming too fast. I need to detonate the explosives now. When the motorcycle bounced to a stop, he was able to stand, pull his phone from his pocket and take a firm grip.

"Hold on, I have no idea what's about to happen." For the longest moments of their lives, they waited. Nothing.

"Oh no, please. This has work. Charlie, this has to work." Before Charlie had time to respond to his dad's desperation, the charges went off. The blast and the settling of the mountain on top of water that had already escaped created a tidal wave that exploded out like a rice field Tsunami. John Evers, his son, and a wounded guard were swept away like insignificant bits of regurgitated flotsam. The motorcycle, the trailer, the two passengers, and the driver were washed hundreds of yards away from each other. Dirt and newly planted rice mixed with computer parts, office supplies, and whatever got in the river's path, also made its way to freedom.

The entire event lasted only a minute. When the wave started to settle the churning water turned them loose. Charlie splashed down to earth and looked up at the sky. He smiled. Miraculously, his dad and the wounded guard were close by, equally amazed at their survival. Charlie's hand had come to rest on a computer keyboard. His mouth was filled with dirt. His pants were gone. And then he started to laugh.

"Dad, the river stopped. The explosives worked," Charlie cried out as he came running to check on his dad. "That was fantastic!" Covered with mud, laughing, slipping, thankful to be alive, Charlie and his dad squished when they hugged. The wounded guard had been flung far from the trailer but was able to stand and join Charlie and his dad in their celebration. With one arm over each of the Evers shoulders, they were able walk/drag the guard and themselves away from the exploding mountain. ChinAlive members had quickly found the caravan of ox carts waiting for them. At the time they were staged, neither ChinAlive members nor the villagers whose farm vehicles had been hired, knew what a stroke of luck it was to have them waiting on higher ground. With the vantage point they had, they were safe from the tidal wave, and easily able to spot the three who had been blown free.

Chapter 64

After the helicopter was blown up, ChinAlive planners had to go to Plan "B"—hiring a dozen ox drawn carts and wagons from local farmers. The passengers would be a most unlikely bunch of freedom fighting refugees. Slowly, the group bounced their way along to safety outside China's borders. After the relief and joy of finding the others, and help for the wounded guard, Charlie was ready with his first barrage of questions.

"Dad what do you really think is going to happen?"

"Oh no you don't." His dad snapped back. "Not until you tell me why you were late coming out of the tunnel. What happened back there? Where were you? We thought you were right behind us."

"I was, but I was curious."

"No surprise there."

"In the split second after I came down from the platform, I looked under the stairs to see what happened to the gunman—I didn't need to worry. After pounding the crap out of him, two of our guards hurriedly tied him to the stairs. He looked unconscious, but as they turned to join me, he slipped a hand free, pulled another gun out of nowhere and starting firing—both our guards went down. It happened so fast. Then he propped himself up to a sitting position and took dead aim at me. Before the gun went off I closed my eyes. When I opened them, he had a bullet in his forehead. The guard who had shot him looked at me with a look of relief and then collapsed. I wasn't sure where he was hit but he couldn't move. When I checked on the other guard, I knew he was dead. I tried to lift the wounded guard who had saved me but he pushed me away.

"Get out, save yourself," he rasped.

"Dad, he laid back, ready for the end. I couldn't leave him. The motorbike and one of the trailers were close by so I hitched them up and loaded him in. The electronic ignition wouldn't work so I had to kick start the thing. I was halfway back to the exit when I heard the river break loose. I couldn't hear myself think. The noise was deafening. I wanted to go flat out but no way would the trailer have stayed on. And then there you were. Next instant, kaboom—coughed up like a volcanic hairball. That's about it."

"So, no big deal," said Jerry. You were, like, trying to ride the big one. Man, that would have been crazy, hanging five on a world class Yangtze wave."

"Yeah, I know, not quite as cool as riding shotgun with a bunch of dirty veggies, but a person has to do what a person can." It took a moment for the comic relief to settle, but when it did, laughter erupted, tears started to flow, and Charlie Evers had his first moment to think about the recent ways in which he had cheated death.

"So," Jerry said, "you going to write the book or do you need a ghost writer?"

"No one is going write about this for a very long time Jerry," said Bill Zhiang. "Much of what we have done will need to stay hidden until a generation of things is sorted out—and sorted out for the best."

"Okay," agreed Charlie, "but what about my question—what do you think is going to happen now?"

"We have tried to imagine every scenario," replied John Evers. "We have had way too many late night discussions, we have agonized, and we have prayed. I do not think, based on past experiences, there is any way to underestimate the anger and loss of face many in power have suffered and will continue to suffer."

"But remember," said Bill Zhiang. "We knew that, and we did everything we could to give the CCP a way to save face, share power, and do the right thing."

"Are there fleas in here?" Jerry grumbled. "Do you feel things crawling on you?"

"Shhhhh," said his mom. "This should be a piece of cake for you, Mr. Survival Boy."

"But I thought we were each going to have our own wagon," Jerry said.

"What, you don't like cabbage and being close to each other?" John Evers laughed. "The axle broke on one of the wagons as it was heading to pick us up."

"Seems strange for people who just changed the course of history to be making their getaway at point one kilometer an hour, fighting off squishy cabbage and bugs to boot," Charlie said.

"Back to your question Charlie—I think the first reaction will be swift and brutal, although a great deal more measured than in past crackdowns. In the past they would have arrested thousands from every corner of the country. But with the whole world so closely following the government's every move, and with so many tourists from around the world as witnesses, it will certainly be more difficult to repeat the brutal measures they have counted on in the past.

Many of the dignitaries we lined up are either in China or where the votes are being counted. Press from around the world is already here—they will have one eye on the government's response and the other on the Olympics. The whole world will be holding its breath to see how these two monumental events influence each other. Let's talk more when we come to a stop. I keep eating dirt and slime every time I open my mouth." All the cart's passengers swatted flies away, smiled through the grime, and were content to slowly wind their way along a dirt road, seldom used – a road that would bring them to the Red River, freedom, and their final escape.

"How much longer Dad?" Henry asked.

"I think we're about to stop for the night son." From his perch near the front of the wagon Henry could see a village approaching. Their hosts and guides were happy for the extra income, but had no idea what this group was all about. They were told that the strange foreigners were out to see a side of China far away from regular tourist destinations.

ChinAlive members were not surprised when the famers asked about the floodwaters – and the damage done to their crops. A contingency fund had been set aside to address any such last minute expenses. After a few minutes of bargaining a settlement was reached and everyone was relieved that the fund had been enough to adequately compensate the farmers for whatever loss they suffered.

After resting awhile, the group sat down to a dinner of fried pork, dumplings, and tea. As they all gathered around an outdoor cook stove, Mr. Liu outlined the rest of the journey they planned out.

"We have about fifteen hundred kilometers to get to the border. Mid-morning tomorrow we will reach the Red River where we will board two river boats that will take us to the northern Vietnamese province of

Lao Cai. The river runs through the province and will take some of us to Hanoi."

"Some of us, Dad?" Henry asked.

"Yes son. Along the way we will say goodbye to most of our ChinAlive friends. Some will go to Laos, some to Thailand. All of us have been individually briefed. Again, it is best that our plans are shared with as few as possible.

"Even now?" Jerry asked. "You think they're after us?" Bill Zhiang looked at his son and mused at his bright boys naiveté.

"Hard to say Jerry. They may not know exactly what or who they are looking for, but the net for any and all of us was thrown out as soon as Ms. Wu began her speech. The only people you need to know about are the Evers, Ms. Wu, your mom and me. We're all catching a plane out of Hanoi for the States."

"But what about Henry and his family?"

"That we shouldn't discuss now, but they will be safe and well cared for."

Knowing that their time together was soon coming to an end, the boys huddled together on the edge of the encampment and tried to figure out a way to stay in touch. After only being allowed an hour together, all project members settled in for the night while guard duty was assigned to the security people who had had the same responsibility in the cave. It was a restless, warm night, but sleep came quickly to most of them.

"A couple of more things Dad?" Charlie asked.

"Go ahead."

"You must have known how the government would be suspicious of all your activities. And if you knew, how could you and Mom carry on, talking about all the negative stuff about the Chinese Communist Party? And all those discussions we had about my project, and corruption, and…on and on? Dad, we slammed them every day, all the time. How could…?"

"Charlie, think about it. How far did we actually go? There are thousands of expats living in China making these kinds of observations every day. Believe me, your mom and I did not go beyond the kinds of things you and I talked about."

"You mean you were going only as far…?"

"As far as I could take it Charlie—we needed to sound believable. You can be sure they had much more dangerous conversations to monitor. I bet we never became more than a tiny blip on their radar."

#

To the amazement of the entire world, ChinAlive gained monumental new footing in its efforts to bring Democracy to China. Cooler heads prevailed in the CCP (Chinese Communist Party). The Department of Propaganda—which had recently changed its name to the Department of Publicity—quickly formulated a plan to see the government through its worst, unimagined nightmare. The voting continued, uninterrupted, as the people of China cast their cell phone ballots. After six hours, it was over. The final vote read like a monumental decree—400,901,223 for democracy, 73,324 against. A third of the people of China had voted. The technology worked. The ChinAlive project had not been discovered and offers of help in establishing a democratic state came pouring in from all over the world.

During their darkest hours the government tried to project an aura of evenhandedness and understanding. Yes, they would listen. Yes, they would abide the will of the people. And then they would try to reestablish order in the way they had done in the past. Little did they know the vote would be overwhelming and universally accepted—the old regime's legitimacy to rule would be forever undermined. Never would they have guessed that one of the architects of this well thought out policy was a member of ChinAlive—an elder Chinese statesman who had waited decades to play a role he had only dreamed about. The days of old were about to end.

Epilogue

Three thousand miles from ChinAlive headquarters, the Standing Committee of the Politburo of the Chinese Communist Party held an emergency, all-night session. Security personnel had been told to keep all Chinese athletes segregated from the other athletes but the orders were ignored. Athletes from around the world joined hands with their exuberant Chinese counterparts. Overnight, Tiananmen Square, as it had been in 1989, filled with over a million, exuberant, celebrating, Chinese citizens.

When Lieutenant Rong Choi, along with many of his comrades emerged from their bunker under Tiananmen Square, they were completely disarmed. Crowded together with thousands of their countrymen, barely able to balance in this celebrating swarm of humanity, the men and women were quickly relieved of any vestige of their official attire. No police or military presence was in sight, only a massive multitide of people celebrating, dancing, and hugging one another. As Rong walked and stumbled to a prearranged meeting place, his heart filled with emotion and pride for a mother and father he never knew, a grandfather who had risked everything, and a step family who had done the same—and he wondered if the day had truly come.

The velvet revolution that had swept Communist regimes from Eastern bloc countries was finally being felt in one of the last Communist strongholds. When it was announced that Politburo members had agreed to see representatives of ChinAlive, the thunder that was heard this time was not from guns or tanks, but from Chinese citizens celebrating with supporters from around the world.

Acknowledgements

The first draft of this novel was written during a gap year between posts in Beijing and Hong Kong. It was written on the move, with never more than a few days in one place. For never letting me relax, for demanding proof of my efforts, my great thanks to Roland and Marie Smith—they snapped the whip from afar. For Roland's advocacy and volume of work in turning kids into readers—your continuing inspiration helps me get it done.

My great thanks also goes to Nancy Spalding, Patty Walhood, Steve Sampson, and Chikae Yamatin for slogging through and offering invaluable advice. Thanks to Rhody Cohon Downey for her excellent editing and formatting help and to John Stevens, for his absolutely perfect cover art. To the cadets at the Shanghai Public Security Bureau College—you are truly the generation that will make the biggest difference in China's future. Thank you for the privilege of being your teacher and friend. And a special thanks to the Hillsboro branch of Washington County Libraries—a fantastic institution, a place that made me proud to be a librarian every time I sat in a quiet spot to look out over the duck pond while rewriting this book time and time again.

To Simon Winchester for his book, *The River At The Center Of The World : A Journey Up the Yangtze, and Back in Chinese Time*—thank you. The "first bend in the river" was the initial inspiration for *ChinAlive.*

And finally, to the lovely Susan, who has heard it all, read it all, and made it bleed—several times. The book is so much better because of your love, encouragement, and amazing editing skills.

Bob Jonas has been a school librarian for seventeen years—four in Beaverton, Oregon and seven in China—Shanghai, Beijing, and Hong Kong. In South America he worked for three years in Santiago, Chile, and then three years in Riyadh, Saudi Arabia. Currently, Bob is working as a school librarian in Erlangen, Germany.

As a storyteller, writer, and librarian he has motivated, inspired, stimulated, stirred, cajoled, provoked, and done what was necessary to instill a love of reading in kids on four continents.

ChinAlive is one of three novels he has written for young adults in the past decade. Four books for the illustrated market are still off the grid, in deep cover as well, but not for much longer. Learn about these and Bob's worldwide perspective on writing, reading, travel, and adventure at: http://www.thevagabondlibrarian.com

22740239R00152

Made in the USA
San Bernardino, CA
19 July 2015